"You called me Amy."

Crawford's eyes flew open, and he focused on her in one last effort to dissuade himself—and her—from what he was sure was totally dangerous territory. But reality conspired against him. Her eyes, luminous from tears, shone with seductive duskiness at him, and her mouth, half-parted with confusion and innocent invitation, drew him. He felt as if he was drowning in her. The line he hadn't wanted to cross was already fading into oblivion. She'd pulled it out from under him.

"A slip of the tongue," he breathed with ironic heaviness.

His warm hands slipped up her back and came into contact with thin fabric. Heart pumping, he tried again, and this time his hand came up under the fabric, finding naked, silky skin.

Her lashes drifted upward as she shivered under the caress of his fingers and the smoldering look in his eyes. She wanted to experience more of him. "Is *your* name Samuel?"

"Yeah." Crawford swallowed hard. Why did such a simple fact seem so intimate?

Dear Reader,

Hot days, hot nights and hot reading—summer's really here! And we truly do have a hit lineup for you this month. For example, our American Heroes title is by Naomi Horton. *Hell on Wheels* is a very apt description of the hero, as well as the name of the truck he drives. But when he meets our heroine... Well, all I can say is that they'd both better prepare for a little taste of heaven!

Award-winner Justine Davis checks in with *Target of Opportunity,* a sexy bodyguard story with a hero who's absolutely scrumptious. Lee Magner's *Standoff* is set in the rugged American West, with a hero who's just as rugged—and a whole lot more romantic. Frances Williams brings in *Passion's Verdict,* with a hero on the run and a heroine who's along for the ride of her life. Christine D'Angelo's title says it all: *A Child Is Waiting.* But for the heroine, finding that child is going to take the help of one very special man. Finally, welcome new author Victoria Cole, whose *Mind Reader* has a psychic heroine and a skeptical hero on the trail of a missing child. Something tells me that you'll want to get hold of each and every one of these books!

And in months to come, look for more great reading from favorite authors such as Emilie Richards, Marilyn Pappano, Suzanne Carey and Linda Turner, to name only a few of the talents contributing to Intimate Moments, where excitement and romance go hand in hand.

Enjoy!

Leslie Wainger
Senior Editor and Editorial Coordinator

A CHILD IS WAITING

Christine D'Angelo

Silhouette® INTIMATE MOMENTS®

Published by Silhouette Books New York

America's Publisher of Contemporary Romance

SILHOUETTE BOOKS
300 East 42nd St., New York, N.Y. 10017

A CHILD IS WAITING

ISBN: 0-373-07509-X

First Silhouette Books printing July 1993

CHRISTINE D'ANGELO

has been a successful commercial writer for over twenty-five years and has won awards for her campaigns and slogans. Prompted by her husband, she turned to writing fiction a few years ago. Because of him, she says, she believes that romance really does exist. Not only is he the strong, silent type, but, more practically, he bailed her out of debt the day they were married, and he's still doing it, she confesses. She admits that *A Child Is Waiting* comes from the heart. From her stepfather, to whom she dedicated this book, she learned that parenthood is a question of love, not circumstances.

To Richard John Adams.
Dad, this one can only be for you.

Prologue

Somewhere in the mountains, a child slept, her perfect hands and feet flexing restlessly. Around her was mud, earth, twigs, branches, nature's dubious bounty fashioned to create a home.

It was cooler in the mountains than in the rest of Marita, but the air was still stifling, heavy with the humidity that rose from the tropical forests below. Out of exhaustion, her foster parents had spurned the prospect of climbing higher where it might have been cooler yet.

A film of perspiration coated her young, tiny, naked body. But underneath the sheen, her skin was rough—the result of a diet prescribed by poverty. Everything that cradled her was primitive—from the prickly grass bed to the cave she rested in. But still, around her there was raw beauty.

Outside on a ledge, a condor with its immense wings tucked against its body watched the distant horizon. Cocky in its dominance, it barely deigned to regard the rugged path that led to the child's home. It puffed out its chest, satiated. Unlike the child, it had eaten full meals in the last two days.

Against a night sky, the mountains' stunning black majesty caught the blazing silver-white light of a full moon. The silence was brilliant. No traffic, no voices, no whirring buzzes from crackling city wires intruded.

This child's foster parents were prepared to give her up. Not because they didn't care about her, but because they already had eight children of their own, and parents in Marita had precious little. They knew it was the practical thing to do. They also knew that the money they'd received for her would make them, by Marita's standards, rich. With their new wealth, they could feed their other children, perhaps even educate them. The new government had promised more schools, had even promised to make formal education mandatory for its small citizens. To take advantage of that was their dream.

But they had still shed tears at the prospect of losing her. All life in their opinion was to be revered. Why else would they have rescued the little one from the burning village? Why else, with trembling hearts, would they have taken her from the arms of her dead mother? Of course they didn't want to give her up, but the letter from another world had been filled with hope, joy and a gentleness that had touched their hearts.

So, the couple who nurtured the child who wasn't theirs, therefore, dreamed of educating their children—and of delivering the child who would pay for that rare and wonderful gift into a cocoon of love and privilege.

What the child dreamed of, no one could know. But in her innocence, one could imagine she might be dreaming of an angel. An angel who would cradle her in something other than grass and mud. An angel who already loved her.

Her angel. Her special angel.

She slept on, secure in that dream.

Chapter 1

My God, was that her?

Sam Crawford sucked in his breath as he saw the woman with the identifying rose reach the top of the antiquated airport ramp. He felt his gaze glinting with a hard, resisting light as it traveled the full length of her.

Mrs. Amy Blake was a pint-sized knockout.

She wore a mint-green dress that featured tiny straps caressing creamy skin. The rose that he'd suggested she wear was pinned to the sundress. The dress in turn clung to a breathtakingly lithe body. It was the body that stopped him cold in his tracks: every man's fantasy, small, but curved everywhere from bare shoulder to rounded hip.

His eyes slitted. Maybe he shouldn't have been in such a hurry to get to the airport. This kind of temptation he could do without. He waited for her to descend the ramp, in no rush to greet her. He'd already been waiting an hour. Another few minutes would hardly make much of a difference, he reasoned.

He let out the breath he'd been holding and closed his eyes briefly. He'd gotten to the airport early out of habit. Even though he knew its boundaries, its nooks and crannies, its secret problem areas, he never took anything for granted. Life was a constantly changing canvas. It was always better to leave a margin for error.

Whiling away time, he'd recited lesson number three from the beginner's driver manual under his breath as he'd taken shallow drags on his cigarette. Driving, he'd discovered, had a lot in common with life. Ignore a yield sign and you could lose your life. Especially in a place like Marita.

Then with feigned casualness, he'd kept an eye on the soldiers sporting their AK-47's. They were touted as the saviors of Marita, but he'd always been wary of guns, no matter whose hands were clutching them. In his experience, revolutionary philosophies often didn't translate well into reality. They could spawn other, more devastating realities. But he'd made a living from revolutions and their aftereffects in more countries than he cared to tally, so why should he complain? he'd thought. These days it was hard to tell the good guys from the bad guys, anyway. Goals got muddied after the first shot was fired.

Narrowing his gaze, he'd then continued to watch the passengers disembark from the recently landed aircraft, until she'd appeared, drifting into view like a soft, tiny, dark-haired goddess.

Out of place, but definitely worth the wait.

He opened his eyes and refocused, giving her his full attention.

She reached the end of the ramp and glanced around, but he still made no move toward her. Better to know what he was really up against, he thought.

He frowned as his gaze lifted steadily upward from the rose. No relief there, he realized as his eyes fixed on a cloud of thick, raven hair framing pale, fine features. He paused, momentarily frozen by her aura of loveliness. If he'd wanted to take a woman to bed, his imagination couldn't have conjured up a more perfect angel . . . even from twenty feet away he could tell she was delicate, but with that body that could mold itself to a man's easily, there was suggested passion. . . . Startled by the sudden image that had sprung to mind, he cut it off in a hurry.

He hadn't wanted a woman like her in too long to remember. He shouldn't now. Women with those kind of foxy, classic looks belonged to his old life—a life he'd distanced himself from both by choice and circumstance. A life with no roots, no sentiments, no needs, no desire to strangle you....

Anyway, the woman had a husband. He wasn't sure if he was grateful or regretful of that reminder.

He forced himself to concentrate on the reason she was here and to analyze what her chances were of pulling it off. Hiking up the Tackazan Mountains was no picnic. Now, looking at her objectively, he seriously doubted she could make it.

Her skin was porcelain pure. *That* would burn in no time— three hours, tops, he decided. Her hair was heavy and shining. *That* would dry out under the relentless sun. He experienced a moment of genuine regret for that, however. There was precious little in life he still revered. Natural beauty, though, was something that still awed him. And hers was as fresh and clean as a spring meadow.

He blew out an exasperated ribbon of air. She belonged in an English garden somewhere, sipping tea, with the only danger an occasional wasp.

He wondered what her husband was like. Rich, old-world Boston, he imagined. And just as useless, he decided arbitrarily. Absently, he reflected on why they hadn't been able to adopt a child back home. Her patrician looks told of privilege and money. Money could buy anything. Why not that?

He took another drag on his cigarette, this one deeper as another question posed itself. Where were the husband's brains when he allowed a woman like her to come to a war-devastated country like Marita? Sam sure as hell wouldn't have sanctioned such a move.

He remained surveying her from a distance, still not moving toward her. He had to grant her a grudging respect. She had class, and an innate sense of self that he admired. Her shoulders were straight despite the long, gruelling plane trip. He had a feeling she knew exactly what she wanted. She glanced around curiously but without judgment. She was, he concluded, no ugly American. He exhaled a sigh of relief. The trip would be tough enough without that added into the mix. Maybe she had a chance of making it after all.

He tilted his head, giving her a final once-over. It was likely to be the last he'd get, unnoticed. He felt he could indulge himself. He ran his fingers through his mahogany hair. Since his self-imposed exile, he hadn't seen anything as entrancing as she was. She reminded him of satin, and silk, and perfume that smelled like wild roses. . . .

He blinked hard, seeing her jump as the soldiers began circling. At least she had good reflexes. He muttered resignedly under his breath, "You're going to need 'em, Mrs. Blake." With that, he started to unfurl himself from his leaning position.

Impatiently, he paused for a moment, waiting to see if her husband would join her. But when no one joined her, and he saw that the ramp had cleared, he decided he couldn't afford to wait any longer. Too quiet in here all of a sudden.

He had a sneaking suspicion that the soldiers were about to pounce.

He tossed his cigarette down and ground it with his boot before he headed toward her. She was half turned away from him. He touched her lightly on the arm to get her attention. "Mrs. Blake?"

He watched as with obvious relief, she tore her gaze away from the pacing soldiers.

"Sam Crawford?" Her voice had a breathless quality. She raised her head, and a pair of emerald eyes peered at him from under long, coal-black lashes. He immediately felt as if someone had delivered a sucker punch to his stomach.

He nodded and she extended a hand, smiling tentatively. "I'd just about given up on you."

"A deal's a deal, Mrs. Blake. I said I'd be here." He frowned, looking past her, over her shoulder. "Where's Mr. Blake?"

Amy cleared her throat. She hadn't exactly told Crawford in her phone calls or correspondence that she was single. Some information, she'd discovered, was best withheld until the last minute. She bit her lower lip nervously. From here on in, with a child in tow, she imagined she'd be hearing Crawford's question a lot. She was going to have to learn how to deal with it. Now she supposed was as good a time as any to start.

"There isn't a Mr. Blake, Mr. Crawford," she answered evenly. "Except for my father. I'm single."

Crawford shot her a slightly distracted look. Out of the corner of his eye, he saw one of the soldiers advance toward a couple in the corner. Being under suspicion in this country was as dangerous as being guilty. He sensed the atmosphere in the airport was becoming charged. Airport workers were drifting away from their posts.

He swore silently. Something *was* going to happen.

Without seeming to, he kept his senses alert to what was going on around him, even while he refocused impatiently on the woman. He raised his brows as he took off his sunglasses. "I'm sorry—did I miss something?"

Amy braced herself, offering him a forced, sweet smile. "Yes, I mean no...." She tilted her head, regarding his surly face.

She hadn't been told by the social worker at the adoption agency who'd recommended Sam Crawford just how much of a renegade he'd be. But one look said it all. She'd never seen eyes as steely, as jaded or as compelling, despite the fact they were also, contrarily, the most vivid blue, the color of a usually friendly sky. They dominated his rough features and contrasted with his bronzed skin. His body was lean, lethal-looking, and taut, as if he always kept it honed, ready to strike. A woman would have to be crazy to trust herself into his care, she thought. He looked as though he'd seen it all and didn't give a damn.

She inhaled sharply. Coming to Marita was the wildest thing she'd ever done. She had a sneaking suspicion that hiring Crawford was the second.

She jerked her shoulders back with a stubborn twist. He was exactly what she needed, she reminded herself sternly. Tough and cool. After all, she wasn't going to be dating the man.

"I just didn't come with anyone, that's all," she finished with a touch of defiance.

He lifted an eyebrow, a sarcastic bite making it into his voice. He hadn't missed that stubborn tilt to her chin. "You mean you're alone?"

Amy tossed her damp hair out of her eyes, the humidity curling its ends, and offered him a broader smile. "Well, I was until a few minutes ago, but now, Mr. Crawford, I have you, so I'm not really alone, am I?"

She held her breath, praying he wasn't going to abandon her. For all her flipness in tone, she was terrified he'd leave her to take off on her own. She couldn't speak Spanish. Her father used to say she wasn't built for strength but for speed, like a greyhound. She was equally hopeless at reading maps. Crawford, she'd been told, knew the terrain and the people like the back of his hand, and could guide her through it blindfolded.

"But he's no barrel of laughs," the social worker had warned her. "He's a moody character, so be prepared."

Suddenly, looking at Crawford and the scowling expression on his face, she believed the woman's comments.

His mouth slanted to the side. "You want to run that by me again?"

She fiddled with the strap of her shoulder bag. "I said, I'm not really alone, because I have you."

She watched him as he stared at her in silence. She took a deep breath triggered by a natural curiosity about what made him tick. What makes a man with a brilliant career in intelligence fall off the face of the earth? Why had he chosen to become an expatriate and soldier of fortune in this place? It occurred to her how little her investigation of him had *actually* produced and how risky it was for her to have hired him on a social worker's say-so. Likely the social worker had never actually met him. Maybe if she had . . .

Interrupting her thoughts, he shook his head, a hard look on his face. "No way, Mrs. Blake. If you're alone, the deal's off."

She opened her mouth to object when suddenly she heard him mutter under his breath.

"Good God!"

Instantly, he grabbed her. Her eyes widened in surprised panic. Next thing she knew he was dragging her toward the hallway.

She felt him throw his body at hers. She was too stunned by his sudden action to offer even a faint protest.

The air vanished out of her lungs as she felt his body pinning hers, twisting and pulling her down. In reflex, she tried to break away as their bodies hit the ground, his on top of hers, but his chest pressed against her breasts, stifling her. Her right shoulder jammed into her shoulder bag and the buckle grazed her bare skin. She cried out automatically as a barrage of shots erupted, shattering her eardrums. Within a second, the airport was an explosion of sounds.

"Oh, my God!" she gasped as fear raced through her. Out of the corner of her eye, she saw flashes of smoking light. A woman voiced the most unearthly cry of pain she'd ever heard. Everywhere there was the sound of stomping heavy boots and screams. Her body started to shake convulsively. The noise was deafening. She'd never been more terrified in her life.

Was the woman dead?

Her entire body started to tremble beneath Sam Crawford's.

"Easy," he murmured in a rough voice, his mouth warm against her neck. "Easy...you're safe—I've got you." He dug in closer toward her, embracing her, protecting her.

She wanted to cry out at his weight and at the horror unfolding above and around her, but didn't dare. What was happening? Trapped beneath Sam Crawford, she could hardly breathe, but, as if fear had heightened her senses, she could feel every hard line of his body. His chest and arm muscles were like tempered steel, hot and hard against her, his legs taut, tensed, easily covering her and holding her captive.

Suddenly, there was a lull, and the massive body crushing her went rigid. Amy's heart thundered in fear for what was next. Using his elbows, Crawford hoisted his body upward.

Amy held her breath as he spoke, not daring to move. Anger and concern showed in his gaze. "They've probably got who they want, but just in case someone gets trigger-happy, we'd better run for it," he said in a harsh voice.

"But—" she started.

"Be ready," he growled.

Amy thought of the beautiful baby clothes she'd brought with her. "My luggage—" she protested in a weak, gasping breath.

"To hell with it," he snapped. "Have you got your passport and money?"

"Yes—" She struggled to get the answer out.

"Then—*now!*" he ordered.

In a split second, he'd dragged her to her feet. She felt herself scrambling, trying to keep up with the long-legged pace he set. A couple of times she stumbled as her sandals slipped on her feet, but he righted her. Scenery whizzed by her in an institutional blur, and then miraculously, they were charging through a pair of doors.

Blazing sun and excruciating, humid air hit her in the chest. She almost reeled with the impact. She felt as if her lungs were being impaled with red-hot arrows. Her legs buckled beneath her.

"Sweet Lord," she gasped, trying to steady herself.

Crawford caught her as she was about to lose ground. Without further ado, he leaned her up against a wall for support.

They both came to a standstill and stared at each other.

Crawford frowned, catching his own breath trying to shake off the scent she wore. It lingered on his skin from when he'd held her.

He'd been right.

She smelled of roses. Wild exotic roses.

Sweet roses. Tempting roses.

He blinked. "Sorry about that. You all right?"

Chest heaving, lungs struggling for air, she took a deep breath noticing that his hands were keeping her arms pressed to the wall. His eyes were so intense on hers. She was uncomfortably aware of the feel of his fingers splayed across her bare shoulders. As her gaze merged with his crystal-blue gaze, she gave a nervous cough.

No, she thought, she wasn't all right. She felt as if she was going to faint. Fear, the heat, his body...

She struggled to compose herself. "Is it always like this?" she managed to say.

Crawford shook his head up and down and then sideways. Her scent seemed stronger as the sun and heat absorbed it. He swallowed back the desires it triggered.

Roses tended to have thorns, he reminded himself.

"Yes and no. The revolution still has some enemies. The military is ever on guard."

Amy was ashamed to realize she hadn't meant the altercation in the airport. She'd been terrified, true, but conditioned by her father's warnings to expect to see such things. After all, it hadn't been so bad, had it? She'd survived. Strangely, she was beginning to feel a peculiar blankness about the whole thing. She must be tougher than she thought. God, she hoped so.

She refocused, discovering they were in a parking lot.

"I didn't mean that, I meant the heat."

Sam frowned, his eyes searching her face. Except for the soft pink tinge staining her cheeks, she looked comfortable and unruffled. His hands dropped immediately. Here he was worrying about her reaction to the airport scene and she was concerned about the heat? The lady had to have ice water flowing through her veins, he thought with disgust.

He ran his hand down the hilt of the knife hooked in his belt, shrugging. What did he care? She was none of his business, anyway. "Yeah, and sometimes worse. C'mon, let's get out of here."

She'd done something wrong, Amy thought, but she wasn't sure what. Crawford's brooding expression had become even darker as she settled in the passenger seat of his truck.

She watched as he wheeled the vehicle out of the lot and onto a dusty, dirt road. His bare forearms looked out of proportion to the steering wheel. As he drove, she could see the corded muscles running in lines close to the bone. A mahogany sprinkling of hair trailed along his skin. She shifted with a strange uneasiness. It wasn't like her to be vulnerable to a man's sex appeal. Except Crawford didn't possess appeal so much as he possessed a savage kind of strutting intensity. She blinked quickly. He made her feel as if she were suffocating.

"Where are we going?"

She saw him check the rearview mirror before answering. For all the activity at the airport, the road was surprisingly deserted, although in the distance, she could hear a siren, likely that of an ambulance. She wondered if it was, but the frown on his face discouraged the question.

His lips tightened around a response. "A private home of some people that I know. Most of the hotels are taken up with military and government. Mercedes and Raoul Mendoza often take in Americans who come here to adopt. Their place is clean and fresh, the meals good, I rent a room there and they're close to the courts and junta headquarters. You'll need that sooner or later."

Amy nodded resignedly. She'd been warned by other adoptive parents who'd formed a support group in Boston what to expect.

"I was told the bureaucracy is horrendous."

"Then believe whoever told you that, sweetheart, because they sure weren't joking."

Amy bristled, beginning to wonder if Sam Crawford hated women or just her in particular. He appeared to enjoy making everything sound so negative.

Did he really hope she'd back off that easily? Just because of bureaucracy? Did he believe that she'd cave in just because he was so rough and rude?

It was on the tip of her tongue to tell him that if he only knew how badly she wanted this child, he would have realized that nothing could dissuade her. She found she couldn't. It was disconcerting to discover that the man she'd hired might become one of the problems she'd have to overcome. She hadn't expected him to take an instant dislike to her, nor had she anticipated this ridiculous tug of attraction she felt toward him. It was stupid, she thought. Normally, only civilized, quiet, nurturing men appealed to her. She couldn't like this man in a million years.

But a racing pulse could just as easily be caused by too much coffee . . . she'd had plenty of that on the plane.

Her mouth set into a stubborn line. "Tell me, Mr. Crawford, just how do you make any money?"

He regarded her arrogantly. "Beg your pardon."

"I mean, how do you make any money when you treat people with such disdain?"

He laughed harshly.

"People need my services, sweetheart, so they put up with me *and* my bad manners. Pure and simple."

Amy's heart turned over. He was right. As sullen and as difficult as he was, she'd have dropped to her knees and begged him to guide her, if need be.

She sighed, her stomach queasy as unexpected tears sprang to her eyes. Without warning, she felt as if some low-level shock was settling in. Suddenly, the woman's screams penetrated the shell Amy had encased herself in at the airport. A wave of dizziness assailed her. She clutched at the handle of the truck door. With alarm, she realized what was going to happen.

"Mr. Crawford," she choked. "I'm going to be sick."

Chapter 2

Of course, he thought. A delayed reaction. He'd been stupid not to think of that. Nice, he'd read her wrong.

"I'll pull over. Hang on." With a screech, he brought the truck to a stop on the shoulder of the road.

Amy flew out the passenger side before he managed to reach her side. Hair streaming behind her, she disappeared like a streak into the bushes.

Crawford went to go after her, then changed his mind. Nobody liked an audience when they were throwing up. He sure as hell didn't. And in the last ten years, he'd done his fair share.

Leisurely, he returned to the cab of the truck, and searching in his supply trunk, pulled out two bottles and a cloth dampened in ice water. Leaning against the passenger door, he waited for her.

Five minutes later, she emerged from the thicket, pale and wan, clutching her stomach. "I'm sorry," she said abjectly. "I don't know what came over me."

Even disheveled, she looked tempting. Her hair was a luxurious tangle of black midnight framing her delicate features. Crawford narrowed his gaze, ignoring the twisting wrench in his stomach as a scowl formed at the lined corners of his eyes. There ought to be a law against a gorgeous female like her be-

ing allowed in public when they looked so helpless. He didn't
want those strings being pulled."

He shrugged. "No problem."

Amy caught his intent expression and flushed, suddenly
aware of the image she was likely presenting to him. She ran a
hand across her forehead, trying to rearrange her hair. Her skin
felt parched in the tropical heat, and she knew her dress was
wrinkled. She was a cool-weather type who far preferred crisp
blankets of snow to sultry, mind-boggling heat. She'd never be
able to think straight in suffocating heat. It rattled her.

She probably looked a mess, she thought miserably, but why
did she even care? The man was nothing to her except an ex-
pediency. Her flush deepened as his eyes followed the direction of her hand. Something about the way he looked at her
made her nerves jangle.

"Something hit me," she said in a halting voice, "and I
couldn't seem to stop it."

He pushed his body away from the side of the truck and extended a hand. "Some shock, I would imagine," he answered
in a voice as raw as the weather. "Here—take this bottle, and
run this wet cloth over your face."

Amy did as she was told, unable to believe she'd actually
thrown up if not exactly in front of him, close to it. Gratefully, she ran the cloth over her hot skin. Physically soothing,
it also seemed to soothe her rising temperature, as well. She
glanced up at him through heavy lashes, noting the strong ripple of muscle as he dropped his hand.

"That woman's scream . . . the shots . . . I didn't think it got
to me. I thought I'd just accepted it and filed it away." She
shivered convulsively.

For the first time, she saw his features soften with compassion.

"You never get used to violence, even if it's inevitable," he
said. "In World War II, a lot of hardened soldiers got sick
when they were forced to watch executions."

Amy shivered again as she drew the cloth away from her face.
"I think I remember reading that, but I probably blocked it
out."

"Don't feel bad. You're a novice at this." He smiled cryptically. As smiles went, it would hardly light candles but for some

reason, it made her heart flip-flop. "Rinse," he ordered, the smile spreading.

Amy had almost forgotten the bottle in her hand. She glanced at it absently, then regarded him wide-eyed. The glass was a familiar amber. "Is that what I think it is?"

He grinned. "Good old American beer. It'll take that awful taste out of your mouth. Rinse, and then bottoms up. It's safer than the water." He held up his own bottle. "Cheers, Ms. Blake."

An hour later they drove into the center of town. It wasn't much by American standards, as it only boasted two hotels, a restaurant, a barbershop, a drugstore and a minisupermarket. To Amy, though, it represented a civilization—of sorts. She breathed a sigh of relief at having left behind the dry, yet thickly-brushed countryside that had brought them from the airport, but the relief soon evaporated as she remembered what Sam Crawford had said to her at the airport. *"If you're alone, the deal's off."*

Sooner or later, she had to broach the subject of his guiding her. She wasn't going to let him abandon her without a fight.

He brought the truck to a stop outside a small brick house. Wild red flowers as high as its windows brushed against the exterior. Since they were obviously at the home of Mercedes and Raoul Mendoza, she had to bring up the subject now.

He turned off the ignition, taking the words literally out of her mouth. "Well, we're here. I'll take you inside and introduce you to the Mendozas. After that, you're on your own."

Amy took a deep breath. He was back to being brash, she noted. Maybe she'd imagined he'd fallen off the wagon back there and actually imitated human behavior. In this heat anything was possible. "Mr. Crawford, we need to talk about that."

He gave a hoarse laugh, taking off his sunglasses to regard her with humorless eyes. "Nothing to talk about," he replied. "I don't guide single women, and that's that."

"But I've given you part payment in advance. What difference does it make? One person is likely easier to guide than two."

He fidgeted with a pack of cigarettes in his right hand, his look straightforward but glacial. "From your perspective, maybe. I'll return your advance, Ms. Blake, but to answer your question, two men are better than one on a trip like this. Usually, I count on the husband helping the wife while I keep to my guiding.''

Amy's eyes flashed. She was surprised at the emotion this man could trigger in her. Normally, she was mild-mannered to a fault. ''That's chauvinistic, Mr. Crawford. Men have been using that excuse to exclude women from all kinds of things from time immemorial. I refuse to be penalized by you for being a *woman alone*. You'd better have other reasons than that.''

Crawford's fingers stopped moving as his eyes turned deceptively sleepy on her. So the angel had a bite. Thorns and teeth. Risky assets in a woman.

Twisting his left hand around the wheel, he jerked the keys out and said evenly, ''I do.''

''Well, then, out with it.''

Crawford's head snapped up at her tone, their gazes clashing. ''For one thing, you're too small for this kind of trip.''

He watched while her eyes turned incredibly dark. He imagined them smouldering in another situation. Too bad, he thought, that of all the rules he did break, escorting single women wasn't one of them.

''Good grief, Mr. Crawford! If kids can climb up into those mountains, then so can I.''

Crawford dropped the cigarettes onto his lap and leaned his arm along the back of the cab. He'd never have thought a woman who was so gorgeous could be so annoying.

''That's not the same thing.''

''Well, *do* kids climb up into these mountains, Mr. Crawford?'' she pressed.

God help him. *''Yes.''*

''You see.''

He suppressed a frustrated sigh. He didn't see anything. He especially didn't see why a woman without a husband wanted to hike not just some mountains, but the Tackazan Mountains in order to adopt a child.

He shook his head with irritation. ''The army is everywhere, Ms. Blake, in case you hadn't noticed, and these days, it's more than a little jumpy,'' he commented with dry understatement.

Her stubborn gaze fastened on his. "You saved me once, you could save me again."

Crawford suppressed a sharp intake of breath, wondering if all the men in her life were that accommodating. Manfully, he resisted asking.

"Tell me, Ms. Blake, have you ever hiked?"

She shook her head.

"Done any climbing?"

She shook her head again.

No kidding, he thought.

"How about camping?"

"No—but back home, I ski and I walk five miles a day."

"And," he was continuing sardonically, "what if we get flooded out? Do you feel up to pushing my truck out of the mud or burrowing your way out of a landslide?"

She clamped her mouth in mutinous resolve. "I've researched what's ahead of us, Mr. Crawford. I know the rigors. I've brought all kinds of medication with me. The rest is up to you, to make sure we don't get stuck. So..." She angled herself sideways against the leather seat. "You said there were a number of reasons. Is that it? Are you finished trying to scare me off?"

"Not quite."

"Please, Mr. Crawford." She shot him a withering look. "Let me have it all."

"All right, Ms. Blake," he ground out, his hand clenching on the seat. "The main reason I don't like to escort women alone is that the last time I was such a cavalier, I ended up accused of, for want of a better description, unwelcome advances."

An excruciating silence fell as his comment lingered in the air between them. It crackled in the confined interior of the truck.

Amy felt a ripple of repulsion snake down her spine. The heat, the shoot-out at the airport, throwing up, the delayed shock had left her shaky. For a moment, she just wanted to get out of the truck and find somewhere fresh to clear her mind or to head back to Boston on the first air-conditioned flight.

But she wanted this child so desperately.

She glared at him. He had to be making this story up, to frighten her.

She took a deep, strained breath, determined to be reasonable even if it killed her. The man could try a saint. "Mr. Crawford, I am not of the school that automatically believes all women are innocent and all men are guilty, by virtue of their sex, so let's just clear the air, shall we?" She raised her gaze to his. A brooding challenge glistened in his. She spoke slowly, "Were you guilty, Mr. Crawford?"

His jaw set into a hard line. "No."

The coil inside her stomach started to relax. "And did the courts agree?"

"The lady changed her mind and dropped the charge."

Her lashes flickered, mirroring her relief. "Then that's that, isn't it?"

Crawford raised his brows in skepticism. Nothing in life, he'd discovered, was that easily resolved. But for the time being, he let it pass.

"Walking the picturesque streets of Boston hardly equates to trekking through this godforsaken country."

Amy's eyes danced fire at him. "Mr. Crawford, get real."

His right hand knuckled white with aggravation as he sensed that somehow if he wasn't exactly losing the arguments, he was losing some kind of ground. He'd never reacted well to nagging. His response was usually to walk away. For some unknown, ridiculous subconscious reason, he was letting this woman keep him on the hook.

His scowl darkened. He supposed he could always remind her of the fact that she'd thrown up all over the countryside after seeing what had happened at the airport. But he would have expected that of any civilian, and in truth, it was beneath him to bring it up.

But only just, he thought.

He frowned, barely capping his temper at his self-imposed nobility.

"Do you have any idea what's *really* ahead of us? Mountains with changing elevations that can flatten you. Impossible terrain, debilitating heat. You're bound to lose ten pounds in a question of days, and you don't look like you're carrying any extra to spare...."

Amy only just kept a lid on her temper as his gaze traveled insolently over her. It didn't look as though he had missed any virtue or flaw.

"Mr. Crawford, don't insult my intelligence," she said, glaring at him.

With a forced shrug, he said, "I'm not."

He ran a hand through his hair. "I still don't want to escort you into the mountains, Ms. Blake, your show of confidence notwithstanding." His mouth twisted into a cryptic smile as he bowed his head and looked up at her from under dark lashes. "This is a hard trip. It's hard even for me. I don't honestly think you can handle it, no insult intended. I wouldn't want to see you get hurt."

Amy stared at him thoughtfully, noticing the cryptic smile did not extend to his gaze. *It* was hooded, dark, unfathomable. Maybe he was genuinely concerned for her safety. The social worker hadn't said Crawford was careless or cruel. Suddenly, her curiosity was piqued again. What went into the making of a Sam Crawford? The man couldn't have been born abrasive!

She said very distinctly. "If you don't guide me, I'll get someone else to do it. Look, Mr. Crawford, I know I'm not the big, powerful Amazon you'd prefer—I'm small but I'm tough. I can handle this. If I didn't think I could I wouldn't have come. Furthermore, the very reason I'm hiring you is so that you can compensate for all my supposed shortcomings. You've got the brawn and the expertise, and—" she smiled wryly "—the arrogance to pull this off. If I could do it alone, I wouldn't need you, Mr. Crawford, don't you see?"

He regarded her with a measure of respect. The woman never gave up, he had to grant her that. Whatever she wanted, she went after with a passion. He thought about the other guides that Marita had to offer and felt queasy. None of them were savory by any stretch of imagination. They'd take one look at her money and those glorious eyes and . . .

He took a ragged breath, knowing the outcome.

She could kiss both her virtue and her money good-bye.

"Aren't you afraid that I might jump you in the middle of the night?" he asked in a sarcastic voice, not prepared to give in too easily.

She regarded him with mock sweetness, "Why on earth would you do that, Mr. Crawford? If you need a woman so badly, I'll increase your fee so that you can take care of those physical needs before we leave. I'd hate for you to go with-out."

Temper immediately flared in Crawford's eyes. "I beg your pardon," he said incredulously.

A wisp of a smile curved at the edges of her mouth. For once, she thought, she'd gotten under his skin. Serves him right. "Sorry, I guess that was a little out of line—"

"Way out of line," he interrupted, his jaw clenching. This woman exasperated the hell out of him, yet in some private corner of his mind, he realized that was in part because he was attracted to her cool, feminine beauty.

This was ridiculous. He ought to back out now while he had a chance. He blew out a heavy sigh. For some reason, he had a feeling it was too late and he'd blown all his chances.

She flicked back a strand of dark hair. "You had it coming, Mr. Crawford, with your macho posturing. I was just trying to loosen this conversation up. I've had a couple of shocks too many for one day. My father taught me that sometimes humor helps in tense situations."

"I don't approach sex with any kind of humor, Ms. Blake," he snapped.

Amy's eyes shadowed with brief amusement. "No, Mr. Crawford, I would imagine you don't."

What exactly she meant by that, he wasn't about to pursue. The topic was a bit too sensitive to him at the moment to risk discussion.

He jammed his hand on the steering wheel. "Look, could we get off the topic of my sex life?"

Amy leaned forward and touched her fingers to his bare arm. He almost jumped at the jolt that shot through him.

All traces of humor had left her face. "Mr. Crawford, it's to you I am entrusting my life and the life of the child I've come here to adopt. I can't afford to spend time worrying about anything else other than those two things, and I certainly don't expect you to have designs on me. Frankly, the thought hadn't even occurred to me. So which is it—yes or no?"

Crawford debated with himself, sensing he'd live to regret his decision. She was beautiful and elegant and terribly tempting, although she was too calm and persistent for his liking. He preferred his women far less talkative, but he'd been without her kind of woman for so long that even just looking at her caused a sharp need inside him. She conjured images of soft sheets and whispery fabric against bare skin. She made him homesick for the country he'd left ten years before. She made him think of apple pie. She made him think of ball games. She made him think of sex in the afternoon.

She made him want her.

Right here and now.

Damn.

He inhaled a dry, dusty breath, his throat aggravated by the cigarette he was smoking.

All of the above, he reasoned irritably, he could likely live with but she also made him want to prove her wrong. She'd never go the distance. Not in a million years, but if he were paid, what difference would it make to him? He did, after all, need the money. He always needed money.

He ringed an exhalation of smoke. Who knew, maybe she'd turn out to be a real mountain goat and prove *him* wrong. In a way, maybe he'd even prefer that if it gave her what she wanted. She seemed to want it badly enough. Although why the hell she should, he couldn't fathom. Cantankerously, he felt it might give him some satisfaction to help her get it.

Human nature, he thought with disgust. It was always unpredictable.

He shrugged. "You win."

Her face broke into a smile. "Wonderful."

"Yeah, right." He caught the brilliance of her smile and swallowed a groan. He *was* going to regret this. He did already. His eyebrows drew together. "By the way—are you a lawyer, by any chance? I feel like I just got off the witness stand."

She laughed. "No, but my father is."

Crawford shook his head, shuddering.

"Like father, like daughter."

Her laughter turned to a chuckle. "My father would enjoy the comment, Mr. Crawford. He always wanted me to follow in his footsteps, but I'm afraid I let him down. I just own a small flower shop."

Crawford tossed his dying cigarette into the truck's ashtray, and drew in a sobering breath. He for one was glad she'd decided to stay out of courtrooms.

Refocusing, he turned toward her.

"So—you've got all the papers?"

Amy nodded, relieved. One hurdle overcome. She began rummaging in her purse. "Right here."

"That's okay," he said, waving her offer aside. "I don't need to see them. Where's the child now?"

Amy pulled her fingers out of the bag, "In the mountains, that's all I know. Mrs. Cordova said she'd tell me exactly where when I see her."

He nodded, recognizing the name of the lawyer who handled foreign adoptions and approving of Amy's choice. In his opinion, Giselda was the only game in town *he'd* trust. Other agents weren't nearly as reliable. Since Marita had opened its doors to foreign adoptions, a proliferation of fly-by-night entrepreneurs had emerged, their only interest a fast buck. Children for dollars, he thought with disdain.

"When's that happening?"

"She said to drop in any time tomorrow. Apparently she's in court all of today."

At least twenty-four hours gave him a chance to get some perspective on how Amy Blake made him feel. Maybe by tomorrow, he'd have it and himself all under control. He closed his eyes in brief, distracted reflection. He certainly hoped so. For both their sakes.

His head throbbed as he forced his eyes open. Even with her safely pressed against the passenger door, he felt she was too close for comfort. He valiantly tried not to think of sleeping bags, and the forced proximity facing them.

"Okay, then, let's get this show on the road. I'll introduce you to the Mendozas, then I'll go stock up." Thinking ahead or as much as he wanted to, he paused, shaking his head again. "This is a real act of faith you're embarking on, Ms. Blake."

Amy pushed the heavy bag back as far on her shoulder as it would go.

"Life itself is an act of faith, Mr. Crawford—haven't you noticed?"

Amy drew in a deep breath.

The Mendozas' house was divinely and surprisingly cool, the shade from the outside trees offering precious relief from the beating sun. She stepped inside, grateful to be out of the glare.

A beaming Mercedes and Raoul greeted them the moment Sam escorted her into the foyer of the house. Sam barely got out the introductions before Amy was whisked into the center of the hall by the Spanish woman.

"Señora Blake...welcome..."

Mercedes stopped in front of Amy, her hands reaching up to touch Amy on the cheek. Then, a string of rapid-fire Spanish erupted from her mouth as she directed her comments to Sam. Holding on to Amy's arm, she continued her elaborate one-way conversation for a full minute before her husband interrupted with a laugh.

"Mercedes, please, let them get in the door, first." Raoul held up a hand to Mercedes. Amy got the impression he was long-practiced at the gesture. Turning toward Amy, he grinned. "Please forgive my wife, she is big talker."

Amy smiled spontaneously, instantly liking the Mendozas. They were a handsome couple, dark and dramatic-looking, their heritage clearly evident in their flashing eyes, strong features and thick black hair. She judged they were in their mid-thirties, but their charm seemed classically ageless.

Laughing in a soft voice, she said, "Believe me, it's nice to get such attention, but I'm afraid I don't know any more than five or six words in Spanish. What did your wife say?" she asked curiously.

Before Raoul could respond, Crawford cut in, loosely translating. "She said you were lovely."

Amy twisted toward him sharply. She didn't trust the bland expression on his face. "Really?"

Crawford shrugged blithely, ignoring the barely veiled provocation in her tone. He wasn't about to translate Mercedes's lecture that he should find an American wife just like Amy and stop supporting the local professionals.

Not that he did or ever had, but on principle he never argued the point.

Deliberately, he kept a straight face. "It's an effusive language."

Amy raised her eyebrows dubiously. She doubted it was *that* effusive.

Taking a frustrated breath, she turned her attention back to the Mendozas.

"It's very kind of you to let me stay with you," she told the couple in a husky voice. "I'm sure this will be much nicer than a hotel."

Mercedes grabbed her hand in a proprietary fashion. Amy had a feeling she'd been adopted by the other woman. "You have biggest room—front of house—huge bed for you and your husband—" she waved her hands expansively "—made for a king ... my husband buy in America ... maybe you make your own child while you're here...." She teased with sparkling eyes.

Amy flinched, stupidly embarrassed. Suddenly somehow, she felt as if she had committed a sin by being single.

"I'm afraid I'm not married, Mercedes," she said in a strained voice.

The other woman's eyes widened in amazement. "But..." Her confused gaze shifted between Amy and Crawford, then she again rattled off a string of Spanish. Just as rapidly, Crawford replied.

Amy frowned at Crawford. God only knew what he'd dreamed up.

"Dare I ask what you just said?"

He smiled cockily. Obviously his earlier translation or lack of it had left her suspicious. Score one for perception, he thought.

His smile turned into a grin. "Relax. I merely told her that it was a long, sad story, and you didn't want to discuss it."

A long, sad story.

Amy felt as if the air had been sucked out of her lungs. How could he have known to hit so close to the truth? Her legs felt weak beneath her. Her sudden reaction didn't surprise her because buried pain was like that, she'd discovered. Without warning, a small comment, a picture of a place, an aroma, anything, could trigger the memory that caused the pain. Her doctor's words—"I'm sorry, Mrs. Latimer, but because of the accident, you'll never be able to conceive again"—feathered through her brain.

She blinked quickly as she pulled herself together. "I see. Thank you."

Crawford lifted an eyebrow when the expected rejoinder didn't come. He'd only known the woman an hour or so, but in that space of time, he'd learned she was rarely at a loss for words, roadside nausea excepted. So, he'd hit a raw nerve.

"Sorry. Did I say something wrong?"

"No." She shook her head emphatically. "Not at all."

He saw that whatever had upset her, she'd managed to control it in short order. His gaze narrowed in admiration. He liked a man or woman who could bounce back quickly. Whiners had never been his cup of tea. Score two, for resilience, he thought.

So far, he conceded reluctantly, the lady's balance sheet wasn't doing too badly.

He grinned at her. "Good. I hate to upset a client."

"*Señorita,*" Mercedes interrupted, "is not our business...come, please, you must be tired, I show you your room."

Turning, Amy smiled thankfully at the other woman. The pain blessedly was subsiding. "Thank you. I'd like to freshen up and rest a bit if you don't mind."

Mercedes immediately sprang into action. "Raoul?" Imperiously, she directed her husband toward the one carryall Amy had managed to retrieve from the airport. "I give you a tour first," she told Amy. "Then later we all have dinner. I fix something nice."

Amy nodded as Mercedes directed her up the stairs. She wondered if the "all" included Sam Crawford. She moistened her lower lip nervously. She was going to practically be living with the man for the next few weeks. What was one more dinner?

For some reason, the thought didn't calm her nerves.

She shook her head, suppressing a quick surge of panic. Sam Crawford reminded her of an untamed jungle animal. Big, tough, swaggering. She imagined he'd be insolent in the face of danger. Not a man she'd ever care to spend time with under normal circumstances. But these weren't normal circumstances.

She shivered. Somehow she felt at cross-purposes with herself where he was concerned. She needed him desperately, but she wished he'd disappear.

She straightened her spine. All that notwithstanding, a twinge of more than politeness dictated that she say something to him. He had, after all, saved her life—although that, she suspected, was due more to his caveman instincts than to any concern for her. Reaching for the banister, she turned toward him and said stiffly, "Thanks...for everything."

He shrugged his large shoulders, obviously ready to leave. "No problem. Will you be okay for a while? I've got a few things to do."

She nodded as he rammed a pair of sunglasses over his eyes, masking their incredible blue. Without the saving grace of his changeable gaze, he looked altogether hard and ruthless. Out of reach. Yet the aloofness added to his appeal, and she felt an unusual lurch in her stomach.

"Sure."

A rueful smile played at the corners of his mouth as if he'd been aware of all the crazy things she'd just been thinking. "By the way, if it's any consolation to you, Mercedes isn't crazy about the fact that I'm single, either." Turning like a big cat, he headed for the front door.

A second later he was gone.

Hearing Mercedes close the door behind her, Amy resisted the urge to cave in on the spot. And the tour of the house had only taken a few minutes. Compact and fairly Spartan, consisting of four bedrooms and a communal washroom, it nevertheless gleamed with cleanliness and smelled not just of pine-scented soap but also of something deliciously like a stew. Obviously Mercedes had started cooking the evening meal early.

She glanced around the room Mercedes had given her. An oak wardrobe and one small chest shared space with a bed that was, as the Spanish woman had said, indeed king-size. A rag rug in soft hues of blue, white counterpane, and lace curtains gave the room an overall sense of airiness.

Dropping her purse and carryall on the bed, she walked toward the window overlooking the street and pulled aside the lace curtains.

Past the dusty, old-fashioned streets, she could see the world-famous Tackazan Mountains soaring like magnificent sculptures of slate. Piercing the brilliant sky with their peaks, they nudged under banks of clouds. She had heard that they were dazzling. And they were.

She inhaled deeply. So, this was the city of Santa Clara in Marita, the country of her father's fond memories.

She blew her dark hair out of her eyes and flexed her leg and back muscles, aching from the flight. Since the car accident, sitting wasn't very comfortable, and the events of the past twenty-four hours were finally catching up with her.

Tearing her gaze away from the mountains, she looked down to the street, seeing the ever-present heavily armed soldiers leaning against doorways and patrolling. She repressed a shudder as she recalled the soldiers in combat gear at the airport and the woman's screams. She'd been lucky, she now realized, that a stray bullet hadn't found her. If it hadn't been for Sam Crawford . . .

She shivered.

A child was waiting for her here. A child to fill her empty arms . . . her *very* empty arms, she amended with glistening eyes. For a brief moment, she thought of the other child she'd never seen, never held . . . of the children she could never bear and of the husband who hadn't cared.

Pain sliced through her. You have to move on, she told herself sharply. Nothing can bring back the past. Think of the future and what you have to do.

What she had to do, she thought, was get to the tiny, waiting baby that she'd negotiated for, for so long and so hard and with such fervor.

She ran a hand down the side of her neck. It was going to be no mean feat, she knew.

With a shake of her head, she pushed the recurring negative thoughts aside. She had to make it. And she was going to. Her dream wouldn't let her give up. But she knew she couldn't do it alone.

Her eyelashes flickered pensively. Thank God that she wasn't alone and that she had Sam Crawford.

If anyone could get her up into the mountains, past stragglers of the vanquished army, over hundreds of miles of rough roads and through primitive, possibly unfriendly towns, it was Sam Crawford.

She might not like the man, but she certainly had no doubts about his competence. None of the information she'd collected on him had cast any of those kinds of doubts, either, although creating a file on him hadn't been easy. . . .

She shut her eyes tiredly, thinking of what she'd learned about the man with whom she was entrusting her life. The private investigator she'd hired found Crawford was one of those people who was well known, without much actually being known about him. He was thirty-eight or forty-two, depending on which source one wanted to believe. He was what was euphemistically called a "soldier of fortune," but as far as she could tell, Sam Crawford wasn't making a fortune. Not according to his last income tax statement filed with the IRS.

She'd learned that in the past fifteen years, he'd only set foot in his native United States once, and that was to undergo surgery for the removal of three pieces of shrapnel in his body. He hadn't waited for the full ten-day healing period before he'd disappeared again, this time to Marita.

As a young man, he'd been recruited from Yale to work in intelligence. She hadn't been able to find any documentation on him for the following five years, so she assumed he'd gone undercover. Then he'd reemerged as an intelligence adviser to a number of Fortune 500 companies whose activites spanned the globe. But then something . . . what? she puzzled over . . . had happened to abruptly take him away from the corporate world and back into the field. One source said he was married. But her private investigator hadn't been able to track down a marriage certificate. Crawford, though, had to be smart and ruthless to work in intelligence. She had to give him that.

Her expression turned thoughtful. Of course, there was always an intangible quality that couldn't be captured in statistics or written up in reports. That something about Sam Crawford made her physically on edge. She recognized it for what it ridiculously was—an attraction. How? Why? she wondered. He wasn't the kind of man who usually interested her. He was too much of a primitive. Too rough-and-ready. She liked her men with a little more polish and reserve. She opened her eyes, squinting as sunlight burned her eyes, trying to block out the memory of his body pressed against hers as he'd dived to protect her. Sinewy, hard, stirring, like no other body she had ever felt. . . .

She walked away from the window and back toward the bed, still lost in thought. She'd done her homework on him, and now she had to let him do his job. It was difficult, though, not to wonder just what he was really like. She was going to have to spend a week alone with him, traveling up into the mountains. The isolation, the physical rigors and the dangers were daunting enough. Although she had hidden her reaction to Crawford, she had been surprised about the morals charge, but she had been even more surprised that he'd volunteered the information. His admission had surprisingly given her a measure of confidence. Obviously, the man had some kind of ethics.

Determinedly, she shook the other reservations aside. Sam Crawford was supposed to be the best—the best at maneuvering a reluctant bureaucracy, the best at winning the confidence of people living in the villages, the best at knowing when to play bluff poker and when to play for real and . . . the best at winning.

"Buy quality, sweetheart. It's cheaper in the long run. Don't be afraid to pay the price." Her father's words rang in her ear.

On the one hand, she recognized that as a woman, she didn't feel the least bit safe with Crawford, yet on the other, she felt totally safe. It was all that modern-day warrior stuff, she supposed.

She sighed. What price would she finally end up paying for Sam Crawford's help? Life had a nasty habit of costing, and she worried that this time she'd pay far more than she'd anticipated. But if she had to put up with him, she would, she thought resolutely.

She exhaled a ragged breath, fisting her fingers around the toothbrush she'd been looking for. Sam Crawford might not like it, but he was stuck with her. A child was waiting for her here. Her child. If it nearly killed her, she was going to do this.

No matter what the price.

Chapter 3

This he could do without, Crawford thought contrarily. He drew in a breath of heavy air as he got into his truck and turned the key in the ignition.

Why hadn't Amy Blake stayed at home?

Women that looked as good as she did and possessed such willpower, such blindsided purpose usually spelled trouble for a man.

He steered the truck into a U-turn, frowning. That persistence of hers suggested that beneath it burned a passionately tender woman. Under any other circumstances, he'd bet his last dollar to test the theory. And possibly his last nickel.

She sure looked the part with those burning eyes of hers. And nobody willingly traveled the Tackazan Mountains without being driven by something. He shook his head in confusion. He understood childless couples going to any lengths to adopt. He didn't understand a single woman doing it. He didn't object, not in this day and age, he just didn't understand.

Mind you, he thought, he admired her for whatever conviction was behind her decision. She obviously made up her mind and stuck to it, through hell and high water. After the subtleties of intelligence work, of which he'd had more than enough, he appreciated that kind of approach to life. And after the complexities of revolution, he also admired the simplicity of purpose. Although he doubted that Amy Blake was simplicity personified. He'd never met a woman worth her salt who was simple. His ex-wife had taught him that lesson in five harrowing years of marriage.

It'd be interesting to unravel the mystery of Amy Blake and find out where that hint of passion led him.

Too bad he couldn't.

He closed his eyes as he came to a stop sign, suddenly tired.

He didn't trust women, he reminded himself bitterly. Or the look in their eyes. That too was a legacy from his wife. Corruption in high places and a faithless woman were the reasons he was here in the first place.

The first he never forgot; the second he would have a hard time remembering.

Anyway, Amy Blake was a forever kind of a lady and he was a rolling stone. Too late for the leopard to change his spots.

He squinted against the bright sunlight as his thoughts spiraled inward. Maybe he should have retired after the revolution. He remembered having considered it after the Maritan revolution, but he also remembered why he hadn't. What else could he do that didn't involve his being in a straitjacket of some kind or another? Hadn't he tried intelligence, thinking it would keep his restless energy and fertile imagination gainfully occupied? And hadn't that been okay for a while until he'd become disenchanted? And how different had being a suit for the corporate world been, anyway? The objectives might have been different, but the careless disregard for human life hadn't been.

So, for ten years, when he hadn't been fighting bad guys of some sort or another, this is what he had done. Not a great life, he'd be the first to admit, but a lot better than returning to the kind of world Amy Blake came from.

He shook his head realizing how ironic it was that he, who had strove so hard to have a normal life and lost, should now be so involved in helping other people find a child to love to complete their family. He'd likely never hold his own child in his arms, yet he helped other people to do just that. It was a true jest of the gods.

He inhaled a gulp of heavy, sultry air.

Now the question was whether he could handle the risks of taking another single woman up into the mountains. Sounds like a hit tune, he thought, as the supply store came into view.

He pulled easily into a parking space outside the store. Marita wasn't overcrowded with vehicles. Parking was never difficult.

Turning the ignition off, he reached into his pocket to pull out his checklist of supplies as he mulled over his choices. Something disturbed him about Amy Blake. What was it?

He scowled, stretching. As if he didn't know. Chemistry. The woman appealed to him, and so temporarily, he couldn't let her go. He guessed it was fate. Men were forever tempting themselves that way.

Getting out of the truck, he stepped onto the veranda of the store.

Maybe he shouldn't get involved in this.

He pushed open the door with a bang.

The proprietor looked up, anger flashing in his eyes as he prepared to give whoever had walked through the door a lecture on noise control, but the anger dissolved as he recognized his favorite client. A wide smile spread across his face.

"Crawford, you old bag of worms. The usual?"

Crawford nodded abruptly. "Yeah...and make it quick. I'm running on empty."

"When aren't you running on empty, Crawford?" was the reply.

Amy felt better after brushing her teeth and taking a sponge bath, but there was the problem of her abandoned clothes, she realized, frowning. She glanced at herself in the mirror. All she had was what was on her back. The sundress would hardly be enough for three weeks, not to mention the fact that she would need underwear, as well.

She wondered if Mercedes could direct her to a store. There must be some place where she could buy a few comfortable items that would see her through the trip. It was worth a shot.

Heading down the stairs, she suddenly remembered that Sam Crawford had said he lived here, too. Somehow the small, neat house seemed too tiny and confining to contain his kind of suppressed energy. Like caging a lion, she thought. Which was his room? Safely distanced from hers, she hoped. She gave herself a mental shake. She was becoming far too curious about Sam Crawford for her own comfort, she told herself soberly.

She ran her hand along the banister rail with appreciation. The wood fairly glowed. Halfway down the stairs, she heard the doorbell ring, and seeing Mercedes make her way to the door, she smiled. The woman was a bustling streak of energy. "You must be working all the time, Mercedes," she complimented as she reached the bottom step. "Your house is beautiful."

"Sí," Mercedes laughed, nodding, her hand on the knob. "A woman's work is never..." Her words halted as she opened the door.

Amy immediately sensed her surprise.

She looked beyond Mercedes and paused, too, as she saw a tall man framed in the entrance. Automatically, she tensed as she recognized an army uniform.

"General Garcia," Mercedes acknowledged.

The tall man smiled graciously. *"Buenos días,* Mercedes." Stepping inside without an invitation, he paused just past the threshold and looked down at the diminutive woman. "I'd like to have a word with your guest if you don't mind."

Mercedes moved aside slowly, wiping her hands on her apron self-consciously. *"Sí..."* Turning, she led the man into the house and with hooded eyes introduced him to Amy.

"Señorita Blake, this is General Garcia of the People's Army," she said hurriedly.

Amy instantly knew who he was from his name. He was one of the three-man junta now running the country. The man stopped in front of her and Amy looked up into a pair of piercing black eyes that crinkled slightly at the corners. About thirty-eight years old, Garcia was meticulously turned out, trim with not one ounce of fat beneath a navy braided uniform. His mouth wore a practiced smile, but she sensed that he was deadly dangerous. Clever, too, she suspected, as she saw intelligence burning behind his eyes.

She extended her hand with polite wariness. "General Garcia."

He gripped her hand firmly in response, bowing his head. "Señorita Blake, welcome to Santa Clara and Marita." Straightening up, he said in polite, precise English. "I wonder if I could have a few moments of your time."

Her temples started to pound with nervousness. All her papers were in order, she thought frantically. What could this be about? A horrible, sinking suspicion bottomed out in her stomach. She forced herself to regard him calmly. "Of course."

"Good." His white-toothed smile was even. "Thank you, Mercedes," he said to the Spanish woman. "I'd like to be alone with Señorita Blake, if you don't mind." Even though it came out like the gentlest of requests there was no doubt that he had given an order.

Mercedes nodded and with reluctance walked toward the back of the house. At the doorway, she paused, a worried look on her face.

The general nodded reassuringly at her, laughing in a low voice. "It's all right, Mercedes. There's nothing to be concerned about." She raised her eyebrows resignedly and slowly disappeared.

Amy took a deep breath, facing the general squarely, even though her heart was beating a wild rhythm. She wondered where Crawford was. All of a sudden, she'd give anything to be able to lean on him. Accepting the presence of the army philosophically was one thing. Dealing with the reality was another. She suddenly felt bombarded with too much reality. Crawford, where are you?

As best as she could, she hid her nervousness from Garcia. "What can I do for you, General?"

Garcia hooked a thumb into his belt, his gaze wandering over her in leisurely fashion. "Did you have a good trip, Señorita Blake?"

She nodded uncomfortably, feeling a trickle of sweat spiral down her spine. The man's eyes made her feel as if she were squirming under a microscope.

"Yes, thank you."

His gaze moved upward probing hers. "I understand you are here alone."

"Not quite, Garcia. The lady's with me."

Crawford's voice drifted toward them, starting like a growl and turning to a purr. Whirling with heartfelt gratitude, Amy saw him glide into the foyer from the kitchen. She swallowed back a sigh of relief. His bulk and style might irritate her, but there was no denying the feelings of safety and confidence they also generated in her.

Garcia also turned. "Ahh...Crawford." The general's eyes narrowed. "The lady usually *is* with you, I'm afraid." He shook his head in mock exasperation. "I've often wondered what it is exactly that they see in you. I myself have never been able to fathom it."

Crawford grinned. "Good old American charm, Garcia. Works every time."

Garcia snorted delicately. "You and charm. To my way of thinking, that's a contradiction in terms."

Crawford smiled wryly, drawing closer and putting his arm around Amy's shoulders protectively. She stiffened at the gesture, surprised that her pulse instantly jumped like a jackrabbit's. "You never did think too straight, Garcia, but I'm sure you didn't come here to discuss my charm. What's this about?"

Garcia waved with elaborate carelessness, but his eyes remained alert and hard. "Merely routine, Crawford. I was only checking on the reason for Señorita Blake's visit to our beautiful country. It would appear I missed her at the airport," he finished ironically.

Crawford's eyes met Garcia's head-on. "The airport was a little busy for our tastes, General."

Regret, real or fake, shone in Garcia's eyes. "So I gathered, but as you can see, *señorita*—" he offered as he slanted his gaze toward her "—we here in Marita can be very accommodating. Since I couldn't make contact with you at the airport, I have come here to see you."

Amy nodded in acknowledgment of whatever he'd intended. If there was a game to be played here, she'd play it...carefully. "Thank you," she murmured in a soft voice.

"Look, Garcia," Crawford interrupted with impervious disregard for caution. "Get on with it, will you?"

Garcia's eyes glittered. Amy could see the man was trying to keep his temper under control. As a general in the revolutionary army, she imagined he was rarely if ever challenged. Was Crawford mad? she wondered. She shot him a furious look, which he blithely ignored.

The general smiled tightly, feigning a frown. "Such charm...but...such impatience, Crawford. Señorita Blake and I had barely started our conversation when you came on the scene. If you will permit me—" he bowed mockingly "—I have some questions for her."

"All right—go ahead," Crawford replied arrogantly, dropping his hand from her shoulders and moving aside a few steps. With languid ease, he crossed his arms and leaned against the banister, regarding Amy and Garcia like judge and jury. "But make it snappy."

Amy's jaw muscles tensed as she glared at him. She could have gladly throttled him. Her safety zone was diminishing at an alarming rate. He was going to get them both killed.

"*Thank you.*" Garcia's voice dripped with ice.

"Please, General," Amy said. "What do you want to know?"

He inclined his head as if understanding that temporarily she was on his side. "I merely wondered, *señorita,* what is the reason for your visit?"

She replied in an even tone. "I've come to adopt a child. I have all the papers if you'd like to see them."

He waved his hand a number of times, slowly. "No, that won't be necessary for the time being. But . . ." He paused, fixing his eyes on hers intently. "You are not married, are you, Señorita Blake?"

She fought back a rising flush, aware that Crawford's interest had suddenly also increased. "No, that's correct."

Garcia regarded her, his chiseled features sharpening more. "That's somewhat unusual, wouldn't you say? Now, I have to wonder why would a single woman be in the market for a baby? Especially here?"

Amy opened her mouth to speak, but Crawford cut the words off before she had a chance to say them.

Stepping forward, he unfolded his arms, a scowl on his face. "She's an American and free to do as she pleases within the law, Garcia. None of this is any of your damn business."

Garcia shot him a warning look. "Careful, Crawford, before I throw you into one of our luxurious jails."

"Give me a break, Garcia. I fought on *your* side, remember?"

Garcia's eyes darkened. "I remember only too well, Crawford, just as I also remember that you are a soldier of fortune. Your loyalty is something people buy with money. That hardly fills me with much respect. Now, please—let me do my job."

Amy glanced between the two men, getting annoyed with both of them for their macho one-upmanship. But she had to remain calm, she knew. "Please, obviously none of us are enjoying this. I'm willing to answer your questions, General. Mr. Crawford is merely being overly protective."

Crawford looked prepared to dispute that in no uncertain terms, but she silenced him with a pointed, murderous look. He shrugged and moved back to his position against the railing. Amy let out a frustrated sigh. "Continue, General, if you don't mind."

"Your father is Trevor Blake?" Garcia asked mildly.

She nodded. "That's correct."

"And what does he do for a living, Señorita Blake?"

Amy hesitated. He knows, she thought suddenly. He knows who my father is, and he wants to see if I'll tell him the truth.

"He's a lawyer," Crawford snapped.

This time, Garcia almost seemed pleased that Crawford had interrupted. Turning toward the other man, a slow smile spread across his face. "He is also a senator and chairman of the Committee on U.S. and Maritan Affairs—were you aware of that, Crawford?"

Crawford couldn't stop an instant look of surprise from flitting across his face.

"Ahh . . ." Garcia said with satisfaction. "I see you did not know and are startled by the information."

He wasn't startled, Crawford thought, he was furious. He made a mental note to himself to wipe the floor with Amy Blake for withholding not only vital, but dangerous information.

He squashed his anger in front of the general. "On the contrary," he replied with lazy sarcasm. "I'm not surprised by the news, I'm just surprised that your intelligence is aware of the fact. I hadn't realized it was capable of anything that sophisticated."

"But what difference does it make what my father does for a living?" Amy interrupted in a quick voice.

Garcia redirected his gaze at her. "Forgive me, *señorita*, but surely you cannot be a senator's daughter and be so naive as to think that you would not be noticed in a place like Marita?"

She had thought of it. She'd thought about it before she'd sent in her application, she'd thought about it all through the waiting period for approval and she'd thought about it on the plane, but she'd been trying to ignore the implications.

"I hadn't placed undue emphasis on the fact, General," she said carefully. "I try to stay out of politics."

Garcia stared at her with probing eyes. "Agents from a number of countries appear to be suddenly interested in our activities. Were the shoe on the other foot, would it not strike you as strange that such a man's daughter, who is single, should suddenly come to Marita for the purpose of adopting a child? On the surface, I'm sure you'll grant me that such action is suspicious, particularly to the new Maritan government whose relationship with the U.S. is as yet . . . undecided."

Crawford frowned. He had been thinking exactly the same thing but he wasn't about to let the good General know that.

"Get with it, Garcia," he growled, before Amy could respond. "Were she married, it would be an excellent cover for the gathering of information and were her father not who he is, a superb cover. But seeing as how the lady is single, CIA or whoever does that kind of dirty work these days would hardly pick someone whose cover had such holes in it."

Amy's heart started to pound at this turn of events. She had hoped that her father's position would not be a factor in her treatment here. Obviously, she'd been wrong. "I'm not a spy, if that's what you're thinking," she protested.

His bomb dropped, Garcia shrugged, absently adjusting the buckle on his belt. "You may well not be, *señorita,* and Crawford here might for once possess some logic that makes sense. However, Marita is not stable at the moment, and the army cannot afford to take any chances. Tomorrow, I will take a look at your papers, and if I decide that you are indeed telling the truth, then you can be about your business. But until then, you are to do nothing." His hard expression was intractable.

Incredulous, she returned his look, while Crawford swore under his breath.

"You mean I'm confined to quarters?" she whispered.

"A quaint expression, *señorita,* but no, of course not. You are free to roam the center of the town at will. Please, enjoy it. The sunrise and sunset in Marita are magnificent." He waved with expansive graciousness. "And tomorrow morning, you will have breakfast with me. While you are here, I would like to show you that *Maritan* men also possess a certain kind of charm." He glanced over at Crawford, his mouth twisting into an ironic smile. Sam rewarded him with a murderous glare.

Laughing softly, Garcia offered Amy a different kind of smile. One filled with a sudden, sad appreciation. "My driver will bring the car around at seven o'clock sharp. Please be ready, Señorita Blake, and bring your papers with you. It will be a most amicable breakfast, I assure you."

Bowing, he turned and crossed the foyer with smooth grace. He paused, his body angled sideways as a guard opened the door. Ignoring the man who held the door ajar, he inclined his head to Crawford, saying in a low voice, "By the way, Crawford, my instructions also apply to you. No disappearing into the mountains, if you don't mind. I would be most pained to hear you had done that."

Nodding curtly to the guards, he disappeared through the open door.

Crawford exploded. "What's going on here?"

Amy stood frozen to the spot, her limbs trembling. All she wanted to do was adopt a child that nobody else in the whole world wanted. Why did politics have to enter into it? Before her mind could conjure even a reasonable explanation, Crawford grabbed her. "I ought to have you horsewhipped," he snarled, dragging her out of the foyer toward the kitchen.

Amy snapped out of her dazed state, pride rising to the surface.

"Stop that! What do you think you're doing?"

"Getting you the hell out of here, sweetheart. You and I are going to have a talk."

Amy wanted to scream as he forcefully guided her into Mercedes's domain. The Maritan woman looked up in confusion and disapproval as she saw Sam pushing Amy past the stove toward the back door. She did not condone fighting in her well-run home. "Señor Crawford—"

"It's all right, Mercedes," he answered in a surprisingly even voice. "Señorita Blake and I have some things to work out. Don't worry."

Holding the door open with one hand and still holding Amy with the other, he shoved her outside.

Hot, dry air attacked her lungs. She closed her eyes in reflex. She was going to cut him into small pieces and deliver them back to Garcia! Nothing would bring her greater pleasure.

Crawford spun her around so that they were standing facing each other, his ice-blue eyes merging with her furious green ones as he tilted her head upward to look at him. "Lady," he snarled. "You owe me an explanation."

Amy found she was more than ready for him. "You show-off, *you* owe *me* one. Were you trying to get us executed back there?"

"Me?" Crawford's eyebrows lifted into a dark V. He tried to ignore the fact that her cool beauty turned into something hot and smoldering with her anger. "Are you crazy? You're the one who just about landed us in front of a firing squad."

Amy gave him a scathing look. "And to think I actually felt safe when you first arrived on the scene," she said, her voice dripping with sarcasm.

Crawford struggled to keep his fists from clenching and un-clenching. Hadn't she any idea how scared he'd been for her when he'd seen Garcia's car parked outside the Mendozas'? His heart was still in his throat. The thought of her in one of Marita's jails had made his stomach churn.

He shuddered, his gaze slitting defensively to a searing blue line of fury.

He knew he should have stayed away from her.

"That was the whole point, Ms. Blake. Garcia needed to know you had a little muscle behind you. I'm not apologizing, so forget that."

Amy might have lost her temper but certainly not her mind. He had to know he was the one who'd jeopardized them, not her. She felt his fingers digging into her bare arm. Jerking it away, her eyes flashed.

"Stop manhandling me, Crawford. I don't respond well to this kind of treatment."

Crawford's jaw tensed as he measured her with his eyes. She was a hell of a lot more fiery than her soft looks implied. And a hell of a lot too desirable . . . Crazily, his body was stirring in a way that even reality couldn't suppress.

Suddenly, he remembered Garcia's invitation and her acqui-escence. The recollection caused his gut to wrench. Garcia was handsome and tough. In Marita, he was the catch of the year. He knew it was only slightly less than ludicrous even to think of Amy and Garcia in the same breath, but the image was too vivid to be comfortable.

He needed to calm down.

"Ms. Blake, you lied to me."

"I did not!"

Crawford's head snapped back. The tension in his jaw jammed its way right up to his temples. What did he care if Amy and Garcia had a good old roll in the hay? Good luck to them.

He forced himself to concentrate on the business at hand.

Finding a cigarette, he jerked it out of the package. When he spoke, his voice was harsh. "Look, where I come from, with-holding important information falls into the category of sins of omission. Admit it, angel, you deliberately did not tell me you were single before you came here, and you certainly didn't give me your father's curriculum vitae. That's lying, no matter how you cut it."

Amy straightened up. As a politician's daughter, she'd learned never to go on the defensive.

"Oh? And you're perfect, are you, Mr. Crawford? Playing your macho games with General Garcia, strutting like an arrogant peacock. How dare you suggest that I'm the one at fault here." Her anger made her eyes glitter like emeralds. "I'm here as an unofficial guest of this country. I'm not here to launch a missile attack, although the way you acted could have easily suggested that. Your aggressive behavior was despicable. It put us both at risk."

Crawford inhaled sharply. Five seconds in the country, and she was telling him how to handle himself. He blew out a thin line of blue smoke between tight lips, his annoyance increasing. "My behavior was exactly what is called for in a place like this. You have to be aggressive in Marita, or you get rolled over by any convenient torture toy. If you're too hard to break, the military leaves you alone for easier prey. It's like being in the jungle—stamp your feet hard enough and the other guys take off."

It was fairly close to the way she would have described his actions, she thought perversely. The jungle animal pounding on his chest, kicking up dirt, staking out his territory. Her own chest heaved with frustration. But panic nipped at her heels. She couldn't let herself believe that Garcia was a genuine threat. If she did, she'd stall at the starting gate.

"General Garcia was gracious to you," she retorted.

He snorted with derision. "Garcia is military. The 'General' says it all, sweetheart. On his orders people were killed in the takeover. He's a thug. They're all thugs."

Amy's eyes widened. The man was unbelievable, she thought, a throwback to the Middle Ages. Self-righteously convinced that what he did was all right, but what everyone else did wasn't.

She regarded him with a haughty tilt of her head. "I thought you helped the revolutionaries."

His mouth clamped around his response. "I did."

"Oh, but *you're* not a thug, I suppose?"

Crawford's hand toyed with the cigarette pack. He knew he'd left himself wide open for that one, but her comment stung a little more than he might have expected. He hadn't been overly proud of the way he'd earned his living in the last few years, but he hadn't exactly been wallowing in regret, either. He was a lot more careful about the causes he hired himself out for than he actually let on. He had some shred of decency left in him, but not much, even he had to admit.

He opened his mouth to reply, then shrugged arrogantly.

Whatever shreds were left weren't worth debating. He'd given up defending himself years ago. "Sure, I'm a thug, but the difference is, I don't pretend not to be."

"What a relief," she replied dryly.

He took a long drag on his cigarette and blew smoke out impatiently. "Look, Ms. Blake, as much as you might think discussing my sex life and my ethics is highly entertaining, I don't share your enthusiasm for the subjects, unless I'm more actively involved in the former." A wry smile tugged at the corners of his mouth as she colored at the reminder of their earlier conversation. "So, I would suggest that we get onto a topic that matters, like the real reason you're here and your father's role in all of this. Why didn't you tell me everything?"

Amy glared at him. "The reason I didn't tell you anything other than what you already know is that I didn't think it was relevant. What difference could it possibly make to anyone whether I'm married or not? If the guardians of the child don't care and the courts don't care, then it never occurred to me that anyone else should care. There's nothing subversive about my trip here if that's what you're thinking. My father didn't send me here. I came of my own free will to adopt a child, Mr. Crawford. That's all there is to it."

He regarded her, squinting dubiously. That air of innocence and naive bossiness annoyed him no end, but for her to be a spy... although maybe Garcia had a point, as ridiculous as it might sound. Why would she want to adopt a child alone, without benefit of a husband? Hadn't he been wondering the same thing? What little secrets bubbled behind those entrancing eyes? Maybe she was an operative? Then again, maybe she had something against men? He recalled her sad look in the Mendozas' foyer. Some detail was still missing here, he thought.

Frowning, he said, "Look, there's got to be a connection here between your father and your trip. It's too circumstantial, and I don't believe in Santa Claus or the tooth fairy. If I'm going to be guiding you into the mountains, I need to know where the land mines are so I don't trigger them. You're going to have to level with me, sweetheart—pure and simple."

Amy's mouth set into a stubborn line. "I *have* leveled with you."

Crawford rolled his eyes heavenward, trying to control his legendary temper. "Really? Then I must be hard of hearing because I sure don't remember you telling me about your father. Is he head of the committee like Garcia says?"

He watched as her eyes flashed in response to his inquisition. The late-afternoon sunlight slanted across her hair like gold dripping on shining velvet. It formed a breathtaking ebony halo. He wondered what it would feel like if he reached up and took a strand in his fingers. He blinked hard. The idea was crazy. As sexy as she was, she tried his patience.

Finally, she nodded her finely shaped head. "Yes, he is."

He tore his gaze away from her hair, narrowing his eyes. "So where does he stand on the recent coup, then?"

Amy replied in a prim voice. "The U.S. is ambivalent at the moment about which side to support."

Crawford laughed hoarsely at the political answer. He knew a lot about ambivalence. He'd often been left out to hang and dry because of it.

He took a jerky drag on his cigarette.

"All that means is that the powers that be are going to wait and see whether it's in their best interest to support the new government or not—right?"

Amy bristled at his mocking tone. "That would appear to be the unofficial position, yes."

Crawford shook his head in frustration. Either she was the most naive woman he'd ever met or the most accomplished spy or just plain crazy. Right now, his bets were riding on the latter. Anyone else would be able to tell how much danger they were in. "You still haven't answered my question," he said roughly. "C'mon, angel, spill it. What's your father got to do with all of this?"

Chapter 4

Amy drew in a hesitant breath. She hadn't thought her wanting to adopt a child in Marita would turn out to be this complicated. Somehow, what had started out as something wonderful was turning into something tainted. But what was the point of trying to explain the subtleties to someone as insensitive as Crawford? She felt herself losing steam.

Tiredly, she replied, irritation tinging her voice. "All right . . . all right. He worked here about ten years ago as a volunteer. He loves this country. For years he's watched all the turmoil, hoping that some of it would break the tyranny of its dictators. Time and again, he's told me that the children are the ones who are the most tragic victims of this kind of chaos. So, when I decided to adopt a child, this seemed to be a good place to come." A flash of temper rekindled. "Satisfied?"

Crawford hadn't expected that answer. It made him pause. He believed her. Ten years with the CIA had taught him a thing or two about recognizing when people were telling the truth. So, the only tricky thing about her was what she did to his insides.

He tossed his cigarette into a nearby flower bed before glancing back at her curiously.

"Other countries have similar victims," he pointed out.

Amy's eyes shadowed. "Yes, I know, and it was hard to pick a country. The decision was eventually made easy by the fact that my father already had a connection with Marita. My mother died ten years ago. My father was filled with grief and came here looking for something to restore him. But when he was here, he also caught a virus and the villagers nursed him, so not only did he come to terms with his grief here but the Maritans saved his life. I feel I owe this country something. As for adopting from other countries ... Romania was out of the question. It cut off international adoptions awhile back, and in the U.S. adoption, even private adoption, is unbelievably difficult. Furthermore, preference is given to married couples. The fact is, Mr. Crawford, I don't stand a chance against those kinds of odds. It's so hard to think of children in all of those countries ... wanting ... needing...."

She fell silent, a small, involuntary catch in her throat snagging her words as she thought of another child...another child who hadn't had a chance.

A veil of tears misted her gaze as she forced herself to raise her eyes to Crawford's. This child *would* have a chance.

If Crawford hadn't changed his mind. So much depended on his cooperation.

Without realizing it, her vulnerability showed in her eyes as their gazes merged.

She took a deep breath, concluding, "That's all there is to it, nothing more complicated than that."

The raw look on her face belied her words and took him by surprise, but what surprised him even more was his own reaction to it. An instinct he hadn't felt for decades stirred to life inside him. The gut-wrenching, reason-defying instinct to take her in his arms and comfort her.

He'd wanted lots of women in his time, but it was a long time since he'd wanted to hold a woman and protect her from the horrors of the world. Or to hold a woman and absorb some of her softness.

He'd done it once in his lifetime, he thought, as he brushed some imaginary dust from his khakis. He'd never do it again.

He folded his arms in front of him. "Why not just marry and wait for nature to take its course?"

She stiffened but defiance overcame her distress. "Because, Mr. Crawford, I tried it once, and it didn't work out. Okay?"

So they were both losers, members of the walking wounded. He shrugged, shaking his head. "Okay, sweetheart, sounds simple enough. Here's hoping it stays simple."

"Look, Mr. Crawford, I'm sorry for the emotional outburst, so let's get on with it, all right?"

He dropped his arms, watching her. So, she didn't like to show her true feelings, either. "Sure, fine with me. Never happened."

She smiled wryly. "I'm usually quite a no-nonsense type."

An ironic smile spread across his face. "I hadn't noticed."

She gave a quiet, deprecating laugh. The sound of it was clean, fresh and childlike. She wet her lower lip, a pensive sigh whispering through. "I don't think there's anything you don't notice, Mr. Crawford."

She was right, he thought, with a rueful intake of breath. And right now, he was noticing that the tip of her head came just about to the middle of his chest and it wasn't hard to imagine what she would feel like snuggled against him. Something primitive was coming to life inside him. At a pace that was dangerous for both of them. He swallowed a curse under his breath.

"Forget the 'mister,'" he corrected brusquely. "Crawford's good enough."

Amy paused, slowly raising dark, luminous eyes to his. "Crawford." She repeated his name as if testing it on her lips. "So..." She took a long, elaborate breath, obviously worried about something. "Now that you know everything, do we still have a deal, Crawford?"

It was her running the tip of her tongue along the edge of her lips as she murmured his name that did him in. He'd been very good the last ten years walking away from temptation, he told himself, but this was one offering he'd be damned if he'd pass up. In one decade he was entitled to at least one taste of heaven, he reasoned. It was insane, he knew, to be turned on by her, but he knew it was too late to stop that. It was even more insane to agree to take her into the mountains, seeing as how she made him squirm every time he looked at her. He was begging for torture if he even took one more step with her. But he sure as hell wasn't going to abandon her to the likes of Garcia.

He'd handle it, he thought. All it would take was a little willpower. And if he kissed her now, he'd get this damn ache out of his system.

It wasn't as if he *had* to care. Or that it had to lead anywhere.

He shifted slightly, drawing closer to her. His last rational thought was to wonder—had she really believed he'd abandon her now? The thought hadn't occurred to him. But he'd deal with her error in judgment later. Now he had other things on his mind.

"We've got a deal," he said hoarsely, and before either of them realized it, he'd lowered his head and settled his mouth on hers.

He felt her surprise beneath his touch. Mentally he tensed himself, waiting for her resistance but . . . it didn't come. That fact startled both of them. For a moment each hesitated, then his lips slowly shimmered over hers . . . testing . . . suddenly wanting more than he'd imagined.

She ought to break away, Amy thought. What was possessing her? Somehow she couldn't seem to move. Curiosity, she told herself. It was natural to want to know what this big, sexy man tasted like. That's all she was doing, satisfying some perverse curiosity. But the mild, budding fascination he held for her suddenly exploded as she got her first warm taste of him. Her legs turned to jelly. The texture of him was undeniably glorious. He was both rough and smooth like a carving, half-polished, half-unfinished. His lips were warm, firm, sensual. Closing her eyes, she gave in to pure sensation, letting it wash over her, willing to test it, knowing it was only one moment in her life. Why not savor it? she reasoned. Why not even help it along?

Slowly, she parted her lips, a small moan catching in her throat.

Crawford heard the sound and caught it with his own breath. Puzzled but heated by her compliance, he wasn't about to fight it. Instead, he felt himself caving in, drowning in her softness, his tongue leading the way, searching, yearning to be deep inside her. The symbolism of it all struck him with full force. He could strip her naked, taste and touch every inch of her satin skin and bury himself inside her and never think of anything real ever again. He felt like a young hotshot. His chest constricted as her mouth welcomed the invasion. Automatically, he brought his arms around her and gently pressed at her lower back so that she slipped easily into the haven he created around her. As her breasts rubbed against his chest, he started at the explosion that instantly spiraled through him. He was too old now to settle for kisses. And too painfully hungry.

He shouldn't have started this, he realized. He'd only want more. She had that kind of hot sweet power that could make a man forget everything. Still, though, he couldn't bring himself to stop. Forgetfulness suddenly seemed wonderful.

She smelled not just of roses, but of blazing sunlight that dazzled him. She was natural, earthy, real, but it was all over-laid with an incredible, elusive sweetness. He sensed he could chase after that sweetness for a lifetime and never quite capture it. The yearnings she'd conjured in him earlier for the passionate innocence of his youth crystallized into a driving need for the kind of softness he'd missed for so many years. But wanting her meant returning to something he'd abjured a long time ago.... Slowly, as reality pricked at him, he knew he had to stop. He knew he had to pull himself away from her and call it quits before he weakened too much, before *his* vulnerability showed....

But she felt so good.

Too good.

Abruptly, he released her and drew himself back, need still rocking through him. With supreme discipline, he drove it down. He ought to know better, he thought. Women like Amy Blake weren't one-night stands, any more than the college girls of his youth intent on marriage and permanence had been. Somehow, they managed to ensnare a man's emotions, as well. Women were adept at that. He felt his past rising up, turning on him, choking him, cooling his ardor, dampening his exultation. He felt dizzy and conflicting memories of glorious passion and cold, hard bitterness. None of it Amy Blake's fault.

One kiss, he thought, and all that hits me.

He watched as her eyes flew open. In them he read her surprise and the glimmering pain of rejection. He mutely berated himself, guilt creeping into his consciousness. It was his fault he was aching, not hers. He'd initiated this, not her. She deserved better than he could ever give. He was only interested in taking. It was all he could do anymore. The giving side of his nature had frozen years ago. But women like Amy Blake didn't settle for that.

Her gaze merged with his, wounded and startled. The look in her eyes made him want to cringe. He ignored it. If he didn't, he knew he'd lose his resolve.

"Don't tell me you're at a loss for words, Ms. Blake," he said roughly.

In truth she was. This flip, arrogant, no-values soldier available to the highest bidder shouldn't have made her heart turn upside down. But he had. Her limbs were trembling, her breathing uneven. She was shaken to the core. He'd unleashed something wild inside her, and it had taken her totally by surprise. He was no one she would ever want long-term. And yet, he'd stoked longings inside her. For one brief moment, she'd wanted him so badly.

She shook her head in dismay. How could she? Especially now that it was obvious he regretted the moment. Hurt raced through her at the cavalier expression on his face.

Her breath still ragged, she struggled to bring her dazed emotions under control. That look would be with her a long time, she thought, suddenly feeling angry. How could he? How could he make her feel so much, then just thrust her aside with a careless comment?

Pride warred with hurt, pride winning out. She stepped back away from the warmth of his body, feeling its loss. A chill hit her.

She shivered but met his eyes head-on. "No, Crawford, I'm not at a loss for words, but I'm not sure you'll want to hear what I have to say. The fact is, I'd appreciate it if you'd keep your hands and your mouth to yourself from here on in. That's *not* what I'm paying you for."

With that, she turned on her heel and headed back to the sanctuary of Mercedes's kitchen.

"*Señorita,* you want some tea?"

Amy forced a bright smile to her face as Mercedes greeted her in the kitchen. She hoped the other woman couldn't see how flustered she was. Next time she was alone with Crawford, she was going to lay down some ground rules. She heard Crawford behind her, but she deliberately blocked him out of her consciousness. He could go to hell for all she cared, she thought mutinously. She was even willing to assist in sending him on the trip.

"Thank you, that would be a godsend. By the way, I lost my luggage at the airport, I was wondering if there's somewhere I could buy some clothes."

"Ahh..." Mercedes commiserated, her gaze shadowing. "*Sí*, down the street. I show. Crawford, you want tea?"

Crawford paused, shifting his gaze between the pair of them as he remembered the lost suitcases. Mercedes's question barely registered. So the lady didn't have any clothes. Fine with him, he thought immediately. But the image the fact conjured—of a naked Amy Blake—had him inwardly groaning two seconds later. He looked over at her, scowling in frustration, but the lady seemed to have turned her back on him. She was annoyed with him. He could tell from the firm set of her small shoulders.

He exhaled a sharp, stinging breath, setting his shoulders into a rigid line.

That, too, was fine with him. Even better. It put distance between them.

Shaking off his trance, he muttered half under his breath. "Too tame for me, Mercedes. See you both later." He saw Mercedes raise puzzled eyebrows as he turned abruptly, but he didn't stop. He had every intention of heading for the only bar in town. And dousing the fire in his gut.

Why did the woman have to be so appealing? He tossed his head back as a wave of Maritan heat rose up from the earth.

What he needed, he thought, was a stiff drink. The stiffer, the better.

Five minutes later, he found himself in the bar. Sixty seconds later, he had a scotch in front of him, with a beer chaser.

Raising his glass elaborately, he took a deep, uncomfortable breath.

Here's to you, Ms. Blake. May you find a hundred gunnysacks to hide yourself in. We're both going to need 'em.

With that, he downed the burning scotch.

In the dry goods store, Amy found some baby items to replace the ones she'd lost, plus more than enough clothes to tide her over for the trip up the mountains. Because she was so small, she was able to buy a couple of items in girls' sizes. But

the fact unsettled her. The reason the store had a plentiful stock
was that the women and children of Marita couldn't afford to
purchase slacks, dresses or blouses. Vestiges of the old regime
still lingered on. The revolution hadn't brought instant wealth
to Marita. It was too new for that. Any money the local peas-
ants might have probably went for food. Just as always.

Some things, unfortunately, took longer to change than
others, she recognized sadly.

She paused once she'd reached the entrance to the store as the
proprietor held the door open.

The woman beamed at her. *"Gracias, señorita."*

Amy tucked one of the bags under her arms. The owner had
already thanked her a dozen times for the sale. Amy imagined
that no one had bought as much as she had in one day, in one
year, with the possible exception of other foreign adoptive
parents. The disparity made her feel embarrassed and guilty.
The only consolation she had was that at least the proprietor
and her family might benefit from what she'd spent.

"Buenos dias," she said, giving the woman a soft smile. That
was almost the total extent of her Spanish vocabulary, but she
hadn't needed to know any more. The proprietor had immediately grasped what she'd wanted through sign language and
Amy's repetition of *"los vestidos."* The latter had been courtesy of Mercedes's instructions.

The Spanish woman was grinning now. *"Buena suerte, señorita, hasta luego."*

Amy stepped out into the hot air, heading back toward the
Mendozas', lost in thought. *Buena suerte.* That was another
expression she did know. Good luck.

She tossed back her heavy hair trying to find some relief from
the gritty heat.

She was going to need more than good luck to survive the
next week with Sam Crawford.

She recalled the cool look in his eyes when he'd drawn away
from her. How could a man do that? Kiss a woman as if he
were sharing his deepest needs with her and then pull back as
if nothing had happened? Surely she hadn't imagined the passion in him when his hard mouth had moved so seductively over
hers?

She shook her head bitterly. She must have, just as she'd once
imagined that David loved her. Maybe she wasn't destined to

have any luck with a man. Maybe she was, as David had said, too starry-eyed about love, family and hearth. Too old-fashioned.

Maybe she was, after all, just too tame for a man like Sam Crawford.

Tears unwittingly sprang to her eyes. She realized her anger with Crawford had evaporated long ago, giving way to self-doubt and embarrassment.

Damn him anyway for making her remember the pain and humiliation of rejection. Damn him for reminding her of how fragile her emotions still were after her failed marriage.

And double damn the man for making her realize that against all odds, she was attracted to him.

Something was in the air.

Crawford raised his head suspiciously as he checked the dining room and found it empty. Going through to the kitchen, he headed toward the terrace, hearing someone in the basement of the house. The sound didn't alarm him, although a year ago, when the revolution had been in full swing, it might have. Mercedes or Raoul, he surmised, was raiding the wine cellar.

Once he got outside, he paused on the brick terrace, breathing in the hazy air. A slight breeze ruffled his dark, thick hair.

He started to walk to the left where the Spanish couple kept a homemade stone barbecue, then stopped. Ahead of him a small table and two chairs were strategically placed under a eucalyptus tree. A huge pot sat on an adjacent server. Candles vied with stars dancing light across the tops of bushes and slumbering flowers. The scent from the pot was tantalizing, but the scent from the garden mingling with it was even more exotic. A sultry, but not unpleasant heat created a heavy canopy over the setting. Nice, he thought, searching for a better description. Pretty? No. Romantic . . . that's it.

Romantic?

His gaze narrowed at Mercedes as she bustled past him carrying a tray with a bottle of wine and two glasses.

"What are you up to, Mercedes?"

She shook her head as if to dispel the accusing note in his voice and placed the wine and glasses in the center of the table. "You and the *señorita* will eat out here," she ordered.

"You single, she single. That's that," she finished bluntly, anticipating his protests.

Crawford's dark eyes locked with hers. "Hold it right there, Mercedes. The *señorita* is a client. I don't mix business with pleasure, remember?"

Mercedes clamped her jaw into a stubborn line. "This—different. The señorita is woman first, client second. You need woman. She need husband. Baby needs father. Señorita Blake pretty. Perfect for you. I like, so I help." She raised her head, flashing her eyes at him in challenge.

Crawford stared at her in wide-mouthed amazement. Mercedes's leap in logic astounded him.

Women, he thought, exhaling with impatience. "Even if I was interested in Ms. Blake, which I'm *not*," he said arrogantly—liar, he thought—"I certainly wouldn't need any help."

Mercedes regarded him the way she often regarded members of his species—as if his brain cells had evaporated at birth. She shrugged off his temper with the same disregard. "Hah! You need plenty help." She rolled her eyes at him. "You eat here, end of history." She brandished the tray, shaking her head as she retreated to the kitchen, muttering as she went. "Plenty help, believe."

Crawford rolled his eyes in annoyance. He was about to take off after her and conclude the discussion to his benefit, when he heard Amy's voice behind him gasping in delight.

"Oh, how lovely."

"Yeah, right." Still frustrated by Mercedes's comments, Crawford whirled around to vent a little more male steam, not too fussy about who the object of it was, but the words died on his lips along with whatever thought processes were engineering them.

He looked at Amy, and his throat went dry. Now he knew how Ulysses felt strapped to the mast as he heard the siren's sweet, haunting call. Tortured, unable to risk more than one sense to temptation.

She was wearing the simplest of outfits, a loose white scooped-neck blouse that draped across her breasts like a caress and a flowered wraparound skirt that hugged her hips and fell to below her knee. His breath stopped in his lungs at the sheer image of fragile loveliness she presented. Damp, shining hair hung around her neck in thick wisps of abandonment, catching the soft evening light.

She looked refreshed and rested, like a glowing gem, fragility and sensuality exuding from every pore. The sensuality was enhanced by a fact he quickly noted and wished he hadn't.

She wasn't wearing a bra under the thin fabric of her top.

A hot twist of desire tore at his stomach and embedded itself inside him. He could graphically imagine what was underneath the blouse.

Maybe they *ought* to lash him to a mast.

"It looks like a fabulous picture postcard." Amy stopped in front of him, smiling. "What a great idea to eat out here. Do I have you to thank for this?"

She looked like a pleased child, but there was nothing childlike about her body, he thought. Imagination gave way to reality when, as she tossed back her hair with her hand, she inadvertently afforded him a view of pert, small breasts pressing against the fabric of her top.

It's a mistake, his body couriered to his brain. A mistake to spend more than ten seconds in this woman's presence.

He took a deep breath as his head remembered something else. He was committed not just to ten seconds, but to a week.

"Mercedes," he corrected in a dry voice. "I don't have this much finesse." Folding his arms, he gave her a sardonic shrug.

Something immediately shut down in her. He saw the sparkle flicker and die in her eyes. He regretted that he'd caused it to disappear.

"Well, at least you're honest, Crawford."

He offered her a self-deprecatory half smile. "Honesty pays, haven't you heard?"

Amy frowned, tilted her head so that her hair could catch the warm, stirring breeze. She'd been honest with David, and it hadn't done her any good. If she'd waited and given him the chance to get used to the idea of having a child, perhaps things would have turned out differently. Perhaps in her own happiness, she'd jumped the gun....

"Sometimes—" she murmured softly, momentarily lost in time "—it doesn't."

Crawford studied her sharply. This was the second time she'd drifted off to another place. Where does she disappear to? he wondered.

He raised his eyebrows. "So how did the shopping trip go?"

She appeared to refocus quickly. "Fine, I think. What do you think?" She swished the skirt in a way that made the fabric crinkle as it brushed up against the bare skin of his legs. The sound cut through him, causing a bittersweet shaft of need to dig deeper inside him. He wanted to trail his hands along that naked skin the way the fabric had, that's what he thought.

But obviously what he thought wasn't appropriate for repeating.

He stepped away from her to relieve a pressure building between his thighs. He shrugged. "Hey, lady, if you're happy, I'm happy." He started to walk toward the table, doing it very slowly.

He stopped at the edge of the table, glancing at her over his shoulder, of necessity keeping the lower part of his body turned away from her.

"How about some wine?"

Amy's temples tightened. Three hours away from him had convinced her that the attraction she'd felt for him had been caused by overwrought nerves. Having settled that in her own mind, she'd come down to dinner determined to be pleasant. Within a minute, his cocky manner had set her teeth on edge again.

She cursed him under her breath with more imagination than she thought she possessed.

"Okay."

"Red or white?" he asked in no rush to turn and face her.

"Whatever."

Crawford's mouth twitched. Obviously, he wasn't the only one feeling testy. Too bad it wasn't for the same reason. He reached for the bottle. There was only red wine. But he didn't tell her that. He needed to stall.

"Two red coming right up."

Amy exhaled a strained breath as she waited.

Why did she always feel off balance with him? Why did he still seem determined to treat her offhandedly?

Maybe she was being overly sensitive. She was older and wiser now, she reflected, not so likely to let a man dictate her emotions as she had once been. Although this afternoon, just for a moment, she had to admit, she had had a lapse.

But... it shouldn't matter that she and Crawford didn't get along, or that somehow they rubbed each other the wrong way. All that mattered was that he could guide her to the baby she already loved. A child could fill the void inside her. A man couldn't. Ever.

Crawford came toward her, carrying two glasses. He handed her one.

Things settled in her mind, she took the glass and met his gaze squarely. "Thanks, I could use a drink."

I'll second that, Crawford thought, grateful that the pressure in his pants had finally subsided. He raised his glass in a salute.

"Cheers again, Ms. Blake. Hungry?"

As she came up beside him, Amy drew in a deep breath of the delicious aroma wafting through the garden. Her stomach growled a response before she did.

She curved her fingers around the glass, grimacing. "I could probably eat a horse."

"Army requisitioned all those." With his free hand, he pulled out a wrought-iron chair. "I think lamb and salad are as good as you're going to get. So, Ms. Blake, take a load off your feet."

Somehow they made it through the meal without sniping at each other, and once they'd finished, Amy sat back feeling as if she could burst. She focused on the burning end of Sam's cigarette. To her surprise, he'd actually made an effort to be gracious. He'd turned out to be a much more entertaining companion than she would have imagined. His moodiness still unsettled her, but she'd discovered that he was intelligent and could be bitterly funny when he chose. Yet for all his humor, she sensed a depth in him that he seemed to hide behind irreverence. Many a truth in jest, her father used to say. She remembered the comment now and judiciously filed it away.

Over the flickering candlelight, she said to him, "You look like you're getting a lot out of that. Makes me want to try it."

Crawford stopped inhaling long enough to say, "Don't. It's a bad habit."

"Then why do it?"

"It's an addiction. I guess I have an addictive personality."

Amy frowned, inhaling instead the enchanting night air. Was he also addicted to danger? she wondered. Is that what he was doing in Marita?

The moon now sat high in the clouds, adding age-old majesty to the terrace and garden. She let the breath out slowly, her gaze straying back to him. The scene might be enchanting, but he was the one who looked vibrantly male, she thought ruefully. The edge he had only seemed to add to his fascinating sexiness. It wasn't fair that he could look so wonderful, she thought.

All through dinner she hadn't been able to keep from noticing what a lithe and easy grace he possessed. Like a jungle cat, he hunched his shoulders, bent his hands, flashed his eyes, played with things on the table as he talked. There was a natural restlessness to him, yet she'd also realized he could be incredibly physically calm, as if his CIA training to listen and observe were still very much ingrained in him. He could probe easily when he chose to, despite the fact she'd resisted discussing that part of her personal life that was still raw. But then, he hadn't offered much, either. Mostly she'd talked about politics and how her father's position had affected her upbringing, and about her flower shop. He'd talked about the Latin countries he'd lived in for the past years.

All safe topics. It was as if the kiss this afternoon had created more barriers than it had breached.

Good, she thought, that's what she wanted, wasn't it? But then, why did her thoughts keep returning to the life Crawford had chosen for himself? She took a deep breath. It was natural to wonder about a man like him, she told herself. Why had he buried himself in a place like Marita? Now that Russia had dismantled its old regimes, the CIA would likely become more mercantile in nature. Crawford already had years of experience in industry. In fact, he'd been ahead of his time. His assets would be in even more demand now than ever before. That would fascinate anyone.

She gave up second-guessing herself and gave in to curiosity. "Do you ever think about going back to the CIA or the corporate world?"

Crawford grunted, tossing his cigarette into the ashtray. "Never."

Amy toyed thoughtfully with her wineglass. "Why not?"

His mouth thinned as he leaned back in the chair. "Because I once trusted institutions—government, corporations. You name it, I was a sucker for it." He shook his head in disdain. "Now, no more."

"What about the institution of marriage?" she couldn't resist asking.

For a brief moment, she saw an unguarded expression flash into his eyes.

Then his features hardened. "Especially that."

"Were you ever married?" she asked slowly.

"Once. It didn't work out."

Well, at least they had that in common, but she wondered if he also wasn't warning her not to be interested in him. Remembering his earlier, cavalier attitude, she also wondered how many other women had experienced the kind of wanting he'd made her feel. How many women had been fascinated by those changeable, seductive blue eyes and lean, hard body, and been left in the lurch? Studying him now, she was certain the number was legion.

He'd polished up nicely, her father would have said.

Gone were the professional camouflage khakis and in their place were a natural cream-colored cotton shirt that showed off his dark looks dramatically and a pair of hip-hugging beautifully tailored black slacks. She shouldn't want to but she was tempted to run her fingers along the vee of the open shirt where fabric touched male, weathered skin. The night had a kind of magic that made the thought seem right. Maybe she should do it, she thought, her heart thumping at such a daring idea. What would he do if she did? she wondered.

She couldn't. She was amazed she'd even thought of the idea.

Deliberately, she jammed both hands into the pockets of her new skirt and changed the subject to safer territory.

"That was an incredible meal. I wouldn't have thought Marita would have an abundance of meat."

Crawford blew out a wisp of smoke. "It doesn't. The Mendozas have had hardly any meat themselves for over a month. They negotiated for a week to get the lamb for you. They wanted your first meal to be a special one."

Amy's eyes flew wide open. "I didn't want them to do that for me," she protested.

Crawford shrugged. "Too late, but don't tell them that. They'll be insulted."

"I didn't mean that, either," she corrected in an icy voice. He was reverting to type again. "I appreciate what they did, but I'm certainly not comfortable with other people going without so that I can have. It's not right."

Crawford's face seamed into a rueful smile. Silk for breakfast, discreet diamonds for lunch, check-writing for a charity dinner. That's how he'd had her pegged, and the image could fit except for one thing. He'd listened between the lines as she'd talked, and Amy Blake's social values seemed surprisingly real. That had impressed him.

Still, he continued to test the waters. "It's okay, Ms. Blake. I know what you meant. Anyway," he said insolently, "don't worry about it, the money you're giving them should soften the lack considerably."

Amy stared at him, appalled. Is that what he thought of her? That she tossed money around like a guilty aristocrat? The meal in her stomach churned dangerously. So much for his table manners and spruced-up looks. The man was still impossibly insensitive. She clenched her fingers around her wineglass, leaning forward.

"Crawford, I don't believe that money is something people should use to ease their consciences. Nor do I believe it can buy anything," she said, her tone insulted.

Crawford wondered if she realized that her position offered him a tantalizing view of the cleft between her breasts. Or that the dip and what it led to aroused him so quickly, his heart had started to hammer. He really didn't want her to be noble on top of that. He'd be done for if he thought too hard about that kind of goodness packaged in such tempting curves.

"It's buying you a child, isn't it?"

Her eyes flashed green fire at him. "That's a low blow, Crawford, even for you."

Reluctantly, but of necessity, he tore his gaze away from the creamy swell of skin nudging above the white blouse. He knew he ought to apologize, but reason and civility weren't his strong suit at that precise moment.

He bowed his head dramatically. "You're probably right. Touché, Ms. Blake."

She tossed her hair back with suspicion and disappointment. "Crawford, how can you be so hard?"

When those huge, green eyes turned on him with such disapproval and anger, he had a difficult time not feeling like a jerk. She had a way of making a man believe he should be, could be, a hero. But it was easy to read on her face exactly what she thought of him. And she was probably right.

But . . . it was better this way, he reminded himself.

Seven days from now, she'd be going back to her fancy, civilized, well-to-do world, a world that he'd abandoned years ago. And he'd still be here. With her lovely looks and conservative ways, she belonged there. But he didn't. He couldn't breathe in that world of hers. He didn't believe in it.

Lazily, he arched his right elbow onto the back of the chair. "It's a hard country, and it *was* a hard revolution. You should have been here when your friend Garcia waged bloody war from the mountains. You'll discover how free of illusion it can be here, if he decides to stop you."

Amy finally acknowledged a moment of genuine fear.

She'd been fighting panic ever since Garcia's visit, thinking it was better to ignore it rather than give in to it. But if it hadn't been for Garcia's instructions, she might now be on her way up the mountains . . . she might now be getting closer to the baby she so helplessly yearned to hold in her arms.

Garcia had the power to stop her.

Anxiety burned in the back of her brain as she realized what she'd done. She'd taken all her pain, all her anguish and turned it into hope.

Almost blindly, she'd transferred all the pent-up emotions into this dream. Maybe that had been a mistake. One shouldn't want so desperately. You only set yourself up for pain. If Garcia stopped her, what could she do? How could she return home, with empty hands and heart? What would happen to the tiny child whose mother she already felt herself to be?

She closed her eyes over the awful thought, then opened them again. Crawford's rugged features drifted back into view as she forced herself to focus. She had to be stronger than this.

"Do you really think he'll stop me?" she murmured.

Crawford arched his eyebrows in a reflex action. Beneath her cool demeanor, he read rising alarm. She had every reason to feel it. By coming here, being who she was, she'd walked into a potential lair. But she really wants this child, he thought, frowning. Her desire cuts deep. Why?

He felt a peculiar tug of compassion. He'd long ago given up dreaming, but why shouldn't she have her dream? At least she'd taken a chance.

"Look," he said candidly, respecting her desire for the truth. "I'll be honest with you, I don't know *what* Garcia will do. He's a brilliant man, and supposedly honorable, but politics and armies tend to make men like him a lot less frank and a lot more cautious than they might normally be. As far as I can tell, he has no reason to stop you..." He paused before taking a chance with the sixty-four-thousand-dollar question, "...unless, of course, you really *are* a spy, in which case he'd already have done it. Don't worry. Everything's going to be fine."

Her face still remained pale, but in the same instant, he saw her usual spirit return. "I am definitely not a spy."

He held up his hand. He didn't need convincing any longer, but he knew the uncertainty bothered the general. Garcia knew the CIA wouldn't be above negotiating with the vanquished government and supplying them with arms if that's the way they felt the wind should blow. And Garcia knew the agency also wouldn't be above using someone like Amy as the messenger.

"Okay, relax ... but there's nothing you can do about what Garcia may or may not think. You're just going to have go through with it. Hightailing it out of here isn't going to work because Garcia's office has to approve all travel plans in and out of the country. You're going to have to tough it out."

Her eyes shadowed. He watched as she brought her attack of nerves under control. From under dark, long lashes, she met his gaze honestly. The lady's got some guts, he thought.

"I guess I'm a little afraid of what will happen tomorrow," she said sheepishly.

Crawford liked the fact she could admit that. He knew all about fear. It was nothing to be ashamed of.

He cleared his throat before answering. "Don't worry about it," he finally said cockily. "Remember, you've got me."

Amy laughed spontaneously, grateful for once for his verbal swagger. Maybe that's why he was the way he was, she thought

with new insight. Maybe, as he'd said earlier about her first
meeting with Garcia, you had to be aggressive in situations like
this.

She smiled. "I guess you think I'm a real fool, not taking
Garcia seriously before, don't you?"

Privately he wondered what would have been gained by her
agonizing about Garcia. At first, he had to admit, he had been
angered by her apparent disregard and the position she'd put
them both in. Now he was calmer and reconciled. Her way was
likely better.

Sometimes innocence had a habit of winning out.

"I think you should be aware of the danger, but don't wal-
low in it. Being scared in front of Garcia isn't a great idea." He
found himself saying something he hadn't expected to say.
"You handled yourself well today, you'll handle yourself well
tomorrow."

Amy had herself under control now, but she could hardly
believe her ears at such largess.

"I can hardly believe you said that."

He grinned with self-mockery. "Neither can I. C'mon. I'll
walk you back to your room." Standing up, he lifted the chair
as he moved it backward so it wouldn't scrape on the grass.

A few minutes later, he stopped at her door, holding it open
for her. His arm still stretched out, he paused, looking down at
her, but not saying anything.

Amy held her breath, half-backed-up against the wall. There
was no artificial light in the hallway, only a sliver of moonlight sneaking its way through a small end window and slanting silver along the walls. His gaze had turned to a deep, intense
sea-blue. Slowly, he reached up and with an enigmatic expression on his face, brushed back a stray strand of her hair. His
fingers grazed her cheekbone.

She almost jumped at the jolt that shot through her. She was
sure he had felt it, too.

For a second, he almost seemed like a different person. In
flashes, she felt she'd somehow seen glimpses of the real Sam
Crawford but was still missing the whole picture. Then the
brashness returned as he dropped his hand, drew back and
adopted an arrogant expression.

"Sleep well, angel. We've got a big day ahead of us tomorrow."

With that, he turned and sauntered down the hall.

Watching him, Amy let out a sigh of relief. She'd been convinced he was going to kiss her again. And she hadn't been ready for it. Her heart jackknifed at the prospect. Somehow, though, she felt strangely bereft and cheated.

But she was glad he hadn't kissed her . . . wasn't she?

Chapter 5

Amy raced down the stairs once she saw Garcia's limousine draw up outside the Mendozas' house. It was hard to believe that given her concern over Garcia's decision, she'd actually slept in.

Too much wine, she thought ruefully, and not enough sleep.

Too much Sam Crawford was more like it, she amended, grimacing. How could she have actually dreamed about him? She flushed as she realized that not only had she dreamed about him, but the dreams had been vividly erotic....

Like worried parents, Mercedes and Raoul hovered anxiously in the foyer.

Mercedes hurried toward her with concern. *"Señorita..."*

Amy shook off her confused exhaustion with a toss of her head. "I know, I'm ready," she responded in a rushed voice. Quickly, she glanced around. Where was Crawford, anyway? Her eyes flew toward the kitchen entrance. He was nowhere to be seen.

Her heart did a peculiar somersault. A stab of disappointment shot through her. For all his blunt ways, she never imagined Crawford would let her go off and face Garcia without even a word of support. If nothing else, she'd at least have ex-

pected his ego to motivate him into making a strutting appearance for the general's benefit!

Her mouth set in a grim line. So much for male concern. Her
husband hadn't been much different.

She blew out a breath of suppressed air. "Mercedes, I'd better go, but thank you for the lovely dinner last night, and also
thank you for the wine."

The Spanish woman's eyes relaxed a fraction. "No thank me,
Señor Crawford smuggles wine and beer in when water system
not function too well. Whole town depend on him. Sometimes
he also smuggle in powdered milk for babies."

She wondered how much he was pocketing for *that* little
venture that the IRS didn't know about.

"I'm surprised the Maritans can afford black-market
prices," she replied tersely.

Mercedes waved a hand. "Oh, no, Señor Crawford never
charge. Good will, he call it. Anyone who asks, he give. I store
wine and beer in the cellar for him. You come back, I show."

Amy's head reeled with lack of sleep and anxiety. The gesture didn't fit with her image of the hard-bitten Crawford. She
pushed a stray strand of hair out of her eyes. This was too much
to think about on top of her appointment with Garcia.

"Mercedes," she attempted with a frown, "I'm afraid I don't
under—"

The other woman interrupted, hugging her anxiously. "No
time now. Good luck with Garcia, and may God be with you
and your baby. Is good thing you do."

May God be with you and your baby.

Amy's heart wrenched. "Thank you," she whispered in a
rough voice. "I want this baby very much." Mercedes nodded, her eyes grave as she looked at her husband.

Raoul took a step toward Amy and put an arm around his
wife. His eyes were dark, caring and honest as he addressed
Amy. "We know that *señorita,* but you must hurry. We'll be
here when you get back . . ." He hesitated, then added as if answering her unspoken question, "And so will Crawford."

"But where—?"

Raoul released his wife and patted Amy's arm. "*Señorita*, do
not worry. Crawford will not let you down. Now, please, go."
His voice turned urgent. "Right now, it's Garcia you need in
order to get your baby."

Everything else flew out of Amy's mind at that point.

She closed her eyes, a silent prayer beginning a litany inside her. Please, dear God, she pleaded, let Garcia say the words she desperately needed to hear.

"I'm gone," she murmured, and clutching her documents, she jammed them into her bag. A moment later she tore out the door.

A chauffeur and a guard, both in uniform, led her through the Palacio, to Garcia's suite. Once a hotel and now the temporary headquarters of the junta, it still retained the old-world Spanish charm of stucco walls and heavy dark beams, but she noticed it boasted little furniture. Requisitioned for other purposes, she imagined.

Garcia rose the moment she entered and came toward her from behind his desk. In the full midnight-navy uniform with the gold braid he'd worn the previous day, he cut an impressive figure as he dismissed his male receptionist and then turned to her.

"Ahh, Señorita Blake. How lovely to see you, and how lovely you are . . . a sight for these very tired eyes." He waved toward a bank of chairs facing the desk. "Please sit down."

Everything Garcia did was measured and gracious, yet those very tired eyes were fiercely bright with ruthless courage, she reminded herself warily.

Her hands trembled as she selected a seat and waited for him to sit opposite her. The fact that she was completely at his mercy struck her with frightening force. Beneath her Marita-bought outfit, she grew hot and cold. Garcia could forbid her to travel any further in the country should the whim take him. He could also rescind her adoption approvals.

Would he?

"General Garcia . . ." She started to speak the instant he began to move away from her.

"Americans . . . always in such a hurry. Here, let me pour you a cup of coffee first," he said, extending a hand toward a tray on his desk.

"Sorry," she murmured, giving herself a mental shake and a reminder that she was, after all, a senator's daughter. Until now, she'd been reasonably competent at the lessons she'd learned from her father even if her own direct nature had often put her at odds with them. This, though, was different. This involved a personal dream. That was all the more reason to handle herself well.

She exhaled a shallow breath. "I guess I'm a little nervous."

He handed her a cup of coffee, his mouth still twitching. "That's to be expected, *señorita*. My apologies—we have very little cream and sugar at the moment, but I do have some. Please help yourself." He indicated a small jug and bowl, then returned to sit opposite her again. The movement gave him back his power position. Without hurrying, he leaned back in his seat and steepled his hands together, regarding her with thoughtful eyes.

Her pulse jackknifed again. With an effort, she squashed it back to normal. For something to do, she added sugar to the coffee and twirled it, then forced herself to meet his gaze.

"General, I really am anxious to get going. Would you mind looking at my papers now?"

Garcia sighed, blinking.

Dropping his hands, he lay them on the desk. "All right. We'll do this the American way. Please, *señorita*. Let me see them then."

Heart pounding, Amy dug into her bag, pulled them out and handed them to him.

Without a word, he reached over and took them. She held her breath as he read them slowly. The turning pages set her teeth on edge.

Please God, don't desert Carmela and me now.

Finally, after what seemed an eternity, Garcia smoothed the papers back into position and raised his head. His eyes were icy cold and his manner all business. It was hard to believe that seconds before he had been smiling compliments at her. He rested his arms on the desk, every bit a revolutionary General.

"Señorita Blake, I *still* need to know why a single woman would choose to adopt a child on her own."

Sweat poured down Amy's back. That question again. She wondered why it seemed to concern everyone so much. Perhaps, though, to be fair to Garcia, its very peculiarity did suggest something subversive. She swallowed hard, but her eyes met his directly.

"I can appreciate the fact that it's unusual enough to warrant some attention, but I have very personal reasons for wanting to do this. I prefer not to discuss them, if you don't mind."

Garcia frowned. "Such secrets can be dangerous in a place like Marita," he pointed out in a low voice.

A growing panic began to take seed in her. He was going to stop her. He was going to take some stupid little technicality and use it to shatter her dreams, unless she told him the truth, a truth she had never, ever vocalized for anyone, because it hurt so much, because in some ways she was actually ashamed of her failure... Stubbornly, she refused to discuss her private life with a general of the revolutionary army. Her jaw tensed as she formed words tinged with defiance.

"General, I have no intention of making contact with any members of the previous government or negotiating with them for American aid if that's what you're concerned about. Please, just tell me—is there something wrong with my papers?"

Garcia's gaze flickered. For a long moment he sat there watching her, his pitch-dark eyes probing. The silence was enough to convince her she'd made a tactical error. Her body flushed with hot alarm. She supposed that if she had to, she could swallow her pride and her natural sense of privacy and tell him....

Finally, he spoke with deliberate, slow evenness. She held her breath.

"No, *señorita,* not that I can tell. Your papers appear to be in order."

Amy couldn't believe her ears. Her insides caved to cotton batten. "Really?" Her voice came out barely more than a whisper.

He nodded abruptly. "Yes." He emitted a tight sigh. "I suspect you pique my curiosity more than my suspicion, *señorita.*"

She squeezed the words out. "You mean I'm free to adopt Carmela?"

He nodded again, more curtly. "You may adopt your child, provided you adhere to all the regulations. You are, I presume, aware of them?"

At that point, she would have sung them if he had asked. She answered in a grateful rush. "I must remain here for four weeks with the child before I'm allowed to leave the country, the courts must be satisfied that the foster parents are willing to give her up and I must agree to let her be visited every six months by a social worker."

"That is correct. There is, however, in your case, one additional condition."

Amy stiffened, a thread of caution tensing inside her. "Which is?"

Garcia stood up, dark eyebrows drawn together, and began to pace the floor with long, tense strides. He stopped a few feet from where she was sitting, and stared down at her. "America is a very powerful and wealthy country, and there's no denying that your father is an influential member of the elected elite. Wouldn't you say so, Señorita Blake?"

She nodded.

"Marita will need financial aid to move it from an agrarian society to an industrial country..." As if suddenly aware of something, he stopped midsentence and waved his hand toward her cup. "Please, *señorita,* drink your coffee."

Amy glanced at the cup on the desk, then tilted her head back in his direction, confused at his abrupt concern over the coffee. "Yes, of course, I will, but—"

"*Now*, if you don't mind."

It was too much of an order for her to ignore. Still puzzled, she picked up the cup and took a few sips. Surprisingly, it was delicious.

"Good." He smiled incongruously. "How is it?"

Amy wondered what was going on. "Actually, it was quite lovely. Mellow." She felt like an idiot discussing the coffee.

Seriously, he regarded her. "We want it to be one of our first exports as a free country."

Amy suddenly began to understand. "Oh, I see."

Garcia smiled. "I would like you to tell your father that Marita will not just ask for aid, but will seek partnership with American industry and/or government to produce products such as this coffee for export." He waved his hand toward her cup. "We have no wish to be parasites but to take our place in the new order of world economics."

"But you can go through diplomatic channels for that."

Garcia shook his head. "Of course. I am aware that diplomats can tell your father the same thing, but those same diplomats did not recommend that your country intervene in our struggle for freedom, so we have reservations about that route.

You, though, are a different story. You are in effect *our* chosen diplomat. You will be seeing firsthand, without political guides, the real Marita and the Maritans that ambassadors and politicians do not see. No one will monitor what you see and what you hear. You will be free to go wherever you wish. In return, I ask that you request your government through your father for recognition of Marita as a democracy. From there, Maritans can inch up the ladder with pride." He held out his arms. "It is a small price to pay for a child, would you not say, *señorita*?"

Amy sat, moved by the request. It was a simple one, and not difficult for her to deliver. There would be no controls on her, and she would have her heart's dream.

"No, General," she said in a soft, sincere voice. "It isn't much to ask. But my father has always favored a Maritan democracy. And how do you not know I would have done what you're asking anyway?"

Garcia smiled wryly. "We know of your father's feelings, but he has not been here for ten years, and recently his information comes to him from professionals. The committee will need to be swayed. Granting him a granddaughter and treating you with courtesy will give him an additional incentive." His eyes softened with ironic humor. "As for your second question, Americans can be careless, but they rarely go back on their word. I doubt that you will. Now, *señorita*, we need to honor that other American trait, haste. I'm sure you are ready to be on your way."

Amy smiled with relief as he reached for a pen and began signing the documents. "Yes, I am."

Garcia's mouth curved sardonically as he set aside the pen and handed the papers to her.

"There you are, and please, give my regards to Señor Crawford."

Amy toyed with the coffee cup, her mouth thinning. "I'm afraid I didn't see him this morning."

Garcia chuckled. "Señorita Blake, you are a delight. If I don't miss my guess, your Señor Crawford is hidden outside—how do you say—'armed to the teeth,' ready to storm the Palacio to save you if need be. He is, I'm sure, not seconds away."

Amy wasn't as convinced. Why hadn't he shown up this morning to at least wish her well and make arrangements for their meeting with Mrs. Cordova?

Putting down her coffee cup, she stood up, and Garcia escorted her across the office.

She paused at the door.

"General, what happened to the woman at the airport yesterday?"

Garcia's eyes flickered. "She was merely wounded...we gave her medical aid, but now she is in custody."

Disturbed, Amy frowned. "A woman. What a shame."

Garcia laughed with a hoarse, humorless intake of breath. "We do not condone smuggling in Marita. The woman in question was carrying millions of dollars' worth of drugs destined for the streets of your country. Do not be duped by gender, Señorita Blake. Only in the civilized world are women considered the weaker sex. Here, in Marita, we know better."

Panic nipped at her throat. She wondered what would happen to Crawford if Garcia found out about *his* smuggling escapades. There was certainly no love lost between the men. She put the thought out of her head, determined not to worry about it.

She looked at him questioningly. "Do *you* have a family, General?"

Garcia's hard features immediately tensed. His hands clenched by his sides. "I did have—a wife and a daughter—but they starved to death in the last regime."

Amy gasped in horror as sympathy flooded her. For a brief moment, she saw not a revolutionary leader, but a man, who like herself had known bitter and deep anguish that would torment him the rest of his days. Life's tragedies spared no one. Her heart cried out to him. She too had lost a spouse and child. There was no greater torture. But his loss had been far more devastating than hers, she thought. To lose them that way...

She met his gaze with pain in her own eyes. No wonder he was so zealous to forge a new country with a future. A country where what happened to his wife and daughter could never happen again. "I'm so sorry, General. How awful."

He shrugged, although she could tell from the set of his jaw and the rigid stretch of his shoulders under the uniform that he was feeling not just a resurgence of agony, but reined-in anger.

There was also another emotion mirrored in his eyes that she couldn't identify.

"What happened to them was very common. Many Maritans died this way. They were unfortunately casualties of corruption. Ask your Señor Crawford. He knows about corruption."

He held the door open for her, and said softly, "Tell Crawford to be careful. My information is that there are still many soldiers hiding up there, perhaps even Orega. *Buenos dias, señorita*. Do not forget our bargain. I hope you find what you're looking for. Very few of us do." Bowing, he turned and retreated to his desk.

Where the hell was she?

Crawford stood across from the Palacio, nerves taut. Five minutes was enough to review paperwork. Anything more and formality turned into interrogation. He'd seen it happen countless times, not just in Marita but in half a dozen war-devastated countries. It always started with a polite inquiry. "Please, *señor*, let me see your papers. It will only take a moment."

Bingo, he thought. Ten minutes later, you were in jail wondering what the hell you'd done. Wondering where logic and civility had disappeared to in such a short span of time. Then you were screaming as the interrogation segued into something more horrific.

And you were always powerless to protest your innocence, because fanatics weren't looking for innocence, they were searching for guilt.

In his experience, they nearly always found it.

He blew out a choking ribbon of smoke. Underneath his practiced charm, Garcia *was* a fanatic. And Amy Blake had the appearance of guilt.

He closed his eyes uncomfortably. Amy Blake had also been with Garcia for a heck of a lot longer than five minutes.

He tightened his hand on the sawed-off Uzi, calculating his chances of separating her from Garcia's men. They weren't good.

The image of her being manhandled made him physically ill. Fear and anger had him sweating profusely under his fatigues. The thoughts running through his brain made his stomach retch. If that bastard or any of his minions harmed one hair of her head, he'd personally tear the man limb from limb....

He opened his eyes wide, trying to chase away painfully graphic images by staring at the blinding sun. He needed to stay cool and professional. He couldn't afford to think of Amy as anything other than an assignment. But in twenty-four hours she'd become far more than that. How, he didn't know. One kiss and the scent of wild roses. How could that be enough to turn a man into a raging bull? Maybe it was the cocky combination of stubbornness and vulnerability that had gotten to him? What other woman did he know who would risk coming to this place just to adopt a child? Alone, no less. No hothouse flower, she. The lady had some courage and conviction. Maybe he was a sucker for that?

Yeah ... right ... and maybe he was just a fool.

Even if he did want the lady, she sure wouldn't ever be interested in a renegade like him. But if she looked at him one more time with those wide, pleading, green eyes, he might not stop to consider whether she was interested or not.

Rigidly, he forced himself to refocus. Now was not the time to analyze men and women and their foibles.

He gritted his teeth. *It shouldn't take twenty minutes to review bloody minor paperwork!*

Any other adoptive parents he'd taken to the junta for approval had been in and out in less time than it took for a sixty-second TV commercial.

His hands clenched. Damn it, what in God's name was keeping her?

When he saw the door of the converted hotel open, his pulse started to pound. Perspiration from his hands made the gun slick in his grasp. Then he saw Amy being escorted by a guard. His breath gagged in the back of his throat. He swallowed it down as it dawned on him she was smiling at the man even as she was waving the chauffeur aside who'd walked up to them.

He stared, absorbing her casual manner in stunned anger. She could have been conversing with her friends on a Boston street. While he was out here, having a coronary...

His insides exploded with relief, then rage.

In three seconds, he was across the street. Balancing the Uzi with his left arm, he grabbed her shoulder with his right hand and glared at her.

"Just what were you doing in there? Discussing the planetary system?" Furiously, he whirled her around.

Amy's eyes widened in terror. He'd come up on her so suddenly, she'd almost screamed. She gulped back her fear quickly. "Crawford," she stumbled. "Hello."

Crawford could have hit her for her calmness. To think he'd been worried to death about her.

His fingers dug into her arm as his gaze narrowed. "Forget the niceties," he growled. "What took you so long?"

Amy still regarded him in amazement. She'd never seen him look so savage. Surely concern wasn't fueling this display of temper. Out of the corner of her eye, she saw the two other men drift surreptitiously away. She didn't blame them.

Too confused to argue, she said, "General Garcia went over my papers and we talked about Maritan democracy, but that's all. Why? What's the matter?" She glanced around, thinking something might have happened that she wasn't aware of. The streets looked quiet enough, though.

Crawford took a deep breath, cursing himself for being so irrational. He was livid with himself. But he was just as livid with her. He tried to control his raging emotions.

"What do you think is the matter?" he snapped. "You've been in there long enough to adopt ten kids. In case you've forgotten, it's my job to look after you. More than five minutes with the junta and I worry. Get it?"

Amy's fear vanished. She couldn't keep from smiling. So Garcia had been right. All of a sudden, she was beginning to understand this man. And perhaps even like him. No one need ever fear that Crawford wouldn't deliver. For a man she'd believed didn't have a heart, she was finding out she might just be wrong. Happily wrong.

"I think it's great that you would worry about me," she said, grinning, enjoying the moment.

"Great?" he snarled in disbelief. "This isn't a Hollywood movie, Ms. Blake."

She knew it wasn't. The dangers were real. She recognized that, even as she recognized she didn't want to dwell on them, but she also knew that right now she was riding so high on Garcia's decision that nothing could bring her down. But Crawford's concern did touch her more than she was showing.

Her smile softened. "I know, but Crawford, you sure make me think it is," she teased gently.

Crawford's eyes locked with hers in incredulous anger, then he relented. She was obviously thrilled that Garcia had given her the go-ahead. It was written all over her. Amazingly, he found that he was happy for her. She looked like a child on Christmas day, her eyes bright, her skin flushed and her mouth pursed. It was all he could do from taking her in his arms, capturing her mouth with his and sampling the sweet taste of her joy. He'd bet right now that that added to her natural sensuality would have him writhing in two seconds.

He grunted in defense. "That melodramatic?"

Automatically, she found herself soothing his pride. Why she had no idea. He had more than enough to last him past a hundred.

"It's all right, Crawford. I never had anyone go to such lengths to protect me," she said honestly. She hadn't, either, she thought. When had David ever protected her from anything? True, they'd always been in a civilized world, but weren't there other ways a man could protect and cherish a woman? Couldn't he have comforted her after the loss of their child . . . ?

Then again, she was paying Crawford.

"I was scared to death for you," he announced with bald roughness.

She lifted her head up. Don't analyze it, she thought. He'd been willing to risk his life for her. That was enough. Whatever his reasons.

Moistening her lips slowly, she said in a husky voice, "Thank you, Crawford. Thank you for caring."

Crawford drew in a sharp breath as she tilted her head. Her eyes reminded him of fresh, clean grass and her thick, black hair of a midnight cloud. The expression in her gaze was so genuine and trusting and her voice so entrancing, he felt everything inside him turning to full alert.

He *could* take her right now, here on the dusty streets of Marita. Audience or no audience. She was both vulnerable and euphoric over her victory with Garcia. Impressed with his soldier routine. He could capitalize on that.

If he'd wanted to treat her like a tart. If he'd wanted to take advantage of her.

He stepped back.

He wanted her but not badly enough to jeopardize their relationship.

Whatever that was, he thought. The reflection gave him an uncomfortable gut-wrenching start.

"Forget it," he said in a strained voice. "Let's hightail it over to Giselda Cordova's before Garcia changes his mind."

Giselda weighed at least two hundred pounds, but her face was beautifully smooth and her eyes a vivid hazel behind small wire-framed glasses. Her eyes crinkled in a smile as she ushered them into a cramped, small office. Everywhere, papers and folders were stacked in piles—even on the floor.

Amy accepted her handshake. "I'm pleased to meet you."

"So, you are here at long last, Señorita Blake. Please, please, come on in. Move that file off the seat—that's it—on the floor." Dropping Amy's hand, she laughed as Amy cleared a spot and sat on the edge. "You see," the huge woman said, waving her hands expansively. "Lots of room, it's just how you organize it."

Amy couldn't keep from chuckling.

"Well—" Giselda took a seat next to an old wooden desk and leaning forward, finally took time out to snatch a breath. She surveyed them both with astute, sparkling eyes—Amy sitting, Crawford looking around for space. "Look at you and . . . Señor Crawford. One could almost imagine you were a couple."

With that, she stopped and beamed beatifically at both of them.

Crawford picked a wall and leaned against it, glancing down wryly at Amy, who felt dazed by the woman's sheer size and overwhelming personality.

"She's always like this," he confided unabashedly in front of Giselda. "Garcia once said the only reason he would never arrest her is that she would give him a headache, she talks so much."

"Hah! Him!" Giselda snorted. "Garcia may be teasing at times, but he's ruthless and much to be feared. I hear you visited him this morning. What happened?"

Amy's eyes widened on the woman with whom she'd been corresponding for over a year.

"How did you know?"

Giselda's eyes shadowed. "Even lovers' whispers become common knowledge in a place like Marita. Everyone spies on everyone. The revolution has not quite wiped out that scourge....." She shook her head, blinking. "But let's not go into that. What did he say? I assume he wanted to go over your travel and adoption papers."

Amy nodded. Somehow she didn't think it was appropriate to discuss the rest of her conversation with Garcia.

"He said everything was in order, and I was free to travel wherever I wanted."

Giselda appeared surprised at the lack of restriction but like everything else she did, she switched emotions quickly.

Grabbing a file, she pulled it toward her. "Wonderful. Now we can get down to business. The more children we can get adopted, the better I sleep at night." She checked the tab on the file, then with a big hand, flipped it open.

Amy took a deep breath, recognizing intuitively that Giselda's comment wasn't prompted by greed. There was nothing in the almost-ramshackle house to suggest that Giselda was the least bit materialistic. She had been recommended to Amy as a reputable broker and lawyer who was committed to helping South American children find a better life. Amy had unreservedly placed her trust and faith in the woman; now, in person, she was relieved to find that Giselda was every bit as dynamic and straightforward as their countless letters and phone calls had led Amy to believe.

The lawyer looked up from the file at Amy, her gaze taking in Crawford, as well.

She came right to the point. "Carmela has been moved. Her custodians have moved higher up the mountains—do you know the Manion Range?" Giselda directed the latter to Crawford.

He nodded, a brooding expression on his face.

"Well, that's where she is."

Amy glanced sharply at Crawford, wondering about his re-action. "But why has she been moved?" she asked, trying to control her heartbeat. Just hearing someone else say her child's name out loud had caused something wild and wonderful to flutter inside her. "And ... is that bad?"

Giselda addressed the questions in sequence. "There was some rough weather where they were, flooding and very little food. They know they told you they'd wait, but they felt they had no choice but to move to the Manion Range. They have relatives there who have more food.''

Amy's eyelashes fluttered. Something was very wrong here. She felt her earlier confidence eroding. ''But I sent over ten thousand dollars to you. Didn't you give them any money ahead of time?''

Giselda softened her tone. ''Only a small portion. I kept the rest of it in a trust account.''

Amy felt herself growing angry and her hands clenching. ''They deserve that money. They shouldn't have to keep traveling in order to be able to eat.''

Giselda shuffled her ample body in the seat and regarded Amy with penetrating eyes. ''You're right, they do deserve the money—but only *after* you have the child. Do you have any idea how many times North Americans have paid in advance only to discover that the mother or the father or the grandmother or the grandfather or the cousin or whoever had changed his or her mind? What can happen then with many of the couples is that they don't have enough money to look for another child. It can be heartbreaking. I'm sorry if I did something that you don't approve of.''

Amy didn't want to deal with logic. If the family had absconded with the money, she'd have found more somehow, but for the family to go without . . . she shook her head, trying to calm down, realizing that Giselda believed she'd made the best decision in Amy's best interest, but she still wished Giselda had consulted her.

It was a good thing she wasn't in Giselda's position, she thought. She wouldn't be tough enough. Her anger waned, but not her compassion.

''It's all right,'' she sighed resignedly. ''I know you did what you thought best.''

Giselda looked relieved. She opened her mouth to speak, but Crawford interrupted tersely. ''Couldn't the family have brought the child down here?''

Giselda paused, swiveling her chair in his direction. ''No, they have eight children themselves. They can't leave them.''

''How much farther away is the Manion Range?'' Amy asked.

Crawford replied in a tight voice. ''A few days more so it'll be a week's journey either way.''

"Two weeks?"

Amy gasped in dismay, her eyes flying to his. Another week of being in his company, fighting this attraction she felt. Another week of proximity, tight quarters, intimate moments. Another week of watching his lithe, cat-like body flex and prowl, making her want to reach out and touch its sinewy shape....

"Are you sure?" she asked in a hushed voice. Now she understood his reaction. He obviously wasn't pleased about having to spend any more time with her than he had to.

"At the least," he replied dryly, catching the obvious distaste she felt for the extra week in his company. He wasn't thrilled, either. His self-control wasn't that good.

He turned to Giselda. "Have you investigated whether someone could go up there and get the child—like me for instance—and bring her back down?"

"I did. Once I knew you'd been hired by Señorita Blake, I sent a messenger up there, but the family politely refused. They want very much to meet Carmela's mother before they entrust the child to her. These are very concerned foster parents. Carmela's parents were their neighbors in the last town they lived in."

Amy was touched by the family's attitude. It had been their care and caution that had told her she wanted very much to adopt Carmela, but still it meant she really was stuck with Sam Crawford for two weeks.

Two whole weeks. Dear God.

Chapter 6

Perspiring, Amy carried the last armful of groceries from the foyer of the Mendoza house and loaded them into the back of Crawford's truck. Pausing, she stepped back, absently adjusting her unruly hair, and frowned at the equipment and supplies that Crawford had already loaded. It was hard to believe two people would actually use all the stuff piled inside. There were enough supplies in the truck to stock an army—cans of food, tools, bottles of water, coolers of beer, and nestled in one corner, an array of guns and boxes of plastic explosives. She wondered why they needed so many. Was Crawford planning on blasting them through the mountains? she mused wryly.

Tensing, she realized he'd come up behind her.

Passing her without a word, he tossed another blanket in the truck, which made her raise her eyebrows. Considering the sultry weather, the blankets seemed an affront. She opened her mouth to say something, then closed it firmly. Two weeks with the argumentative Crawford was going to sap all her reserves. There wasn't any point in wasting valuable energy.

He shut the door. "That's it," he said, slapping the exterior and turning. "Now let's get the hell out of here before the real heat hits."

Picking up her tote bag and following, Amy regarded his sinewy retreating back incredulously. The day was a scorcher. It was barely nine o'clock and already ribbons of sweat were trickling along her spine, wending down the backs of her legs under the baggy pants she was wearing and gathering in her underarms, creating a sticky film over her skin. *Real* heat. He had to be joking.

She climbed into the passenger side of the truck beside him. "I think you just like giving me bad news, Crawford. Surely, it couldn't get any hotter than this?"

He took off his sunglasses to temporarily run his hands over his eyelids.

"You want to bet?"

She was perversely pleased to see that he didn't exactly look as cool as a cucumber, either, although on him, the heat and even the beads of perspiration sent off sexy, powerful, virile messages.

She arched her brows at him elaborately. "Don't you think you're exaggerating just a little, Crawford?"

"You haven't felt anything until you've experienced high noon in Marita," he replied in an arid voice. "You feel like you're burning up if you're not used to it. Nothing cools you off except maybe stripping right down—" his gaze suddenly dipped pointedly to the front of her blouse and lingered "—but then I see you already had the right idea . . . good thinking to dump the bra. . . ."

Indignation rippled through her. Combative, unwise words were out of her mouth before she could stop them.

"Why? See something you like, Crawford?"

The question startled both of them. The air around them seemed to still.

Their gazes locked in challenge.

She couldn't mean it, he thought, his throat tightening. Slowly, deliberately, disbelievingly, he lifted his gaze to her face. Her skin looked warm, flushed and inviting and her raven hair was snaking around the front of her slim neck in damp tendrils. He could imagine what both would be like to the touch— one soft and satiny, the other lush and thick. His mind, though, was still filled with the realization that underneath the shirt she was wearing, there was nothing but bare, perfect female flesh.... For one brief moment, his throat went dry, then self-preservation kicked in.

"You haven't got anything I haven't seen before, sweetheart."

Amy lifted her eyebrows, her heart thumping as his hard, sensual mouth twisted into a wry slant. Against all reason, she felt herself wanting to feel those same lips against hers again. They'd been tough, compelling, she remembered...but they'd also been incredibly soft and seductive, sweet and heady to taste.

"Please don't be crude, Crawford."

He felt something akin to anger surging through him. Passion? he wondered. If she only knew what he wanted to do with that cool reserve of hers.

"Relax, angel, I was only looking."

Amy took a deep breath as she felt his eyes wandering. Her nipples puckered and strained against the shirt. In silent response, his gaze darkened, then circled in a kind of rolling caress. She felt like sinking through the ground with embarrassment. Then very slowly, he looked questioningly at her face. She steeled herself not to look away, but her breath stopped short of burning the back of her throat. Expecting derision, she met his gaze head-on but was stunned to read a hungry desire in his dusty blue eyes. Confused by the look, she inhaled a shaky breath. The first and last time they'd kissed, it had been *he* who'd pulled away. The hurt of that rejection resurfaced, fueled by pride.

"Since I can't afford to spend all my time worrying about your libido, Crawford, it's comforting to realize I don't have to. So, if you want to know, I just couldn't stand the thing another minute longer. How would you like to wear a jockstrap in this heat all day long?"

His hand tightened in a damp ring on the door handle as he growled low in his throat. He'd wanted to teach her a lesson. Instead, he was getting lectured royally.

The thought didn't sit well with him.

"You don't have to justify your style of dress to me. I'm not much of a fan of bras either—for obvious reasons. They get in the way of a man and woman's pleasure."

Her mouth dropped open. She wished she had something to throw at him.

She closed her eyes, then opened them again, a groan lodging in her throat as she thought ahead to the two weeks they were going to be spending together. If there were any other way to reach Carmela without Crawford, right now, she'd take it.

Impatiently, she waited for him to get right into the truck. She felt frustrated, but she couldn't tell him to get lost. If she did, she knew he'd take her up on it. The look on his face in Giselda's office had told her volumes.

He climbed into the driver's seat and slammed the door behind him.

But before he even had the keys in the ignition, she asked, "How come we've got so many guns in the truck?"

He dangled his large tanned hand over the steering wheel, his expression arrogant. "There's been a revolution here, in case you've forgotten. We might need them, wouldn't you say?"

"An entire arsenal?"

Moving his hand, Crawford broodingly released the hand brake. How could one tiny woman with such an angel face be so annoying? And how could he be attracted to her at the same time? His jaw tensed to his temples. If she knew what she was doing to him, she'd realize she was courting double trouble. He might be able to keep her safe from the vanquished army, but how safe was she going to be from him?

Or he from her?

He blinked hard, his mahogany-dark lashes fanning with exasperation. "Considering that you're a U.S. senator's daughter, we may well be underequipped...."

"Come on, Crawford, there's no need to be so melodramatic."

"Tell me I'm dreaming, Ms. Blake. Nobody can be that naive."

Amy sent him a withering look that she wished could kill. Crawford, she'd discovered, had a nasty habit of introducing reality when she least wanted to hear it.

"It's not naïveté, it's determination. All I'm concentrating on is finding the little girl who's waiting for me." If she was expecting him to be deterred by her expression, she was mistaken.

He snorted, hitting the keys with his hand. "Oh, really! That's very commendable and all that, but if word gets out you're in Marita, you're suddenly going to become very vulnerable to terrorists and if you're vulnerable, then as your guide, I'm vulnerable.'' His eyes narrowed. "That's not my favorite position, Ms. Blake, so I decided to even up the odds with a little firepower."

She saw a hard, almost frightening glint in his eyes. Something told her that he wasn't just being cocky.

"Nobody's going to be firing guns because of me, Crawford."

"The hell they aren't. You're as good as gold to this crew, sweetheart."

She fidgeted with the strap of her knapsack. Maybe he was right. Maybe she was just trying to avoid the uncomfortable truth, and maybe that was part of the reason she was so annoyed with him.

She tossed back her hair with an impatient gesture. She hated the fact that he might be right. "Okay. Perhaps you do have a point."

"Perhaps!" His stomach muscles jerked in reflex. "Don't do me any favors, Ms. Blake. The word isn't 'perhaps,' it's 'absolutely.' I'm *absolutely* right."

Amy's eyes flashed green fire back at him.

"I've agreed with you, Crawford. Isn't that enough?"

He expelled a hot breath of frustration, his brows lifting at the spirit of her delivery. Her face had become beautifully animated, flushed by the heat and her anger. Her soft mouth was parted in a sultry, voluptuous pout as she glared at him. The temptation to grind his own down on it was overwhelming.

Right now, he thought, there were some ground rules to cover. Nerves clawed at his stomach at what could happen to her in the mountains if she took any chances.

Fear fanned his anger. "Look, Ms. Blake, this is my world we're in now. It's a world of guns, violence and very little honor, and there's only one way we can both survive in it—my way. If I have to stop and explain everything we're doing as we do it, not only will we not get where we're going, but we likely won't get there in one piece, either. From here on in, I'm the boss, and no second-guessing from you."

"I'm not stupid, Crawford, nor am I a child, so you can stop treating me like one."

"Then don't act like one."

Amy took a deep breath to control her temper. He was getting to her when she'd made up her mind she wouldn't let him. His eyes were glitteringly determined and his features had hardened into sharp, fascinating planes and lines. He looked rough and conceited, his whole body posture dangerous, but her heart was fluttering ridiculously. He was without a doubt the most arrestingly masculine man she'd ever encountered. She was reacting to that, as much as anything, fighting her attraction to him, couching it in other terms, she realized in amazement.

She unclenched her fists, realizing she had to physically keep from venting her frustration at the very body that was causing her distress.

"I'll try to remember what you said."

Crawford sat stock-still, tensing at the tightly reined emotion coloring her voice. Halfhearted surrenders always brought the worst out in him.

He angled his body toward her, jamming his hand across the back of the seat. Why was it with her, he could never be reasonable? "Not good enough, Ms. Blake. I give the orders and you obey—got it?"

"Don't push your luck, Crawford."

Something in her disdainful tone made him snap. He sized her up as the type to put herself in danger just so *he* couldn't have the upper hand. The image was disturbing. Thinking of what could happen to her tore a hole in his gut. But thinking that he might care more than he ought to upset his peace of mind.

He drew in hot, arid air that burned his lungs. Why the hell couldn't he just keep an objective distance from her? Why the hell hadn't she stayed at home?

He was tired of thinking, he decided. He bridged the space separating them, and with two rough hands seized her shoulders and jerked her forward.

"Damn," he muttered in a harsh voice.

Unprepared for his sudden movement, Amy gasped, her eyes flying open in alarm as he pulled her body around and pressed it into his.

Her lashes brushed upward in dismay as she struggled against him. His fierce strength made her heart turn over. His damp hands were unbelievably sensual as they dug into her bare skin. She tried to draw back, but his grip was a solid, burning vice.

Her head began to swim. Stunned, she could only stare at him.

Crawford paused, also unprepared for the rush of sweet heat that instantly exploded to life as he felt her body crush against his. Cause and effect, he immediately thought. For every effect, there's a cause. She was the cause of these quick flaring arrows of need that were burning his insides.

Their gazes locked.

Amy found her voice before he did. "Just what do you think you're doing?"

Touching her sent wild flares of need through him. He closed his eyes and opened them again, reminding himself that wasn't what this was about.

"Shaking some sense into you. This is no joke, Ms. Blake. There may be some rough stuff ahead of us. When I say to do something, you're going to do it, hear me? Your life might well depend on your doing exactly what I tell you to do. I can't be worried about whether you will or won't obey."

The last word flew in Amy's face like a red flag. She'd given control too many times to her husband to ever want to fall into the trap again.

Her green eyes turned dark. "For your information, Crawford, I'm perfectly capable of making decisions on my own." She went to twist out of his arms, but unfortunately her body pressed closer to his.

His pulse went out of control as he felt the imprint of each curve burn into his consciousness.

In protest, he punctuated his words, his gaze lancing her. "You'll give me your word now, or we don't go. Is that clear?"

Her eyes narrowed with frustration as she tried to pull away from him again and found she couldn't. She shook back her shoulders and discovered that did no good, either. The man's arms must have been molded in bronze. Anger flared up in her.

"Let me go," she rasped.

"Not until you agree that I'm in charge."

She tilted her head in elegant defiance. "I can live without your display of male breast-beating, Crawford," she replied in a tart voice.

She was fire and ice, he thought. Driving him crazy one minute with her smoldering looks, chilling him out the next with her words. Two weeks together, and he was going to be a basket case.

His eyes turned a turbulent blue. He wasn't about to lose this particular contest of wills, however.

"This isn't about macho posturing, Ms. Blake. This is about survival—yours and mine."

"Really, Crawford."

"Angel, you may not value your life, but I sure as hell value mine, such as it is. What the hell is this? You get a kick out of being an ostrich?"

Amy shivered, the quick intensity of his expression unnerving her. He was taking risks for her, she had to admit that.

It cost her, but she managed to ground out, "Okay, I'm sorry—happy?"

His hands tightened on her arms while his eyes registered disbelief.

"Come again? Surely, that's not an apology?" he said sarcastically.

Amy caught her breath at how the simplest change in pressure of his fingers could make her whole body feel fluid and shapeless. She became aware of the lean, muscled body pressed so intimately against hers, and of the confinement of the cab of the truck. She felt the heat from his body flow into hers almost forcefully as if ironically demanding a welcoming haven. The heat matched the man. Tough and consuming. Hard to ignore. Suddenly, she couldn't breathe. She turned uncomfortably as a tiny ache, a twist of need began to smolder inside her. She couldn't remember ever having experienced such a quick hunger for a man. She felt hypnotized by it, unable to let it go as the rough touch of his fingers dug into her bare skin. She wanted to melt into him.

Ridiculous. Insane. Crawford wasn't the kind of man for her to open up to. A rogue like him had about as much sensitivity as a barracuda.

Relentlessly, she pushed the longing down.

She'd contributed to this argument. She'd better finish it, she told herself. "All right. All right. I do tend not to dwell on problems. If I think about them too much, I get petrified. I drive my friends crazy, so I guess I'm bound to drive you a little crazy, too. By ignoring problems, I guess I just hope they'll go away. Call it a character flaw, but that's the way I am. Take it or leave it, Crawford. I'm not backing down any more than that.''

With a final wrench, she broke free of him.

Instinct told Crawford that really was as much of a concession as he was going to get.

He drew back slowly, taking a deep breath. He liked the fact she could admit to having failings. Put her on a more human scale. Although that might not be such an advantage, he realized as he inhaled an intoxicating whiff of sunlight on her satiny skin, laced with an alluring, but faint scent of roses. Barely an inch still separated them. Given the way he felt at the moment, it was a very dangerous and tempting inch.

He jerked his arms from her shoulders and slanted her a meaningful look.

"Some problems you can't wish away, Ms. Blake."

Including him? she wondered, her heart pounding. Was he warning her?

Her lips thinned with determination. One man in her life had already tried to orchestrate her every move. The memory didn't sit well with her. She felt the force of old frustration and pain brimming over into her voice.

"I got this far living my life in such a haphazard fashion, Crawford, so if you don't mind, I'll just keep on doing it, thank you very much."

He wasn't one to retreat easily. Somehow, though, he sensed now was the time. He blew out a sigh. "All right, let's compromise, then. Let me do all the worrying about the problems, and all you have to promise is to follow—" deliberately he stayed away from the more combative "obey" as her eyes flashed "—my directions—okay?"

She was a little taken aback by his civility, but just then Mercedes and Raoul came out of the house and up to the door of the truck.

"Señorita Blake, we have present for baby...." Mercedes stopped by the truck holding up a tiny yellow quilt splashed with blue flowers. They were the same kind of flowers she'd seen in Mercedes's garden and in some of the window boxes gracing the town's houses. Since she hadn't recognized them, she'd assumed they were unique to Marita.

The gesture so moved her that, everything else forgotten, she breathed, "Oh Mercedes, Raoul, it's beautiful."

Her eyes glistened with pleasure as she accepted the present through the open window. It smelled just the way it looked—like a summer meadow of wildflowers misted in sunlight.

She pressed it to her cheek, breathing in the lovely scent. "I don't know what to say. Thank you very much."

The couple beamed. "I make in spare time," Mercedes told her.

What wonderful caring people they were, she thought. She wished she could say something that would convey her gratitude. Her eyes locked with the older woman's. "I'll treasure it always, and I'm sure Carmela will, too, as a reminder of Marita, her country."

Mercedes's head bobbed up and down with pride and pleasure. Amy let out a sigh of relief. Obviously, it had been the right thing to say.

"God be with you, *señorita*," Mercedes replied, touching Amy's hand gently. "And you, Crawford..." Eyes flashing, she brandished a hand at him. "You take good care, you hear...."

Crawford chuckled. "I always do, Mercedes. See you in a couple of weeks." He turned the key in the ignition, gunning the motor.

Glancing over her shoulder, Amy waved farewell to the Spanish couple until the truck turned the corner, heading north toward the mountains.

As soon as she settled in the seat, Crawford's dry voice ordered, "Buckle up, Ms. Blake."

"You know, you could call me Amy," she said as she stretched her arm behind her to reach for the seat belt.

Crawford turned and regarded her cryptically. He thought about the fine line that he'd established between client and woman. About how little it would take for him to cross the line. And how hungry and hot he'd be for her by the time he did it—*if* he did it.

He shook his head.

"No, Ms. Blake, I couldn't."

With a start, Amy sat up and glanced at her watch. It was almost two p.m. They'd been driving for five hours. By her count, they'd also skirted about half a dozen towns, but Crawford had chosen not to stop. Stretching her back muscles, she worked the kinks out of her shoulders. The truck, its shock absorbers worn, gave a bumpy ride.

A wisp of mountain air drifted through the open window and cooled her hot skin. Gratefully, she shifted in the seat, turning her head toward the breeze so she could enjoy its full effect. On its wing she inhaled the deep scent of mysterious mountain foliage.

"Have a nice nap?"

She turned, refocusing on Crawford. His wrists were relaxed on the wheel, but the corded tendons in his arms strained against his taut skin. She remembered the feel of those arms in the airport, in Mercedes's garden and when they'd first started out on their trip. They'd made her feel safe, wanted.

"Fine, thank you. How are you doing?"

He was thirsty is what he was, he decided. He sucked in hard, savoring the same welcoming cloud of mountain breeze that she had. "I'm about ready for a beer."

Amen, she thought. "Make that two."

Crawford stilled. "What, no lecture?" he asked warily.

"About what?"

"Drinking, driving."

"Oh...." She shook her head, her smile spreading. "If I lecture you, I might not get one."

Crawford turned his gaze to her face, catching the sparkle in her eyes and returning her smile, without thinking. How many years had it been since he'd felt enthralled by the teasing lilt in a woman's voice? How many years since a woman's voice had soothed its way down his spine like lush velvet? Too many.

"Okay, we'll stop in about half an hour. I know just the spot."

"Where do you get your milk money, Crawford?" She gave him a curious look.

He half angled his head toward her. "What milk money?"

"The money you use to buy milk for the children, and beer and wine for the adults."

"Oh, that." He wondered how she knew. Mercedes and Raoul, he imagined. "I don't need much to live on, so some of it comes from my salary if I get one. The rest comes from my mother."

"Your mother!"

He chuckled, enjoying her reaction. "Yeah. She's been an activist since the year One. She coerces all her cronies into donations. She also coerces them into giving up their kids' toys. The beer and wine, though, come from my dad. They're both retired from the forces now, so it gives them something to do."

So that was where he got the strong sense of justice that he seemed so determined to deny. "How do you get the stuff in here?"

Crawford laughed again. "My brother's a pilot. He flies in low at night."

She was absolutely amazed. Somehow, she'd have imagined that Crawford was born over forty, with no family ties whatsoever. "I think that's—"

He interrupted her. "Quiet, Ms. Blake. Look."

He turned the truck around a tight corner. Startled, Amy looked forward. What she saw made her gasp in awe. They were at the foot of the Tackazan Mountains. The contrast to the terrain they'd just traveled was startling. For hours they'd been driving through dreary flatland leveled by revolution. Now, the mountains rose in front of them like majestic, mighty survivors. Wide-eyed, she soaked them in.

As far as she could see, the towering natural skyscrapers of slate lanced the horizon, blending with the sky in slashes of dark power. Lush, thick vegetation clung to the base and lower sides while massive trees stretched upward following the mountains' reach for the heavens. Myriad wildflowers and bushes thrived in colorful splendor, cocooned by the trees and shaded by their incredible overhangs.

Crawford deliberately slowed the truck.

He knew what it was like to see the Tackazan Mountains for the first time. They were universally breathtaking. Their silent power still managed to stir even *his* jaded senses. Man never ceased to disappoint him, but nature, so far, had continued to capture his respect—its rules notwithstanding, of course.

"Not bad, are they?"

"Glorious," she murmured in amazement, forcing herself to look away from the range. She struggled for the right words. "They're...magnificent...pure..." As her eyes settled on his granite profile, other words came automatically to mind. Uncompromisingly raw and durable in their essence.

Like him, she thought, fleetingly startled by the comparison.

Crawford pushed his sunglasses back before he picked up speed again.

"Enjoy it while you can. Later on, as we get higher, you'll see a lot of barren land."

"But why?"

"The land's been indiscriminately stripped of its resources." His jawline worked tightly with disgust. "Greedy dictators and the ravages of war know no bounds, Ms. Blake."

She tossed back her dark hair, frowning. As often as her father had talked about Marita, his stories had always been told through the haze of wonderful, idealistic memories. To him, Marita had been an idyllic place filled with peace and basic values. Now, whenever they passed small towns, villages or even simple settlements, she saw flashing evidences of destruction. But also, she saw Maritans clearing away the debris of the war, rebuilding and working the land, taking the first step toward self-reliance. They never seemed idle. Everywhere she looked, she saw backbreaking but cheerful activity and industry.

If sheer work could put a country back on its feet, then the Maritans were halfway there, she thought.

"When my father talked about Marita, he always talked about how rich it was—how you could live off the land if you wanted."

"A lot of damage can be done in ten years."

Her eyes saddened at his words as her gaze returned to the verdant display nestling at the foot of the mountains. To think that greed and war could destroy such natural splendor. This beautiful wild country was her new daughter's heritage, and she was sensing a growing affinity inside her with the nation's contradictions—its turbulent history and yet its natural sense of peace. It was staggering to think of how much it would take to bring the country into the twentieth century, and yet it had so much to offer. Even to her untrained eye, the forestry and mining potential alone should help it achieve some measure of economic strength. And the plants could easily be a treasure trove of herbs and medicines.

She took off her sunglasses and, wiping away the thin line of perspiration that had gathered beneath the rims, asked, "Were you here when President Vernas was ousted?"

"No, that was well before my time, but I've heard about what happened. Vernas didn't have control of Orega, and Orega had control of the army. The writing was on the wall. It was bound to happen." He ran his fingers through his hair, tipping his head to look at the clouds above them, swearing silently at the weather. It didn't look any too promising.

He shook his head absently, continuing, "If whoever's in power doesn't have the backing of the army, then he or she is walking on thin ice. That's why so many generals end up running underdeveloped countries like this. Unfortunately, a lot of armies are corrupt."

Amy pushed her loose blouse back onto her shoulders and regarded him with interest. "What about Garcia's army? Is it any good?"

He shrugged noncommittally. "Time will tell, Ms. Blake."

"How about Garcia himself?"

The muscles in his jaw moved imperceptibly, tightening his bronzed features. "Not bad, I suppose."

Amy took a deep breath, wondering what was between the men. If Crawford had fought alongside Garcia's men, why weren't they at least on civil terms? Crawford seemed simple enough to understand on the surface—basic, primitive, aggressive. Yet she didn't quite believe that was all there was to him. Style wasn't substance. When he'd kissed her, underneath the fire, she'd felt a very deep tenderness. The kind of tenderness she would hardly have expected to find in a soldier for hire.

"Why don't you like Garcia?"

"We don't like each other."

Amy heard the correction and suppressed a smile. She wondered if he protested just out of habit. "Okay...but why not?"

Crawford frowned. Answering questions about himself was not something he did well. Or entertained. Life was better with distance between people, and he'd put thousands of miles between himself and his old world in order to ensure that distance.

He glowered at her. "What is this? Twenty questions?"

"One question, Crawford. We're going to be together for two weeks. We're going to need to talk about something. What can it hurt?"

Reaching for his cigarettes with one free hand, he searched impatiently for his lighter, relenting against his better judgment. "Garcia should have taken better care of his family. If he had, they might be alive today. I think he's a fanatic, and he thinks I don't have any ideals."

She regarded him in stunned surprise. Somehow, she would have expected him to support a freedom-fighting male like Garcia over the family man.

She frowned. "I think you're being too harsh on Garcia, but is he right about you?" she asked quietly. "Don't you have any ideals?"

"I did."

Amy found the lighter and handed it to him. Her father, accustomed to lobbyists and advocates, used to say, "When the strong retreat, everyone loses a little hope, Amy."

Was this a dimension to Crawford that she hadn't seen before? If so, it struck a chord far deeper than physical attraction and softened her view of him. Had he retreated because he'd become disillusioned? She understood disillusionment and the toll it could take.

She kept her voice even. "You fought to help free the people of Marita from a dictatorship and you buy the children milk. How can you say you gave up your ideals?"

Crawford brought the truck to a halt as he saw the landmark he'd been looking for. Taking off his sunglasses, he turned his body and looked her straight in the eye. Deliberately, he squelched down a pile of memories that had emotional baggage attached to them, memories that held some answers even though there were some questions there weren't any real answers to. Some questions, he'd discovered, were too complicated to ever be resolved. And he'd spent years trying not to think of them.

He didn't want to think about them now, either. And he didn't relish some soft-eyed siren analyzing him for the next couple of weeks. He lit a cigarette while he kept one hand draped over the wheel.

"I didn't exactly say I gave up my ideals, Ms. Blake. I walked away from them to be more precise, and to answer your ques-

tion about fighting for the people of Marita, I did that because that's what I do for a living now. I'm a hired gun—
remember? And as for the milk—come on, that hardly consti-
tutes idealism. We're talking kids, here.''

"Yes, but—"

He interrupted through gritted teeth. "Ms. Blake, if I'd had
any idea you were such a chatterbox, I'd have charged you extra. Enough already. Let's just crack open that beer, shall we,
before I die of thirst?''

Walking away from ideals wasn't the same as giving them up,
she thought stubbornly. But judiciously she clamped her mouth
shut.

She wondered, though, if he realized how much he'd given
away by admitting what he had, not just about Garcia but
about himself.

Chapter 7

"We'll stop here for half an hour and have a bite to eat."
Crawford took off his glasses, squinting in reflex against the
blazing sun as he dropped the basket of food Mercedes had
given them onto the ground beside a couple of rocks. Straightening up, he cautiously surveyed the area around them. There
was no telling where stragglers from Orega's army might be
hiding out. The spot he'd picked, though, was in from the road,
a small natural nook, secluded by trees. They should be reasonably out of sight here, he thought. But if news of Amy
Blake's presence in Marita had gotten out, they'd be hardly safe
anywhere. The farther they got from the center of Marita and
Garcia's stronghold, the more nervous he realized he was about
his client's safety.

He sighed with resignation. Nothing like carrying precious
cargo on your back.

Turning, he asked, "Is thirty minutes enough for you?"

Trailing behind him, Amy carried the two beers that she'd
retrieved from one of the coolers in the truck, her head spinning from the pace he'd set. Crawford had driven hard and fast
to this point, barely slowing for ruts or fallen debris on the
winding roads. He'd hiked up the hill with the same kind of
intensity as he did everything else, leaving her to follow, pant-

ing. He obviously wasn't a man who liked to waste any time. Either that or he couldn't wait to deliver her to their destination and hightail it back in a hurry. So he could dump her once and for all, she thought wryly.

Gratefully, she stopped to catch her breath, inhaling hot ribbons of humid air as she surveyed the hidden sanctuary of trees and rock formations. She'd never have guessed the charming oasis was even here. From the road, she'd doubted it had existed when Crawford had stopped, but he'd unerringly led her to it. The social worker hadn't exaggerated his familiarity with the terrain . . . nor his moodiness, she mused. Tearing her gaze away from the picturesque scene, she refocused on Crawford and the basket of food he was opening. Hunger gnawed at her insides. Breakfast suddenly seemed light-years away. For the better half of the trip she'd been ravenous, but she'd been too stubborn to mention the subject of food to Crawford. Now, she discovered she was past caring.

She blinked her emerald gaze against the sun's golden glare, talking to his back, finally answering his question.

"Just give me something to eat, Crawford, and I'll be finished in sixty seconds."

Crawford had crouched by one of the rocks. Glancing up, his blue eyes darkened with a scowl. "No—it isn't healthy. Eat slowly and savor it. I don't want you dropping dead on me from a twisted stomach."

Amy rolled her eyes, her irritated swallow audible in the quiet surroundings. Back on terra firma, the man was a verbal menace again.

Grimacing, she sank to the ground, gingerly positioning her aching back into the curve of one of the smoother rocks. With a beer dangling from each hand, she drew up her knees, tucked her skirt around them and regarded his granite-stern features with exasperation.

"What in God's name is a twisted stomach?"

He regarded her with a bland expression as he unpacked the basket and placed some sandwiches on its lid.

"Dogs get it whenever they eat a big meal, then exercise right afterward. Actually, I think the proper term for it is 'bloat.'"

"Dogs?" Amy's eyes widened on him. The burning sun slashed golden highlights into his mahogany hair as he tilted his head. With his jutting, arrogant jaw and strong cheekbones, she thought he could easily pass for a Roman god. "Gee, thanks, Crawford."

"Anytime." He crinkled his eyes and offered her a sudden smile—a crooked, slanted curve of sensual lips over perfect teeth. Its quick charm startled her.

"I didn't think you had a sense of humor, Crawford."

He grinned cockily. "I have my moments."

And one of them was now, she thought, her stomach suddenly lurching. That lopsided smile of his could melt steel.

Vigorously, she snapped off the caps of the beer bottles, while she tossed back her hair with a tinge of frustration. She didn't want to think about how irresistible Crawford might be.

Holding one beer bottle close to her face, she pressed it against her parched skin while she handed him the other. Savoring the damp, cool feel of the condensation, she rolled the bottle down from her cheekbone, thinking she'd have given her soul for a cool, body-pounding shower. Her green eyes glinted at him through the haze of bright light as she pulled the bottle away and raised it to her lips. The light was so brilliant, it almost seemed like a shimmering smoke screen with him imprisoned in its net.

She paused with the bottle an inch from her mouth. "Do you have a route and schedule worked out that I should know about, Crawford?"

With two fingers he made short work of the beer cap, jerking it off in one twist. Flexing his broad shoulders under the sweat-stained khaki shirt, he took a healthy swig of the amber liquid before responding.

Leaning back on his haunches, he spoke slowly, savoring the beer as the taste lingered in his mouth. "By nightfall we should hit Aruka. It's a small village, but usually someone can spare a cottage. We should be able to bunk down there."

Amy huddled, rooted to the spot, the "we" striking a note of alarm in her. "You mean *two* cottages, don't you?"

Crawford ran his tongue along his lower lip, licking off the residual film of hops. Above the bottle, his eyebrow lifted at the tightness of her tone. "No, Ms. Blake, I mean cottage... one..."

"But surely—"

Crawford chuckled with quick derision. "Surely, nothing. This isn't Paris we're touring here, Ms. Blake, this is a third-world country." He hadn't expected her to be wildly enthusiastic about sharing quarters with him. After the kind of life she'd led and the type of men she'd likely dated, it didn't take any brains on his part to see that he was hardly a man she'd choose to wake up to no matter what the circumstances. But the thought still piqued him every time it occurred to him.

"Here, six people live in space that one North American usually enjoys," he concluded tersely.

"I realize that," she snapped back without hesitation, anger bristling at the condescending manner he always adopted with her. She was getting fed up with it, she thought. The skin across the back of her small hand stretched taut as her fingers clenched the beer bottle and her gaze locked brilliantly with his. "I merely thought perhaps one family might put you up and another family might take me in. I don't think there's any reason for you to keep treating me like a spoiled princess. I'm well aware of conditions in this country, even though I haven't seen them firsthand before."

Leaning over, he handed her a neatly wrapped cheese sandwich and regarded her with sardonic coolness, glad to have something he could use against her as a defense. "A little temper tantrum, Ms. Blake?"

Amy's lips remained open in consternation while she ignored the cradled sandwich in her hand.

As hungry as she was, she wasn't averse to wiping that smug expression off his face first, she decided testily.

She fingered the sandwich as if it were a ring of worry beads and treated him to a wide, scathing sweep of lashes. "Nothing of the kind, Crawford, I'd just appreciate it if you'd quit dumping on me every chance you get, that's all."

Crawford tensed, narrowing his silver-blue eyes at her. For five hours he'd been avoiding looking at her. In the truck, with the road to distract him, he'd felt secure, but out here, he was forced into meeting her gaze head-on. Her hair had become disarrayed from the hot breezes. Thick strands, almost blue-black, like ink, clung to her damp neck. Her mouth, parted with challenging words, was moist and inviting, free of lipstick, yet ripe with color from the heat. He thought of the wild magic those lips could weave under his, and his recalcitrance dug in deeper.

Aggression was his best protection, he decided.

He cocked his head. "I don't dump on you," he lied. "But okay, I'll try to improve my manners if it makes you happy." Amy almost tossed the sandwich in his face.

"What would make me happy, Crawford, is for you to just spill out whatever it is about me that irritates you so much, and then we can both forget about it. Quite frankly, I'm not interested in being your personal verbal punching bag for the next two weeks."

He raked his fingers through his hair, frowning irritably. He might just have deserved that, he thought. "I do not treat you as if you were my personal punching bag."

Amy planted the beer bottle on the ground with a thud, noting the quick flexing of his jaw. It was extremely satisfying to finally be able to nail him on something, she discovered. All her tension to date she put into her barrage of questions.

"Oh, yes, you do. Admit it, Crawford, something about me annoys you. But what I'd like to know is, why? Is it the way I look? Is it the fact that I'm single and adopting a child? Do you think I'm too pampered, not tough enough?" Sarcastic frustration crept into her voice. "Maybe between now and the end of this trip, I could change whatever it is that bothers you about me, but first I'd like to know just what the heck that is."

Crawford's eyes slit to pinpricks of gun-metal blue.

The lady wanted the truth. Okay, she could have it, but he'd bet she wouldn't like it.

"Truth is—I like the way you look. A lot."

Amy regarded him incredulously, shivers of unwanted excitement unfurling down her spine. Beneath the careless comment, she felt a bristling sexual energy in him that made her feel breathless.

A rush of disturbing heat flushed her skin, flaming her cheeks. Forcing herself to ignore the intense look in his eyes, she leaned back against the rock, restlessly shaking out her shirt to encourage air to cool her hot and damp skin. Flapping it back and forth to create a breeze, she countered stonily, "Spare me, Crawford."

Crawford's head snapped up. Her movements caused the shirt to cling more closely to her breasts as the fabric slipped backward. One more flap and he wouldn't be responsible for his actions.

He retreated behind veiled eyes and a ring of smoke. "Just answering the question, Ms. Blake."

Amy's eyes flashed with exasperation. "You're not answering the question, Crawford, you're evading it with smart-ass comments."

He reached for another cigarette, noticing angrily that his hand wasn't any too steady. "Wrong, Ms. Blake. I'm trying to answer. You're not listening. I like the way you look and I even, God help me, kind of like the fact that you're feisty and have a mind of your own. It irritates the hell out of me, mind you, but I like someone who can stick up for themselves. I never was one to go after mealymouthed, simpering women."

Pure suspicion tightened her features. "I'm waiting for the punch line, Crawford."

He allowed himself a cryptic smile, enjoying her aggression. "No punch line, sweetheart."

She didn't believe that for a minute. "Damn you, Crawford, I don't need this kind of tension. Just what is it with you? Do you have something against single women adopting children? Does what I'm doing somehow offend your macho pride and ego? Is that what this is about?"

He could have laughed if the truth didn't hurt so much. It was about chemistry, he was tempted to shout, gut-wrenching chemistry that was making him about ready to snap. Chemistry he hadn't asked for, didn't want and was now stuck with, thanks to her.

Control, he told himself. Stay in control. He shook his head. It was almost nigh impossible to be in control within fifty feet of her. He'd defy any man to say he could do it.

"Ms. Blake, I think you're a lunatic. Only a lunatic with your looks and everything else you've got going for you would spend money and time trying to adopt a child, when there must be dozens of men willing to aid and abet you in your dream to have a baby, but hey, even believing that, I admire your tenacity and independence."

Amy froze, then filled with anger. "I told you before, Crawford, none of that is any of your business. It's a private matter. The subject is closed."

Crawford bit off a harsh, impatient expletive, feeling her block him out. He prided himself on knowing the difference between sparring and treading on people's problems and he also prided himself on having enough sensitivity and class to be able to distinguish between the two. But frustration coiled like a hot fist in his gut. He wanted to know why she was doing this, damn it. Then maybe he could stop being so ridiculously fascinated by her.

He rammed his lighter into the right-hand pocket of his pants, shrugging. "You brought it up, Ms. Blake, not me."

Amy's voice dripped with ice. "All I was trying to do, Crawford, is to get you off my case."

Crawford regarded her lovely, defiant face, shrewdly deciding it was time to back off and eat a little crow with his lunch, even if it gave him indigestion.

"Okay, maybe I have been a bit hard on you. I guess I've been away from civilization too long. How about we declare a truce?"

Only the prospect of two weeks of senseless arguing made her back off. Her eyes slitted. "Only if you keep to your end of the bargain, Crawford."

"When do I not?" He offered her a bland look, then lifting his brows, his gaze fell pointedly to her clenched knuckles. "By the way, were you planning on eating that sandwich or destroying it?"

Amy watched Crawford as he leaned back and lit a cigarette. The aroma drifted toward her. It was awful, but strangely Crawford. Strangely familiar. She frowned. Unfortunately, she was getting dangerously used to both. She let out a deep breath. Somehow, they'd made it through lunch without arguing any further. She considered that a minor miracle. "Now what?" she asked him.

He bunched up the remains of his lunch and jammed them into a paper bag. With one lean hand, he put his sunglasses back on and peered over at Amy.

"Take a few minutes to rest, why don't you? I want to scout around a bit before we leave," he said in a brusque voice. Standing, he picked up one of the two rifles he'd carried to the glade and gave it to her, his hand fitting her fingers around the grip.

"Do you know how to use one of these?"

Amy suppressed a shudder at actually having a gun in her hand. Surprisingly, it only seemed to weigh about five pounds.

Distaste feathered through her. In a place like Marita, she acknowledged the need for protection, but it still frightened her. She wondered how Crawford could live with this kind of reality every day. "Not exactly." Her answer was a total exaggeration. She'd held a gun once in her life. When she'd helped her father move into a new Washington townhouse, she'd taken down his Civil War rifle and packed it for him because the movers had forgotten to take it out of its glass case. She'd shivered then, too, she remembered.

"Well, it isn't complicated. All you have to do is cock this and take aim. Close one eye when you do it, or you'll be off target." Demonstrating, his fingers curled over hers, hot and large. She felt a jolt, wondering if he had felt it, too. She held her breath, feeling his solid, capable strength pressing into her. As he bent closer, his musky male scent teased her nostrils. "Got it?"

She nodded mutely.

"Good." He dropped his hands. "If anyone shows up, point the rifle at them, and cock it—first. Ask questions after, okay?" His dark brows drew together in a warning line. "Whatever you do, don't do it in reverse."

"I could come with you," she volunteered quickly.

He shook his head, his unruly thick hair falling across his forehead. He pushed it back with an absent gesture. "No. This is a simple scouting trip, that's all. You'd only be in the way." He pointed to the rifle. "You'll be okay with that. It's all the company you'll need."

Her heart started to pound. The danger he'd talked about before had become a scary reality. Suddenly, she felt afraid for him and afraid to let him out of her sight. What if something happened to him because of her? Her pulse started to race.

The concern for him startled her. He didn't mean anything to her, couldn't...all they did was fight with each other. She'd be worried no matter who was heading off into the mountains on her behalf, wouldn't she? Surely there was no other earthly explanation for her rush of alarm. No, she thought, panicking, it was more than that. She felt like a woman whose man was about to head off to war, and might not come back...safe, or to her.

She let out a thin breath, her stomach churning. Is this how the women of Marita felt every time they watched their husbands arm themselves? Did they fill with worry that their men would get hurt, or worse, killed?

"Are—are you sure this is necessary?"

He slung his own rifle over his shoulder. "Just playing it safe, that's all. The leader of the former government might be out there. I just want to be sure he isn't."

"I thought Orega was supposed to be dead."

Crawford laughed in a hoarse baritone. "Yeah, so they say, but I don't believe it. The man's a bully. Bullies never die because they're cowards. Cowards always run for cover. If I don't miss my guess, he covered his own hide first. I think there's still a possibility that he's out here somewhere, and we're carrying food and weapons. He'd give his eyeteeth for both."

He deliberately neglected to remind her just how valuable she was. The tattered remains of the former prime minister's army could use a shot in the arm. An American senator's daughter would do nicely. For all he knew, by now Orega or his men could already have put out scouts to detect her whereabouts. He shook his head, feeling a rush of disgust at Garcia. Knowing who Amy Blake was, the general should never have let her travel alone, and without an army escort. But more than that, he realized, he was angry with himself. He could have kicked himself for not insisting that Garcia assign some soldiers to protect Amy. But he'd been so convinced that Garcia himself might incarcerate her, that he'd rushed both himself and his client out of Marita as fast as he could.

He was getting rusty and careless. Or more to the point, letting Amy Blake distract him.

His jaw tightened to his temples. "Whatever you do, don't take any chances, hear me?"

Amy shook her head, trying to block out images of him lying somewhere, hurt and bloodied. The man was raw, arrogant, rude, and yet . . . the prospect of his being in danger terrified her. She couldn't keep the anxiety from showing in her eyes. "You will be careful, won't you?" she murmured.

Crawford paused, suddenly unaware of anything around him except her and the vulnerable expression on her face. For a brief, blinding moment, he could almost believe that what happened to him mattered to her. He shook the thought away, even as he clung to it.

"Hang on to that rifle," he ordered abruptly, then turned and headed toward the slope leading up the face of the mountain.

Amy's fingers were still fastened to the rifle Crawford had given her when he returned. She felt herself shaking as a physical surge of relief bubbled inside her. Every time she'd heard a strange noise, she'd imagined all kinds of awful things happening to him and more than once had almost gone searching for him. Not that she was likely to have been of much help, she thought wryly.

"Everything okay?"

He nodded carelessly, wiping some of the grime off his face. "Fine. It doesn't look as if any of Orega's men have even camped here."

"I was worried about you."

"Afraid you'd get stuck out here alone, Ms. Blake?"

Amy loosened her grip on the rifle, her anxiety turning to irritation. "I'd be a fool not to be, as you've so often pointed out to me, Crawford, but to answer your question, I also happened to be genuinely worried about *your* welfare." She shook her head wearily. "God only knows why."

His lips curled around his teeth. "Well, don't be. Worrying never helped anyone."

Amy fought to keep from testing the rifle on him. "Crawford, what is it with you that you always have to play the tin soldier? Couldn't you try being human for a change?"

Crawford tilted his head in a jerky motion and watched the play of sunlight on her lustrous hair. God, she was beautiful.

Perversely, he wanted to punish her for being so beautiful, for disturbing his peace of mind.

"That might not be such an advantage, Ms. Blake," he drawled meaningfully.

Amy flushed heatedly, the innuendo in his brooding eyes unnerving her as shivers of heat raced down her spine.

"You don't scare me, Crawford."

"Yeah, right." He chuckled harshly. She didn't have a clue what she was talking about. He was very sure that she would run like a scared rabbit from the fierce fire she unleashed in him.

Quickly, he changed subjects, urgently wanting to be off this one. "I think we'd better stretch our legs and then head off again. With Orega's people, it's better to keep moving. Finished?" He held out his hand for the serviette and apple core that she had rolled into a crunched ball while they'd been talking.

Amy shook her head, refocusing. "Do you really think he might be looking for us?"

Crawford shrugged. "Who knows? Maybe he's dead, after all." He started to kick over traces of their stay in the glade, saying over his shoulder, "I'd like to get in about four or five more hours' driving time today, if that's okay with you."

Amy eased herself upward, flexing her shoulder muscles and remembering the truck's uncomfortable bench seat. She suppressed a groan, then bent over to pick up her beer bottle.

Juggling it in her hand, she asked, "Any particular reason for the rush?"

Crawford squinted past her and up at the sky as he tossed the apple core and serviette into a bag. "I think there's going to be a rainstorm. We could end up in a mud avalanche."

Rainstorm.

The words smashed against her consciousness, making her feel faint. She knew a blinding moment of irrational panic.

It had been raining the night she'd crashed and lost her child.

She'd expected she'd have to test herself one day and drive through another rainstorm, but not now, not yet. She blinked hard, trying to fight the memory, but for a split second, fragments of steel shot like fireworks around her and crashing sounds of metal on metal thundered in her ears. She blanched, almost disappearing into that other world of excruciating loss, pain and heartbreak—a world she'd fought so hard to escape.

She struggled to escape it now, but her voice came out little more than a croak.

"But . . . we're in the mountains."

Crawford snapped the basket shut and replied with quick impatience. "A lot of the trees have been stripped at the base of the mountains for lumber. There isn't a hell of a lot holding back the soil, Ms. Blake."

Alarm slipped into her voice. "I meant the rainstorm."

Crawford paused, regarding her with confusion. Her lovely skin, so hot and flushed moments ago with anger, was pale and drawn.

Watching her carefully, he said in a slow, even voice. "It rains in the mountains, too, Ms. Blake."

Amy stared at him, transfixed. She'd temporarily thought about the possibility of avalanches, acknowledged it when Crawford had first brought it up and summarily refused to dwell on it. But life wasn't going to let her get away with this one, she realized with a sinking heart.

"I know that," she said tightly. She hadn't been behind the wheel since the accident. What if they got stuck, and Crawford asked her to drive? What if she turned out to be as ineffectual as Crawford had predicted? What if she fell apart and made a complete fool of herself when the storm hit full force—in front of Crawford?

Her heart hammered in her chest. "What advantage will rushing give us?"

Crawford's head shot up, his steely gaze curious, boring into hers. "If possible, I'd like to beat the storm and try to get to the nearest village. That way we might just avoid getting stuck, if not buried alive."

Casually, he took the beer bottle from her and tossed it into the basket, but his neck muscles flexed automatically as he realized he'd had to practically pry it out of her hand.

"But—"

Confusion more than irritation settled in his stomach. "What is this? You losing your nerve already?"

He saw her mouth drop open and her eyes flash with genuine pain.

He could have kicked himself. He blinked his eyes, remembering that his father had always become aggressive when he was worried about people whom he cared for.

Hell of a time for genetics to set in.

He shook his head, wondering what had caused her reaction. One thing was certain, though. No one could fake that look. Instinctively, he moved forward. "Ms. Blake, I'm—"

"Don't!"

Amy instantly snapped out of her trance and wrenched her arm free. She felt herself returning to normal as she threw him a scathing look. She thought about the child she yearned to hold in her arms, the ache that never went away and the lone-liness in her heart, and as she did, a surge of anger raced through her, helping her claw her way out of her memories. She'd go through hell to finally be able to snuggle that tiny body next to hers. She wouldn't allow herself to agonize about the physical and emotional obstacles. And she wouldn't let Crawford browbeat her about them, either—at least not about the physical ones.

"I haven't lost my nerve," she retorted, her eyes turning as cold as her insides felt.

He held up a hand, frowning. What kind of Pandora's box had he opened? "Take it easy—"

"Is this your idea of a truce, Crawford?" she snapped.

He swore under his breath and his gaze narrowed. "That's hardly fair. You're obviously upset about something. All I'm trying to do is find out what it is."

She refused to listen. Why was he always so quick to think the worst of her? Without knowing anything about her, he was willing to believe she wouldn't and couldn't stick to her guns. It hurt, she thought, terribly. More than she liked to admit.

"You can dish it out, but you can't take it, Crawford. Well, let me tell you, I'm no quitter, no matter what you might think. I can take anything this country can dish out, including your skepticism and lack of confidence." With that, she turned and stalked away from him toward the truck.

Crawford clenched his left hand by his side and swore vigorously.

Giving her a moment to cool down, he watched her retreat, her slim, elegant back stiff beneath the loose clothes, while the sun beat down on him mercilessly.

He should have kept a lid on it. But just what in God's name had he said?

The rain started three hours after lunch. Just a trickle at first but gradually building to a steady beat. Two hours later, it was a horrific assault.

Crawford's hands clenched around the wheel. They weren't going to make it to the town as he'd hoped. But with luck, they might make it to the group of caves he knew they could camp in for the night. The mud was beginning to collect under his wheels. The four-wheel drive was already making very little headway. Soon, they'd be completely mired in mud.

He took his eyes off the mountain road and sneaked a look at Amy again. He'd done that a dozen times since they'd left the glade. Her hands, clasped in a death grip on her lap, were white-knuckled, and the strain around her tight lips told of clenched teeth. She hadn't spoken a word since they'd left. Something told him more than anger with him was the cause.

"Look, whatever I said back there obviously bothered you a lot. I'm sorry for whatever it was."

Amy inhaled a shallow breath. The rain on the windshield pelted a relentless rhythm. It's only rain, she'd been telling herself for hours. Only water hitting glass. It doesn't always carry tragedy with it. Lots of people experience rainstorms and don't lose their babies.

Turning toward Crawford, she somehow managed to croak out a response. "Me . . . too. I guess I overreacted."

Crawford studied her profile from under his lashes. The storm had turned daylight into a heavy grayness that permeated the truck. He could hardly see her in the dim light, but he could feel her trying to conquer whatever was bothering her.

"Care to tell me what the problem is?"

Amy swallowed hard as she forced herself to return his look. She played with the strap of her knapsack. He wondered if she realized she'd tied and retied the straps together every sixty seconds for the past three hours. "I—I'm nervous in rainstorms, that's all."

That's it? Now, why didn't he think it was that simple? Above the hammering rain, Crawford just managed to catch her ragged answer. He swerved to miss a rock on the road. Mud flew back at the sides of the vehicle.

"Then why didn't you just tell me?" he asked blandly.

She flinched. Every time the rain hit, her heart jumped with it. She felt like a fool, a ridiculous, panicked fool. "Because it's stupid to be afraid of something so natural," she replied between tight lips.

Crawford responded in slow, even tones. "I'm terrified of snakes. There's nothing more natural than snakes."

Amy ground her teeth together. It was hard to imagine Crawford being frightened by anything. "I don't believe you, Crawford."

He shook his head. "It's true. Ask my scoutmaster."

She offered him a weak smile, then frowned at the blackening clouds above them and closed her eyes.

Crawford shifted, pressing the small of his back against the seat. He'd left the driver's window open a mere two inches to take advantage of the cooling rain, but he was getting drowned in the process. Drifting rain rifled through his thick hair. Impatiently, he shook the moisture free.

When she didn't respond, he said, "Look, Ms. Blake, I can't make your nervousness go away, but I'm here, remember that. If you want to scream at me or cry or whatever to relieve the pressure, be my guest. I won't think any less of you. Fear isn't something you necessarily conquer. Fear is something you learn to cope with."

Amy took an unsteady breath, opening her eyes again. "How do you do that?"

"You tell yourself that you're not trapped, there is a way out, and you're perfectly capable of putting up with this for a small period of time."

"But we *are* caught in the rain. There is no way out."

"Yes, there is—if I don't miss my guess, we're not too far away from some caves. We can take a break in one of them, and then you'd be lucky if you could see or hear anything."

That was the last thing she wanted, she realized. To run away from this insane panic and to have him help her do it. She might as well face her fears now as any time. "No, I won't hear of it, Crawford."

But her retort got drowned out by the harsh sound of his voice.

"Damn! Hang on!"

Without warning, Crawford's arm shot out and caught her body as she lurched in the seat, suddenly propelled by the collision of the truck with an object. The vehicle came to a thudding halt at the front end, while the back end fishtailed as if on oil. Despite the iron strength of Crawford's arm, she jerked forward and backward with a fierce snap. For a disoriented moment, she didn't know what had happened. Then, for another desperate moment, she actually thought she was back in her nightmare again. Fear rose up inside her in a strangling surge. No! She fought down the terror with an excruciating act of will.

Forcing herself to inhale deep, ragged breaths, she tried to get her bearings. Then, blinking rapidly to focus properly, she remembered where she was.

Instantly, her gaze flew to Crawford in the darkened truck.

He was slumped over the wheel, his head down.

Amy's heart sank like an anchor. "Oh, my God."

Wrenching off her belt, she scrambled toward him and gently shook him, her pulse accelerating with alarm.

"Crawford—"

"Okay...okay..." she heard him mumble. "Give me a minute."

Relief washed over her like a dancing, energetic wave. She could have sung with happiness to hear his gravelly voice.

Her heart was pounding as she put her arms around him and cradled him into a sitting position.

"Easy," she cautioned, as she thought he was moving too quickly. "Are you all right?"

He tossed back his head as if to clear it. "Yeah—wasn't wearing my belt."

"Clever," she replied tartly.

Very clever, he corrected silently as he became aware of the soft breasts flattened against his chest. There was something fabulously sensual about being awakened from a dream or a nightmare or a brief foray into an unconscious world by an administering, magnificently shaped angel like Amy Blake. But it was also risky, he realized, as she dipped her head closer to his. He could feel her warm breath on his skin, fanning it, like a seductive, steamy breeze. Her mouth was only an enticing inch from his... there was that inch again.

Halfway between reality and fantasy, he felt his thoughts drifting and his body hardening....

With iron control, he drew himself out of her arms and pulled himself together. "We have to get to one of the caves, whether you like it or not."

This time she didn't give him an argument. She was too weak with relief. "What do you want me to do?"

Crawford shook off the residue of the crash and replied quickly. "First, we'd better take whatever supplies we'll need

overnight and get them to the nearest cave. The mud's too wet
to fight right now. Got any boots with you?''

"In my knapsack."

"Okay, get 'em out and let's give this a shot.''

Chapter 8

Out of the truck, Amy gasped at the onslaught of rain and wind. Lightning and thunder exploded simultaneously as soon as her feet sank into the mud. Clutching the door handle, she almost jumped as streaks of silver-white light slanted across the truck in jagged lines.

Her heart started to constrict and pound against the wall of her chest. Without the protection of the truck, she felt completely and utterly vulnerable. *The way she had that night.*

She swallowed hard, trying to get her bearings.

With frantic eyes, she searched the ravaged horizon for the cave Crawford had mentioned, but because of the raging storm, she could hardly see an inch in front of her face. Her body trembled in reaction to the jagged lightning.

It's only a storm. Bad things don't always happen in storms she reminded herself again.

She inhaled a steadying breath, but found the litany didn't work as memory throbbed in her brain. She pressed herself against the door, unable to think straight.

Where was Crawford? What was happening?

That question was answered as he reappeared beside her. Shaking his head, he scowled, his eyes dark but bright in the storm's light. His usually loose khaki fatigues were plastered to his body.

A terse growl rumbled in his chest. "The mud's got us blocked in. We'll have to wait until the storm subsides to get out of this. I'm going to check the back."

She nodded, numbed by the deafening sound of the storm as she clung to the side of the door. Crawford returned in seconds. His breath rasped against her slick-wet cheek as he leaned toward her to be heard. He smelled of heavy rain and honest male sweat.

"The back door is broken and most of our supplies have fallen out. I'm going to have to carry the supplies into the cave. We can't leave them out here in case Orega's men come across them, and there's no point putting them back inside the truck without being able to lock the door. Understand?"

She tried to clear her throat as she glanced up at him. A curtain of rain poured down his bronzed face, tensed in concentration. He looked ready to take on an army, whereas she just wanted to disappear into the earth and let it cocoon around her. His words penetrated her fog as she struggled to fight back the panic rising inside her. Squinting, she tried to focus on him through the rain clogging her lashes, her fingers sliding on the door handle.

Dear God, she couldn't just stand here immobile.

With supreme effort of will, she forced herself to concentrate on something other than vivid memories. "I'll help," she cried above the storm.

Without hesitation, he shook his head, dancing moisture in every direction. "No. I can do it." His voice carried like a harsh wave above the tearing wind. "The caves aren't far." He gestured to a spot about thirty feet up an incline. "I want you to go there. Get away from this. But I can't take you. I'll have to work fast. You'll have to make it on your own."

Her gaze swept in the direction he was indicating. All she could see through the tangle of her wet, flying black hair was a gaping black hole on the horizon. She shivered. It looked like anything except sanctuary.

She turned her head away from the side of the mountain and glanced back at him.

Crawford was making it easy for her. Giving her a way out. She should be grateful. Every fiber of her being was tempted to accept, but that meant Crawford would have to do everything alone.

She knew she couldn't let him do that.

Shaking her head, she realized her voice barely carried above the sound of racking nature. "No. I want to help. There's no reason for you to do it alone. Two of us will be quicker."

A gust whipped his hair across his broad forehead.

"Forget it. I don't want you collapsing on me."

His bluntness took her breath away. Anger was an antidote to pain and fear that it would never have occurred to her to use, until Crawford unwittingly triggered it. Now she felt it rising inside her, an ironic balm.

She pushed herself away from the door and took a step toward him, her fury matching the storm's. From the moment they'd met, he'd been dictating to her, like the lord of the manor. The heavy weight of the mud almost pulled her down as she tried to close the gap between them. Frantically, she tried to keep herself from tripping headlong into his arms. She glared up at him, annoyed that his arms were already held out, ready to catch her as if she were a china doll who constantly needed support. She took pleasure in managing to right herself in time.

"Crawford, I'm a big girl. I don't need your permission. I want to help. I can help. I *need* to help."

She watched as his mouth set into a tense line. What little she could define in his face seemed to all boil down to one muscle twitching at the edge of his mouth, indicating frank annoyance and typical Crawford impatience.

Finally, he shrugged, dropping his hands, raising his voice again to be heard above the pelting rain.

"Okay, but you're responsible for whatever happens. If you collapse, I don't want to be facing any damn lawsuits from your father. Let's go." He grabbed her arm with brusque strength, shoving her toward the back of the truck before she had a chance to entertain second thoughts. "We'll have to work fast."

Slogging through the mire, she wondered just how they were going to do that. Just pulling a foot out of the mud in order to put it back down again seemed to take forever.

Slowly, agonizingly, they inched their way toward the back of the truck and she had to squelch a couple of yells as the wild slashes of light and harsh eruptions of thunder seemed to pick up furious energy.

Don't, she told herself, sternly. Don't think of that other night.

The rain was insidious. She bent her head down to try to escape its force, but by the time she reached the back of the truck, she was drenched from top to bottom. Around her ankles she felt the mud caking her boots, slowing her progress. Her muscles protested the immediate tug of the gathering slime as she fought to make headway. Sucking in a deep breath, she choked, succeeding in getting more rain than air in her lungs.

A cry of frustration slipped past her lips when she got to the back of the vehicle. Just about everything had flown out of the truck and was lying in thick, black, rain-sodden dirt. Food, guns, blankets lay strewn as if catapulted by a giant force of energy.

"Oh, no", she murmured, coming to a complete stop.

Crawford turned to regard her with glinting eyes. "My words exactly, Ms. Blake. Come on, let's get at it."

Ignoring the elements the way he ignored everything else, Crawford dropped her arm, and walking away from her, reached down and started to lift up the sticks of dynamite with large hands already well-covered in dirt. Without speaking, he motioned with his head to some plastic bags that had become caught on a bar on the inside of the truck. She nodded in understanding as his gaze moved toward the packages and cans of food scattered on the ground. She began making her way toward the back door.

Crouching over, she started to scramble into the truck. A clap of thunder cracked in her ear. She let out a small scream and froze momentarily, sensing her courage taking a nosedive. Her head whipped around, her gaze darting automatically to Crawford.

His soldier's instincts, ever-alert to the slightest change, had caused him to stop what he'd been doing immediately.

Standing motionless, she forced herself to meet his eyes. Illuminated by lighting, he regarded her, a frown furrowing across his wet forehead. The eerie light sharpened the features of his face, exaggerating the sharp planes of his cheekbones.

Lifting his head, his vocal cords sounded strained against the slamming storm. "You don't have to do this, you know," he shouted.

His voice sliced into her like voltage, giving her the second jolt she needed.

If he could do it, she could do it. She wouldn't give him the satisfaction of treating her like a hothouse flower.

"No way, Crawford. This is *my* judgment call. If my father does sue you, you can browbeat your way out of a lawsuit, like you do everything else."

Without another word, and without waiting for a response from him, she propelled herself into action.

Watching her disappear into the truck, Crawford flinched.

After the sixth trip from the truck to the cave, Amy lost track of time, her fear, her memory and her temper, and wondered if maybe her pride hadn't gotten the better of her. "Pride goeth before a fall," her father had often quoted to her.

She tossed back her sopping hair. Maybe this was one fall she might have almost been grateful for.

She let out an exhausted sigh. The cave hadn't looked so faraway once she'd sighted it, but the combination of mud, jutting landscape and treacherous incline had made each trip a nightmare.

She risked a glance behind her at the still-fermenting storm. It had gathered into an unrelenting fury of wind, rain and unearthly light.

Visually shutting it out, she bent her head under the slate overhang of the cave for the umpteenth time, shaking the water and mud off her body as she hauled in the last load.

Suddenly, her life had been reduced to basics, she realized wearily.

All that had meaning was warmth, food, sleep—and finishing this arduous task. And if she didn't get all four in the next second, she was going to pass out, she concluded.

With the last of her strength, she threw the sleeping bags onto the ground. They hit the hard earth with a thump. Following suit, she collapsed on top of them, and digging into one of the bags, pulled out a towel and began rubbing it over her hair. Pausing, she looked around.

Everything inside her seemed to crumble at once as her eyes drifted from one ragged slate wall to another. A strange kind of euphoria swept over her as she sensed the isolation wrap around her. Now that she had time to notice, she realized the cave Crawford had selected was remarkably dry. And incredibly, wonderfully silent, gloriously separated from the world and the storm. It was blessed peace not to have to listen to the storm, she thought. Only a distant burr seemed to penetrate the cave.

She breathed in the cave's hidden, secretive aroma. There was something almost sacred yet vitally mortal about its hush. How many people had hidden behind these natural walls, perhaps even lived here? she wondered. How many of them had been Maritans trying to escape armies bent on destruction? How many of them had been children, their cries smothered in the night to conceal frightened adults hiding from men without mercy?

Had one of them been Carmela?

Her heart caught in her throat at the prospect. Perhaps Carmela had actually slept here on the stony ground, blanketed with grass and twigs. Was she in fact revisiting her own child's sanctuary?

My two babies. One, lost, never to have lived. One, struggling to survive. She sighed raggedly. Oh, babies. I'm here. I'm trying....

She closed her eyes, wishing she could send a message of comfort to her child. Keep waiting, sweetheart, wherever you are, I'm on my way.

She leaned her head against the back wall, easing her throbbing muscles into a more comfortable position. Her lashes drifted over her eyes, clouding their vision. Closing her eyes was bliss, even if she could only do it for a few minutes, she thought. Crawford had set a steady but punishing pace. She'd never worked so physically hard in her life.

Crawford. She had to give the devil his due, she was forced to admit. He'd worked tirelessly and quickly, with no wasted commands or motions. For her half a dozen loads, he'd done double. She'd actually felt an affinity with him, working by his side against the elements, and surprisingly, it had taken her mind off the night that she had lost her child. Not wanting to let Crawford down had gotten her through the storm. But knowing he was beside her had also helped. If she'd run into problems, she'd trusted him to be there for her. His strong presence had helped vanquish some of the demons.

She could now see, too, why activity was supposed to be good for the soul. She could perhaps even see why Crawford had chosen such an outlet for his energies. Was it possible that Crawford used his physicality as an escape from the world he seemed to hold in such disdain, pouring his frustrations into activity?

She shifted with tired confusion, straining her ears to hear the noises of the storm. But they were muffled now, absorbed by the walls of the cave.

What made Crawford tick? Who was he, really, this complex man she was going to be spending the next two weeks with? She harbored a nagging suspicion that a lot of what she saw of him was affected—the strutting, the disinterested arrogance, the gruffness. But tonight, he hadn't been able to hide the fact that he had a quick sensitivity.

Like a jungle cat, he'd appeared to be attuned to everything around him, and a couple of times, he'd stopped and relieved her of some of her load, and amazingly, she'd felt no condemnation.

Concern, then? Her eyelashes fluttered. If it was, then it was the concern of a guide for his client. She had to accept that, yet now she felt ashamed that she'd bitten his head off. In retrospect, she realized she'd vented some of her fears on to him. Perhaps she wasn't being fair to him. Perhaps she should try to be more understanding with him, less combative. If only there weren't these sparks between them. . . .

She shook back her hair, blowing out a tired sigh. There weren't any easy answers when it came to Crawford, she guessed. And she had no business wondering about him, anyway. Or why something inside her skyrocketed whenever he was near.

Opening her eyes, she ran a hand down the side of her neck to relieve the tension knotting across her shoulder blades. He was still out there, doing what she had no idea, but at this stage, she was too drained for curiosity. She rubbed slowly, circling her head down and around. Every muscle throbbed a gruesome message to her brain.

She hated to admit it, but maybe Crawford had been right—jogging the streets of Boston wasn't much training for this kind of terrain.

Fatigue seeped into her bones, mingling with the dampness. Behind her, the wall offered hard support.

She surveyed the cave again, feeling her skin prickle with goose bumps. Could they light a fire in here? she wondered, as shivers feathered down her body.

Approaching sounds interrupted her thoughts and caused her head to lift. Crawford entered the cave, carrying a can. He walked in quickly, dripping water everywhere as he headed toward her. "That's it," he said.

She raised her eyes and regarded him from under drooping eyelids. It was all she could manage. Everything she owned felt numb.

"Gasoline," he announced to her unspoken question, with a touch of satisfaction in his voice. "If Orega or his men find the truck, it's going to take ingenuity and brains to get the sucker going, neither of which any of them have in abundance."

Amy had to brace herself not to stare. Doing battle with something even as elemental as nature obviously suited Crawford. Despite the wet grime clinging to his clothes, he looked exhilarated, his wonderfully blue eyes brilliant and bright, his lean body bursting with a pent-up energy that seemed to fill the space they were sharing. He stopped above her and put the container down, the tendons in his arm standing out in sharp relief. Careless sexual energy exuded from every pore. Momentarily, she felt rooted to the spot as it dawned on her that she was now alone in this cave with him for a whole night.

"You're always thinking, Crawford."

"Yeah—right," he replied absently.

Running his damp hands down equally drenched trousers, he shook the excess moisture out of his hair and regarded her from under wet spiky lashes. His charge looked like a drowned animal, but her dark thick hair had developed a silver sheen from the moisture. The long strands hugging her neck framed her face in wisps, and her eyes were wide and dark, edged with lines of strain that gave her an enticing, vulnerable look. Momentarily, he felt paralyzed. If he'd been hoping that nature would wrack havoc with her appeal, he realized he'd been terribly wrong.

He clenched and unclenched his hands in reflex.

The muscles in the backs of his legs objected as he crouched down beside her. He shifted slightly to relieve the strain and arched his eyebrows at the jumble of sleeping bags she was perched upon, while he fingered a polyester edge sardonically.

"I think you're supposed to get into those things first."

She blinked at him with jaundiced eyes. "Didn't have the energy," she muttered defensively.

Crawford's gaze sharpened with respect as he allowed himself a few moments' break. She'd surprised him by slogging through the mud like a real trooper. He'd half expected her to collapse after the first load. Whatever fear she'd been battling before they'd started salvaging their supplies, she'd brought it under control.

Guilt stabbed at his gut. Maybe he'd misjudged her, after all, assuming she was nothing more than a pretty powder puff, when all along she was made of sterner stuff than he'd imagined.

Now, to his shock, it dawned on him that the more he was with her, the more he found to actually admire and like. But instead of the realization diminishing his hunger for her, it only seemed to intensify the feeling, adding another dimension to the physical attraction.

In a controlled voice, he said, "You handled yourself well out there, Ms. Blake. You were pretty impressive, in fact."

Habits die hard, she discovered. Before she could stop herself, she'd arched her brows. "I'm breathless, Crawford. I think you're actually being polite."

He smiled wryly, the spell broken. "Not me. Got the wrong guy, sweetheart."

She tilted her head at him. Wrong? What constituted wrong? A man without polish and subtlety? Back there, outside in the storm, and at the Mendozas' when Garcia had first shown up, she certainly wouldn't have wanted someone with those shallow qualities beside her. Crawford was exactly whom she'd needed. Someone tough and strong she could lean on if she had to. The kind of man she'd always wanted but never found, she thought, startled.

"Maybe not," she murmured.

Crawford caught her flush and returned her look in the dim light, wondering how much that little acknowledgement of his

GOOD NEWS! You can get up to FIVE GIFTS—FREE!

If offer card is missing, write to:
Silhouette Reader Service, 3010 Walden Ave., P.O. Box 1867, Buffalo, NY 14269-1867.

FIND OUT INSTANTLY IF YOU GET
UP TO 5 FREE GIFTS IN THE
CARNIVAL WHEEL
▼ SCRATCH-OFF GAME! ▼

Scratch off ALL 3 gold areas

YES! I have scratched off the 3 Gold Areas above. Please send me all the gifts for which I qualify. I understand I am under no obligation to purchase any books, as explained on the opposite page.

245 CIS AJCW
(U-SIL-IM-07/93)

NAME

ADDRESS   APT.

CITY   STATE   ZIP physical prowess had cost her. Wisely, he decided not to pursue the subject.

"So—how are you feeling?"

She could barely move, she thought. "A little sore and wet, but otherwise okay. Now what?"

"We eat, sleep and get dry, but not necessarily in that order."

Exhausted she was all for doing the three activities simultaneously. She stretched her small body from side to side to get the kinks out of it.

"Which order, then?"

Crawford took note of how soaked she was. If she didn't want to risk pneumonia, she was going to have to get out of her wet clothes, fast.

His heart coiled at that prospect and the images such practicality conjured up. It wasn't hard to figure why.

No two ways about it, Crawford, you'd love to be the one who strips her clothes from her. You'd love to run your hands down her damp, lush body, while you warm her pale skin with the heat of your own, and you'd love . . .

He ground the pictures of creamy skin and a perfect body out of his mind and gritted his teeth.

"We have to dry off first. C'mon, you're going to get out of those clothes."

Amy's head snapped up, her mouth dropping open in amazement as he extended his hand. Her lethargy vanished as she surveyed the cave. There was no privacy here. She wasn't a prude, but the prospect of undressing anywhere in Crawford's proximity disturbed her. To take off her clothes with him only feet away . . . Her skin burned inexplicably at the thought.

Why hadn't she thought through these kinds of complications beforehand?

"I . . . I beg your pardon."

"I have to get a fire going, and you've got to change—survival tactics, Ms. Blake."

"But I wasn't . . . I mean, I wasn't going to do it now."

"Were you planning on sleeping in your clothes?"

"No, of course not," she retorted.

Given the wayward direction of his thoughts, he decided that he wasn't up to discussing the issue at any length. Bending over in a swoop, he dragged her to her feet with frustrated energy.

"You heard me—find a spot and get out of the clothes."

Amy let out an immediate gasp of surprise as she felt his hands on her arms yank her upward. Instantly, she became aware of the strength and sinewy lines of his body. As chilled as she was, she could feel his primitive body heat invading her senses, smothering her with its power. She wanted to open herself up to him and damn the consequences. Suddenly, she became pliable in his arms.

Blood pounded to her temples, his fiercely male aura compelling her . . . drawing her against her better judgment . . . digging at something inside her. Alarmed, she went to move away from him but inadvertently found herself pressed even closer to him.

Her eyes widened as she felt the full impact of his big, sleek body imprint itself on hers. Through her damp clothes, she could feel every inch of his taut, toned musculature.

She retreated behind a feigned haughty calm. "Let go of me, Crawford. I just wanted to wait a bit." She tried to yank herself out of his embrace but he held fast. Her lashes fanned imperiously as she jerked again. "If you don't mind."

Crawford's heart was acting ridiculous, beating savagely in his chest. He didn't like this situation any better than she did, he concluded, trying to steady his hands. He was liking it even less as her soft breasts pressed against his chest. The shadows of the cave washed her in a dark, tempting light.

"I do mind, because I'm responsible for you and it wasn't a question, Ms. Blake, it was an order," he snapped. "If you don't get out of your clothes, you're going to get pneumonia, and need I remind you that penicillin is in short supply in this neck of the woods?"

Amy swayed on her feet while she tried to break his hold on her. They were standing so close she could see the beginning of a rough-textured beard. If she reached out, she could easily trace her fingers down his damp skin. She wanted to touch him, she wanted to kiss the rain from his face. . . .

With a sharp intake of breath, she blinked hard, furious at her mental wanderings. She forced herself to remain motionless. Some measure of control was coming back to her.

"Then why aren't *you* changing?" she challenged.

His pulse was steadier now and he rolled his eyes. Overruling her wasn't in his best interests. Why he was bothering was beyond him.

"I'm going to, but ladies first, Ms. Blake, remember?"

She spun ice into her voice. "You're becoming too civilized by far, Crawford."

He scowled as their gazes clashed. Arguing with a woman usually turned him off, but with Amy Blake the exact opposite always happened. His hands impatiently moved up to her rigid shoulders and settled there like dead weights. She was baiting him, and he was falling for it, but he was going to get in the last word if it killed him.

"I can revert any time you like, Ms. Blake. In other words, if you don't take those clothes off your back, I will." He pressed his fingers into her shoulders. "Is that enough of a reversal for you?"

Amy couldn't accept he meant it until she looked into his eyes again. This time, they were burning into hers, filled with a tension she couldn't fathom, but it was almost palpable.

"Oh, for heaven's sake..." she muttered. She didn't doubt for one minute that he would do exactly as he said. She knew enough about him by now to know that he was uncompromisingly hardheaded. With an insolent toss of her shoulders that belied her feelings, she finally threw off his hold, but inside she was trembling.

"I think you're worrying unnecessarily, but all right, I'll do it."

Crawford threw his hands up in the air. "Well, thank God for that. Now, maybe I can start a fire before we both freeze our butts off." Releasing her, he bent over and picked up the towel she'd been using. Tossing it at her unceremoniously, he said, "Here, don't forget this."

Amy caught the towel, which almost hit her in the face. She ground her lips together, barely deigning to reply in a stiff voice, "Thanks."

Shaking, she turned on her heel, and went in search of her suitcase. Her heart was still jackknifing by the time she found it. Surreptitiously, she glanced over her shoulder as she picked the case up. Crawford thankfully was busy trying to get a fire going.

She let out a ragged sigh of relief. He was hunched over, his lean back straining against the damp fabric of the khaki shirt. She'd never seen a more perfect male line than Crawford's. Her whole body flushed. Looking at David, dressed or undressed, had never turned her to mush.

Hastily, she pushed her feet into moving again.

"This is ridiculous," she thought disgustedly, letting out her breath in quick spurts of air as she made her way toward the back of the cave. Why had she looked back, anyway? Had she really expected he'd be leering after her, like a hormone-unbalanced adolescent? And what difference did it make if he saw her half-naked or naked?

Once she'd gone about twenty feet, she sank to the ground and began digging haphazardly inside the case to find a change of clothes.

She wanted to shake herself. She'd lasted exactly five minutes before blowing up at him again. How could he set her off so easily and throw her off balance just as quickly?

She was afraid that she knew the answer. She sat on the ground and pulled off her boots, then yanked off her slacks as she tried to calm the rhythm of her heart. She'd once been attracted to David, so she was familiar with the symptoms. However . . . there hadn't been this wild intensity of feeling whenever she was with him. But then David had been predictable, ambitious, stable and caring. Or so, she reminded herself bitterly, that was how he'd appeared to be in the early months of their marriage.

Crawford, on the other hand, was nothing but dynamite. He didn't make her feel emotionally secure. But he wasn't sneaky or needling the way her husband had been, either. He was stubborn, yes, and irritating, but when Crawford attacked, he attacked openly, treating her as an equal. David had never done that.

She let out a tight breath of confusion.

She couldn't discount the primitive craving Crawford filled her with whenever he touched her. The quick heat he triggered in her didn't remotely resemble the warm but gentle physical yearnings she'd felt for David.

But David had asked her to abort their child.

Tears suddenly sprang to her eyes in a sudden painful rush of memory.

She choked back the gathering lump in her throat. It was old territory, and she'd promised herself not to go over it again. She'd grown up since then.

No man was ever going to hurt her that way a second time.

She toweled herself off with jerky motions, venting her pain and anguish. Then, tossing the towel aside, she pulled on fresh panties and a floral cotton dress.

Somehow, though, she couldn't see Crawford asking her to make the same sacrifice. For all his hardheadedness, she couldn't imagine him visiting that kind of cruelty on a woman. Still, she hadn't counted on wanting him. She was going to have to find a way to deal with her attraction to him.

The sound of his husky voice made her jump as she tied the dress's loose belt around her waist.

"How are you doing back there?"

She stopped, catapulted back into the present.

"Okay, but I'm hungry." As she called over her shoulder, her fingers quickly made short work of the tie around her waist.

"Then hurry up, I'm fading fast."

Her mouth unwillingly twitched at the response as she bent down and bundled her sodden clothes. She grabbed a sweater, tossed it over her shoulder with her free hand and started to make her way through the cave, trying to bring her nerves under control. Maybe she was worrying too much about Crawford, and maybe she was taking everything too seriously, as if she were still David's wife and somehow accountable. She'd left her old life behind the day she decided to adopt Carmela.

For argument's sake, who was to say she couldn't trust Crawford?

She shook herself. No, she thought sadly. She couldn't trust a man again. She wasn't ready yet.

By the time she got back to Crawford, she could see he'd already started a fire. He turned as she approached. He was just doing up the top button of a pair of loose slacks. His chest was still bare. Before she could prevent herself, her gaze strayed unwittingly across its wide expanse. His torso was lean, with rippling muscles in full evidence and three jagged scars. Her throat caught at the puckered, healed tissue. Each scar looked as if it could have once caused a great deal of pain. A jolt of compassion shot through her as the realities of the work he'd chosen for himself struck home.

Hearing her, Crawford paused, tilting his head as he pulled a T-shirt off a ragged piece of rock in the cave's wall.

His gaze merged with hers sardonically. "I thought all those objections before were because *you* were afraid of being ogled."

Chapter 9

"I wasn't ogling. You're right in my line of vision," she protested.

Crawford's mouth twisted into a wry curve. He, after all, had done his fair share of looking.

He dragged the T-shirt over his tawny head, shook his damp hair free, then smoothed the shirt over his taut stomach.

"Good line, Ms. Blake, I must use it some time."

Amy blinked hurriedly, blocking out his gaze. "I think you have enough lines to last you a lifetime, Crawford," she replied dryly. Moving closer to the fire, she held out her hands, savoring its warmth and determined to change the subject quickly. "Why isn't there any smoke in here?"

He moved toward the box of supplies he'd set by the fire, smoothing back his tousled hair impatiently.

"There are enough fissures in the walls to absorb it, and somewhere there's a hole in the roof, so to speak."

Squinting upward in surprise, Amy surveyed the blackness above her. "I can't see anything."

Busy rummaging in the box, Crawford answered absently over his shoulder as he hunched over, balancing his weight on his ankles. "That's because you can't see the top. Some of these caves go on forever."

Amy pulled her hands away from the fire and slid to the cave
floor across from him as he started to pull utensils out of the
box. Suddenly thinking about food, her stomach growled
hunger at her. She huddled on the hard ground, crossing her
ankles discreetly. "What's for dinner?"

Turning toward her, his large hand muscled around a small
container.

He made a face. "Soldier's fare—beans."

She shuffled closer to the fire, its flames mesmerizing.
"Don't you like beans?"

"Not after the hundredth time, I don't."

"Maybe they taste better the hundred and first time."

Reaching into the box, he pulled out a small metal pot.
"Yeah, right. Well, at least they're not straight out of the can."

Her mouth twitched as she leaned closer into the fire, feeling its languid heat wash over her. Its warmth made her drowsy.
If she hadn't been so hungry, she'd have gladly fallen asleep
beside it.

"You're whining, Crawford."

"I'm protesting."

Her smile spread. "So—what can I do to help?"

Crawford paused to glance around at her. "Know how to
make coffee?"

Patience, she thought. Have some patience. "I'm not a
complete incompetent, Crawford."

A cynical smile edged the corners of his upturned mouth as
he caught the challenge in her eyes. Getting the offensive back
always made him feel better.

"Didn't say you were, but this isn't exactly a *House and
Garden* kind of kitchen, you know."

Amy swallowed back a surge of frustration. "Just show me
what to do, Crawford, and I'll do it."

Crawford slitted his eyes at her. She looked relaxed, young
and fresh as the firelight danced brilliant highlights through her
hair, and made her expressive green eyes sparkle. He knew exactly what he wanted her to do and how he would help. But he
doubted she wanted to hear about his suggestion.

He pointed to a can of coffee, a small pot and bottled water.
"Go for it, Ms. Blake."

"I couldn't eat another thing." Amy tossed an apple core
into a makeshift garbage container. Curling her toes closer to

the fire, she picked up the metal coffee mug and hugged it between her fingers, satiated. She sent silent thanks to Mercedes.
The Spanish woman had delivered handsomely.

Crawford leaned back against the wall of the cave, watching
her. For such a delicate, fragile-looking woman, Amy Blake
could certainly pack away the food. Nothing wrong with her
appetite, he mused. His gaze strayed over her petite body. He
wondered where the hell she put it all. There wasn't a single inch
to her out of proportion. He frowned. He wished he could stop
thinking about what was under the virginal dress she was
wearing.

Just once, he thought. If he could just have her once.

"You always eat like that?"

Crawford's surly voice glanced off Amy's nerve endings, but
she was too full and relaxed from the food and warmth of the
cave to take exception. She smiled, arching backward, her eyes
reflecting the firelight as she wryly returned his look.

"Every chance I get, although I suppose one day I'll pay for
it."

Crawford tried to imagine her still tiny but plump and
couldn't. The reality of her svelte, curvaceous body as she
moved was too overwhelming for him to make the mental
transition. He shifted irritably, too aware of her to be comfortable.

He needed to taste and savor *her,* he thought. He needed to
know how she'd feel underneath him.

He needed brain surgery. He grunted noncommittally. "I
thought maybe you were trying to make up for an impover-
ished childhood."

She shook her head, smiling faintly. "Not me. I was given all
the advantages, including food..." She stopped, her smile
fading as the memory of Giselda's comment about Carmela's
temporary family not having enough food resurfaced.

How quickly she'd shoved that to the back of her brain, she
chided herself. Guilt splintered inside her, her own recent meal
churning in her stomach. "I can't believe it. Here I am joking
about food, when Carmela's guardians don't have enough.
God, it's heartbreaking to think—"

Crawford could see what was coming.

"Don't," he interrupted in a gruff voice. "Don't think about
it. It doesn't do any good."

Amy froze, her eyes widening on him as he casually reached for his pack of cigarettes. It was unbelievable to her that he could order away what she was thinking. Did he think that being without food was merely a minor inconvenience? She leaned forward, her fingers trembling on the coffee mug.

"How can you say that? How can anyone fail to think about it?"

Crawford inhaled a sharp breath. "I've seen dozens of towns trying to survive under the same kinds of conditions as Marita in just as many years. You get used to it."

"So the more you see, the easier it gets. Is that what you're trying to say?"

His lips thinned. Caring too much didn't help. He knew. He'd tried it. He lifted a shoulder to shrug. The answer had to sound callous. The truth usually did. "You have to turn it off or you go nuts, pure and simple."

A cold shudder raced down her spine. By his own admission, Crawford had witnessed living conditions that were appalling. Surely, he couldn't be so heartless as to not be affected by what he'd seen?

"How can anyone be immune to the tragedies and hardships that the Maritans and people like the Maritans have experienced?"

Crawford steeled himself against the hurt undertones in her voice.

"You mean me, don't you? How can *I* be immune?"

Flustered, her hands tightened around the mug. "Maybe, I—"

He interrupted harshly. "I know what you meant, Ms. Blake. What you're asking is whether I'm the insensitive bastard you think I am. If I am, it's no win, right, but if I disavow you of the notion, then I become a hero in your eyes. Frankly, neither role appeals to me."

Amy flinched visibly, unable to accept what he was saying. Or that he meant it. That couldn't be all there was to Crawford . . . there had to be more. She shook her head, wondering why it was so important to her. In some tiny way, she thought perhaps it would help justify her attraction to him. Was it that?

"Which do you want me to believe?"

He scowled, his right hand furling into a fist. He wanted to punch at something. Analyzing feelings was dangerous territory as far as he was concerned. Once you got into doing it, there was no way out. The process itself and home truths it identified sucked you under. Worrying about what people thought of you, though, was even worse. He didn't want to care about what Amy Blake thought of him.

"It doesn't matter what you believe about me, Ms. Blake."

"Crawford, I think you do care about people like the Maritans. I just think that you don't like to—"

He interrupted, his mouth clenching. "Look, Ms. Blake, if you want to accomplish anything, you have to learn how to get past being a bleeding heart. Most do-gooders, in my opinion, are more fond of rhetoric than performance. Words just don't mean a lot to me."

Amy blinked back confusion and frustration. He couldn't be that insensitive. She thought about the milk he smuggled in for the children of Marita, and the wine for the adults, and the consideration he'd shown her when they'd been carrying the stuff into the cave. She couldn't have read those actions wrong!

"I'm not talking about words," she persisted. "I'm talking about feelings, about what you feel."

Crawford fingered his drying hair with annoyance. "I'm not paid to feel, Ms. Blake."

Amy's stomach muscles contracted. She could feel an undercurrent of suppressed emotion in Crawford she'd never seen before. Was she getting a glimpse of a darker side to Crawford? Was his facade just a deliberate parody he assumed for the world's benefit? Is this what Crawford hid beneath the swagger?

"Is that what you think *I* am, Crawford?" she asked quietly. "A chatty do-gooder? A bleeding heart?"

She watched while he fidgeted with his cigarette. Their gazes merged as she challenged him.

He regarded her with canny laziness in his blue eyes. He knew full well what she was searching for.

"You could be Santa Claus for all I know, Ms. Blake. Let's face it, I don't know what or who you are. All I do know is that you're in a strange country, traipsing into the mountains in search of a child you want to adopt." Then, without flinching, he moved in for the kill. "And if you don't have to explain that to me, then I sure don't have to explain myself to you."

"That's not fair," she gasped.

He smiled at her through a ring of smoke, pleased to have so easily deflected her questioning. "So, go ahead. Tell me your life story."

Suspiciously, she glared at him. "Honestly, Crawford."

"Listen, sweetheart, you've been analyzing me and probing at me like I was under a microscope since we left the capital. I think it's my turn, don't you?"

"There's nothing to tell, Crawford. In comparison to you, I'm so dull, you'll bore yourself listening."

He chuckled, his eyes centred on her lovely face. "Really? What about *Mr.* Blake?"

She gave him a startled look. "My father?"

He gave a self-satisfied smirk now that he'd hooked her for a change. "No, the guy you married."

"Oh." She flushed, temporarily nonplussed. "Him—David Andrew Latimer."

He drew in a lungful of smoke and lifted his head to look at her wryly.

"Nice name. What was he? A politician?"

She shook her head. "Lawyer."

Figures, he thought, watching smoke from the fire and cigarette drifting upward.

"Want to tell me about him?"

Her mouth twitched with reluctance. "Not if I don't have to."

She wasn't any better at opening up than he was. If she'd had a husband, why didn't she also have the baby she wanted? There were a lot of questions unanswered here, and they weren't all hers.

He tossed his head backward. "Uh-uh. Fair is fair, Ms. Blake."

He waited a moment, then was sure he felt a whisper of a sigh trailing over his skin.

"All right. He was ambitious, attractive, politically correct..." She gave a self-conscious laugh. "You probably know the type, always says and does the right thing at the right time."

Crawford raised an eyebrow. Nothing about what a chump the guy had been for letting her walk out. How did a guy lose someone like Amy Blake, intelligent, beautiful, challenging, complex and probably dynamite in bed? Silently, he drew his own conclusion. The guy was an idiot.

"Sounds like every woman's dream," he commented dryly.

He noted that her hands shook a little as they smoothed back her hair. "So everyone reminded me when I left him. That made it harder... but then I guess it's hard to walk away from any marriage."

Crawford felt a jolt, inadvertently remembering his own experience and the pain he'd felt.

"It's as hard as hell," he muttered in agreement before he could stop himself.

It also hurt, he thought. Almost forever.

"Why'd you get a divorce, Crawford?"

Her question brought him out of his reverie and he gave a hoarse laugh. "It's kind of difficult to carry on a marriage when your wife's left you."

"Why'd she do that?"

It was a long time since he'd thought about this, he reflected. "Her last parting shot was that I was boring."

"Boring?" she asked, surprised.

He inhaled bitter smoke. "Being a CIA agent is only exciting in novels, angel. In real life, it means long absences from home, a job you can't talk about and a driving need for the kind of peace that a stay-at-home wife isn't interested in when you finally show up."

She would never have thought about it that way. "Crawford, I'm sorry."

His mouth slanted to the side. He'd forgotten how women had a habit of worming things out of a man, or how good it sometimes felt to express long-suppressed emotions. Even skimming the surface of them relieved some of the ache.

But this wasn't about him, he reminded himself.

"Forget me. Occupational hazard. Why'd you leave such a paragon?"

He watched as her eyes clouded. "I wasn't right for him, I guess."

That wasn't enough information for him to chew on for even a second, he thought disgustedly. Who better for a struggling lawyer than a senator's daughter?

His gaze pinned hers as his jawline tensed, the stricken expression on her face confirming for him that her husband had definitely been an all-out jerk. He took an inordinate amount of satisfaction in having been right. Perversely, he'd have hated for her husband to have been perfect.

"Works both ways, sweetheart."

He could see that he'd startled her. Gratitude, warmth and tenderness shone in her eyes, making his insides turn over with desire. That, as much as anything, convinced him that bridging the gap with Ms. Blake was risky business. He felt his pulse racing, his heart pounding.

She could do things to him so fast, it made him feel hopelessly out of control. Before she could say anything that would have them sharing any more confidences, he stood up abruptly.

"If you don't mind, I'd like to get some shut-eye. We have a long day ahead of us tomorrow."

He crushed his cigarette under his foot and tossed the butt into the fire as he gestured toward the now-flattened sleeping bags. "Ready?"

Amy straightened her back, surprised at his quick change in mood.

Suddenly though, she remembered that she was going to be sleeping in the same space as he was.

She cleared her throat nervously. "Which one do you want me to take?"

Neither, he wanted to say. Although he wished she would share his sleeping bag, he knew it would be best if she were sleeping a million miles away.... He hunched his shoulders in a way that belied his tension. "Doesn't matter to me. But, I ought to warn you, the best way these things work is if you're completely naked."

Amy flushed. "I'll take the one over there, if you don't mind." She indicated the bag practically hugging the wall.

Crawford evaluated the distance between the two bags. They still looked too dangerously close to him. "Fine with me. See you in the morning. Good-night, Ms. Blake."

Something was terribly wrong. Amy struggled to avoid whatever the danger was, but found she couldn't.

She was sinking farther into the dark abyss. She was in a tunnel.

Groaning, her lashes flickered. She tried to scramble out of the smothering cavern.

Why did she feel such unremitting hurt and pain? Why was so much anger riding with her down this black tunnel? Adrenaline pumped through her, preparing her body for flight. Why couldn't she find her way out of the nightmare?

The premonition turned darker. She could feel it snaking through her with the same ferocity as driving rain smashed against glass. Where was she? What was happening?

She began to shake violently.

Why couldn't she escape?

Her hands gripped what felt like something rigid and cold. Sweat bathed her in a clammy mantle. Lights were coming at her, like streaks of white fire, blinding her, heralding the metal hurtling behind them. She tried to scream but no sound emerged in the darkness of the night, only the relentless whirl of wipers. The scream, with no place to go, turned back in on her, lodging like a suffocating piece of iron in her throat. Then she felt it explode into a silent shriek of terror as something horrible hurtled right toward her in a headlong path of destruction.

In that instant, she knew what was going to happen. She opened her mouth and began to scream again, this time with such force, her body shook convulsively.

My . . . baby!

He couldn't sleep.

Still wide-awake at what he confirmed was three in the morning, Crawford sat hunched against the wall, listening to the quiet of the cave, smoking a cigarette. The quiet was broken only by a very distant blur of rain hitting against the slate walls. Fatigue tugged at his muscles and his brain as his lashes drifted over his eyes, blocking his surroundings from view.

He mouthed a silent curse.

It was impossible to sleep with Amy Blake snuggled in a sleeping bag less than fifteen feet away from him, naked or half-naked—and trying to guess which was definitely driving him crazy. No matter how hard he tried to squash the feeling, he ached to press his body against hers, to feel her writhe at his touch as he made her come alive for him. He was sure that beneath that cool exterior, a furnace raged. A furnace he wanted to unleash.

He shifted restlessly.

And then what, hero? You'll marry her and return to a country you swore you'd never set foot in again. The lady's already been married to one jerk.

He took a long, hard drag on his cigarette, a bitter sigh mingling with the smoke. She made him want to at least entertain the idea. But it was a rotten one. Their conversation had only convinced him of the certainty of that. It had spelled out graphically how a woman like her would view him.

Problem was, he couldn't give her much of an argument, because he *was* too rough now, too uncivilized, too untamed. He could read that in her eyes every time she looked at him.

He watched the smoke spiral upward. No question about it. He was too fond of his independence, too determined never, ever again, to return to that fake world of smoke and mirrors he'd once called his life.

He frowned, remembering what his life had once been like. Phony conversations in sumptuous living rooms. Dealing with corporate and government piracy masking as "third world" aid and protectionist policies.

What would Amy Blake want with a guy like him?

He couldn't play the game anymore and pretend there was any humanity left worth bragging about. He'd seen too much now to have any faith in either side of a battle. Amy didn't need that kind of emotional baggage in a relationship.

Then he ought to stop thinking about her.

He groaned, stumping the cigarette out on the ground. Easier said than done. She was all he could think about. Her and her sweet, breathless laughter, the way she moved her perfect body, that wild scent of hers. . . .

He closed his eyes, regret tearing at his gut. She conjured up pictures of simpler things, long-past and lost to him. And yet, she excited him—her mane of raven hair and sultry, drop-dead looks could bring a man to his knees. She was the kind of woman a man married and cherished, and kept the ugliness of the world away from, while thanking his lucky stars he'd found her. She was all class and elegance but with that tempting, smoldering sexuality pushing at the surface. A man couldn't ask for anything better. An angel on the outside, a siren on the inside. If he had an option he could live with . . . any kind of option . . . then, perhaps . . .

He scowled in the dark. He had no options. He'd tried them all.

Suddenly he heard a sound.

He jerked upward and forward quickly, his mind and body on instant alert. His lungs slammed against his ribs. For a split second, he felt disoriented, thinking he was hearing the cries of Maritan widows again.

Nothing could match the deep-throated, gut-wrenching cries of women who'd lost sons and husbands in senseless war.

He forced himself to calm down. It was eerie the way those cries still haunted him, playing tricks with his mind. Perhaps that's all he was hearing now—their quiet wails locked in his memory.

Stealthily, he moved toward Amy as his fingers sought the cool metal of his Beretta. He caught a flash of tangled, dark hair as she turned restlessly in her sleep.

He breathed easier as his hand found the reassuring weight of the gun. It was still nestled next to his leg in easy reach. Slowly, methodically, his fingers curved around the hilt.

He squinted, his eyes searching the grayness surrounding him.

Pulse racing, he listened, waiting for his vision to adjust to the darkness of the mountain cave. Everything was silent, the fire banked, the shadows on the walls, nothing more than the play of night light. He flicked his gaze in Amy's direction again. Burrowed into the thick warmth of the sleeping bag, he saw the outline of her body twisting as she tried to get comfortable. But she was still there, safe and sound.

Relaxing cautiously, he lay back again and breathed in the cool mountain air. He blew out his breath in silent thanks, sank back against the sleeping bag with care and closed his eyes, waiting for his adrenaline to settle back down to normal levels.

He heard the sound again.

He shot upward in an instant. This time there was no mistaking where the sound had come from.

Amy Blake was sobbing.

Pulling on a pair of shorts, he was on his feet and by her side in three strides, without even thinking. Heart thumping, he bent down toward her, then hesitated, remembering he'd told her it was better not to wear any nightclothes. She moaned again.

He acted instantly. Unzipping the bag, he dragged her into his arms, moving her into a sitting position as he cradled her against his chest. With relief, he noticed that she was wearing some kind of pink nightshirt.

Thank God temptation wouldn't be staring him in the face.

"Take it easy," he crooned.

She jerked in his arms, obviously still in the grips of a nightmare. Her panic wrenched his insides. He tried to rock her gently awake, overcome with a desire to rescue her from whatever was tormenting her.

Words of comfort sprang to his lips. "It's all right, angel, whatever it is, it's all right. I'm here. Wake up, Amy."

Amy struggled to escape the torturous tentacles of her nightmare. She could hear a darkly husky voice yanking her out to the edge of the abyss, drowning out the sights and sounds of the nightmare. She struggled to catch hold of it. For a frightening moment, she felt herself lingering precariously between fantasy and reality. Something strong and firm, though, was molded around her, propping her up. The support pressed closer and in an instant her eyes flew open, locking with two pinpricks of brilliant, concerned blue, but total awareness of reality still eluded her as the fragments of her nightmare shattered into the final throes of a memory explosion.

She reeled with horror, suddenly feeling unable to breathe.

Then, the walls of the cave careened into her consciousness as a terrible emptiness rose up, choking her.

She clutched at Crawford, her fingers clenching at the bare skin of his chest, words tumbling in a quick torrent from her mouth before she could stop them.

She started to shake. "My baby...I lost my baby...."

Crawford could feel her trembling vibrate all through his body. A frown of confusion cut across his forehead, even as he tried to steady her against his more solid weight.

"No, you haven't. We're not there yet. She's waiting for you...."

Amy's cry brushed past his ear to echo eerily through the stillness of the cave. "She's dead, my baby's dead."

Crawford tried to twist her around as she struggled in his arms. "What are you talking about?" He gave her another gentle shake. "Wake up, Amy."

Then, it was as though the nightmare had lost its grip on her. He saw recognition flare slowly in her eyes as she regained her bearings. The wildness faded from her gaze as she focused on him. "Craw ... Crawford ... ?"

He feigned a shrug, tightening the iron grip around her shaking body, muttering softly, "The one and only. You were having a nightmare. Scared the living daylights out of me. You okay?"

Her body stiffened against him. Then, he heard her tortured muffled whisper, her face bumping into his shoulder as she tried to pull away from him. "Fine ... it's just a nightmare I have sometimes."

She went to pull away.

Like lightning, his hands dragged her back. Twisting in his rough embrace, her eyes widened in alarm.

Gently, but firmly, he nestled her in his embrace.

"Sometimes? What's going on, Amy?"

The fire of resistance shone in her eyes.

"Crawford, I'll be all right ... really."

He forced himself to ignore the panicked expression on her face.

"C'mon Amy, you'd better tell me about it."

"No ... I ..."

Swearing, he tightened his grip and shook his head. "Uh-uh, Amy, you're not winning this one."

Amy shivered, suddenly fully awake. No one had held or comforted her after the accident, because she hadn't let anyone get that close to her. Not her father. Certainly not David. Now, she realized how desperately she wanted to lean on someone. She felt the vestiges of resistance go out of her, like a dying flame. Crawford was offering her comfort. It was far more than her husband had offered.

She caved in in his arms, unable to fight the nightmare any longer.

"I ... I felt my little girl die."

"Carmela?"

"No," she corrected in a toneless voice. "Not Carmela."

He tossed back his head, frowning. "I guess I'm not following."

Amy's eyes glazed for a moment with anguish, then refocused on his steadily, but still filled with pain. It was good, she thought, to finally get it out. Somebody had once said confession was good for the soul. Perhaps, after all, it was.

She fidgeted with the polyester fabric of the sleeping bag.

"I—I was in an accident four years ago. I was pregnant at the time. I survived, but my... my little girl didn't...." A broken sob caught in her throat, and she didn't continue as a deluge of memories flooded in on her again.

I felt my little girl die. He had expected to hear that wanting Carmela so badly, the political climate of Marita, and what she'd been through so far had given her an attack of nerves. He hadn't expected this.

"God, Amy, I'm sorry," he murmured in a ragged voice.

"It's all right," she said flatly. "Except for the occasional nightmare, I'm almost over the loss now."

"You said ... you felt ..."

She lifted her pale face to his. "Melodramatic, isn't it?" she replied quietly. "But it was as if I could feel the life going out of her, as if I could sense the moment she was no longer alive."

Crawford unfurled his fists and smoothed his rough fingers over the satin lushness of her hair, trying to comfort her. "Take it easy. Everything will be all right."

"My... my arms always feel empty." Her voice caught.

Oh God, he thought. He pulled her closer, closing his eyes. "I know ... I know."

Amy felt his arms anchoring her, holding her. But as wonderful as it was to have support, guilt tore at her. She dug herself in closer, pressing against his chest, whispering in a ragged voice. "You know what bothers me the most? I—I should have kept her safe inside me, protected her, and I didn't...."

Crawford couldn't believe what he was hearing. "That's ridiculous. You're not to blame."

She forced herself to draw away from his warm, soothing embrace. A blast of cold air hit her. Her eyes were filled with tragic self-recrimination.

"I was to blame. I shouldn't have got into the car that night. The weather was bad...."

Tensing, Crawford experienced a flashback. "There was a rainstorm, right?"

She nodded, her eyes bleak.

Crawford scowled, the look in her eyes twisting his stomach into a knot. He wondered if she'd been beating up on herself this way for the past four years. If so, it was a lot of guilt to get rid of. Enough to fuel nightmares for a lifetime.

"So how are you to blame for that? The last I heard, rainstorms were considered acts of God."

"I shouldn't have taken the chance," she murmured.

Tears suddenly streamed down her face, and she shook all over. For a long time, he did nothing, except hold her to him, comforting her, offering her his warmth and strength and waiting for her to calm. And at last, she finally did, looking up at him. How well he understood her feeling of helplessness. His whole adult life had been plagued by it, by the feeling that nothing he did made any difference, and that wanting something, no matter how right, couldn't guarantee its achievement. The pain burned a hole in the spirit.

"Thanks, Crawford," she whispered.

He could count on one finger the last time he'd tried to soothe a woman's fears. He was amazed at how right it felt with her.

He shrugged, skimming his lips across her temple. "Just a friendly port in a storm," he replied. "You know you should have told me why you were afraid of storms," he chided gently.

Amy shook her head, wiping at her face. "I couldn't. I needed to confront my fear. I haven't driven in a rainstorm for almost five years. I needed to take at least that one step."

Strangely, she didn't object when his fingers tightened on her arms. "Did you get divorced after you lost your child?"

She nodded, liking the way her hair brushed the skin of his face when she did so. It was strangely erotic.

"Just a year afterward. David and I just couldn't seem to communicate after our... baby died. There didn't seem to be much point to continuing the relationship."

Blind fury rose inside him. What kind of a man divorces his wife after she loses their child? Had he blamed her, too? Is that why she carried so much guilt about the marriage?

"I think your husband must have been an idiot," he replied hoarsely.

She tilted her head upward then, becoming aware of how close they were to each other. Heat poured over her in a wave.

Suddenly, too, Crawford felt the atmosphere in the cave becoming claustrophobic. He shifted uncomfortably, his thigh grazing hers. A heady scent of female muskiness and rain ravaged his senses.

He was so hungry for her, he realized.

A groan grew in his chest and tightened. She'd be sweet, oh so sweet. He swallowed hard.

"I feel better," she said, her eyes drifting to his sensual mouth, and the taut temples edging his hairline. Playing with fire, she thought, mesmerized. She'd be playing with fire if she didn't break away now.

She should. She couldn't.

Her hand reached up and touched his cheek.

Her touch set him afire. He growled, not even bothering to conceal the primal sound. Underneath the shorts he'd worn to sleep, his body quickened.

His growl dug deeper inside him as he leaned back his head almost pleadingly.

"Don't touch me, Amy. I'm not that strong."

Neither was she, she realized, as if in a highly charged dream except, unlike the one she'd just had, this one was soul disturbing in a distinctly sensual way. Her name on his lips unfurled a coil of warmth inside her. Something about his suppressed wildness exhilarated her. She felt his heat radiating through her, touching her where their bodies brushed against each other, causing wild anticipation to explode inside her.

She wasn't smart at the moment, either, she realized. His fierce tension seemed to be swallowing her up. But extricating herself was the furthest thing from her mind. She was driven to explore it.

"We're already touching," she murmured.

"That was different. I was trying to comfort you."

"You called me Amy."

Crawford's eyes flew open and focused on her in one last effort to dissuade himself and her from what he was sure was totally dangerous territory. But reality conspired against him. Her eyes, luminous from tears, shone with seductive duskiness, and her mouth, half-parted with confusion and innocent invitation, drew him. He felt as if he were drowning in her. The line he hadn't wanted to cross was already fading into oblivion. She'd pulled it out from under him.

"A slip of the tongue," he breathed with ironic heaviness.

His warm hands slipped up her back and came into contact with thin fabric. Heart pumping, he tried again and this time his hand came up under the fabric, finding naked, silky skin.

Her lashes drifted upward as she shivered under the caress of his fingers and the smoldering look in his eyes. She wanted to experience more of him. "Is your name Samuel?"

Crawford swallowed hard. "Yeah."

Her fingers trailed upward, stopping at the edge of his mouth. "It's a nice name."

He let out a labored breath and rolled his eyes.

Too late. Too damn late.

"So is John F. Kennedy, but I don't answer to that, either."

Inexorably, Amy moved closer to him. She couldn't have stopped if she'd wanted to. "Then, what do you answer to?"

He felt her breasts flatten against his chest, the tips of them hard and tight. "Sam is just fine," he growled.

"Sam . . ." Her lips murmured his name, savoring it as she irrationally worked her way into the broad, hot sanctuary of his arms. His body felt so warm and fabulous next to hers. She felt out of control, on a roller coaster she couldn't stop. "Sam . . . I like that, too." She said his name again, softly, gently, almost with surprised reverence, her tongue softly wrapping around it.

"Tell me, Sam, why do we fight so much?"

Crawford admitted defeat.

Muttering under his breath, he bent his head. He really shouldn't, he thought. But he had to.

"This is why, Amy," he rasped. Then, with thorough deliberation, he brought his mouth down on hers, hard, wild and searing.

Amy gasped as his mouth breached hers, his name on her lips becoming trapped inside her.

Chapter 10

She'd asked for this, she thought. But as soon as his fierce lip captured hers, she was amazed at how natural and how glori ous it felt to accept his ferocity and to answer it in kind. Sh heard him moan under his breath as his hand came up the bac of her neck, trailing shivers down her spine. Then, it tangled i her hair. She gasped as his fingers spread out and his other arr snaked around her, pressing against the bare skin of her back Then, she felt him pull her hard and tight against him. A fir instantly flared to life inside her.

She was stunned by its heat and suddenness and her puls ricocheted in a dozen directions.

She'd never experienced the play of a mouth against her with such demanding strength. But at the same time, there wa a seasoned technique, a giving as well as a taking. Her though spun out of control. She hadn't expected his generosity. It wa as if he were pouring himself into her and then pulling her bac with him, absorbing her. She hadn't anticipated that he woul be so proprietary either, she realized, her heart pounding. Sh felt as if her very soul were being torn from her—wooed, ste len, then nurtured in one slow, hard breath. But at the sam time, he made her feel like a totally desirable woman, som thing she hadn't experienced for years, and certainly not in her husband's arms.

He slanted his lips across hers, forcing her mouth open, dipping into its folds with his tongue, foraging until it found hers, then merging until she felt breathless with the marriage. His lips were moist, tempting, soft when she wanted them to be, hard when her breath caught.

She moaned involuntarily beneath the onslaught, her breasts crushing against his chest. His fingers on her back splayed across hot, sensitive skin and sent shudders of need shooting down her spine. Beneath the thin shirt, her nipples hardened into tight peaks. With a muffled groan, she arched her body, trying to maneuver closer to him.

She wanted more of him, she thought dazedly. As much as he could give, as much as she could draw from him. God, how she wanted him. This was wrong, she thought in a daze.

Then why did it feel so easy... and right?

Crawford sensed her wild surrender and felt an exploding need as her desire clawed at him. He couldn't believe her hot, wild response. She was everything he could have dreamed and beyond. The texture, the taste, the fire, the sheer absolute feel of her compliance tore at him, making him sense that he was losing control. She gave everything. Too much. More than he could handle. More than he knew he could act on in the morning, because tomorrow, he'd have to forget this... and her.

Don't think, he told himself.

He felt her breasts straining against him, and his hand slithered around her waist and up the warm length of her rib cage. His hand cupped one perfect breast. As he rubbed its satiny fullness against the skin of his palm, his heart tightened in his chest at the wave of sensations that washed over him. He heard her whimper as his lips ground down on hers in reaction to the feel of her smooth softness. She was so tiny and small, soft, and yielding in his arms. Inside he raged with the desire to drive himself into her to the hilt of his need. He'd never felt such a strong desire to possess a woman before. It shocked him to the core because it was like nothing else he'd ever experienced. He wanted to not only make love to this woman, but to love, cherish and protect her, even while he yearned for something far more basic. He could feel himself sinking. God, how could he want a woman so badly on so many different levels? In only two days and a night, she'd weaved her way into his consciousness, driving him crazy, exasperating him, fascinating him with her quietly determined ways, but always filling him with this driving need. . . .

Unsteadily, he drew one hand from her back and slid it around to stroke the warm hollow of her neck. Next to his chest, he could feel her inhale with a sharp, primitive anticipation that he understood. His mouth ached desperately to seize the swollen bud of her breast between his fingers and fit it between his lips, just as his fingers itched to move up the silken inside of her thigh.

If he did, he'd be done for, he told himself.

Something inside him began to tremble. This wasn't ordinary. This, he couldn't walk away from easily. This wasn't sex.

This was something else.

This was a yearning to make her his not just for now and not just to satisfy his urges, but for longer than that. Perhaps even a lifetime.

His pulse throbbed against his temples at the insanity of the thought.

The thought implied permanence and stability. His heart somersaulted as cold reality dashed against him.

He felt himself resisting her even while everything inside him ached to succumb. No other woman had ever coiled him so tight so that he wanted to beg for release, but that release was going to cost him, and he had to protect himself. The promise that she held out to him outstripped his fantasies, but he couldn't honor those promises the way they should be honored. He had nothing to offer except his body. For Amy Blake, he knew that wasn't nearly enough.

It wasn't enough for him, either. At one time, a quick roll in the hay for sexual release might have been . . . with someone else. But this was Amy. Fresh out of a nightmare. Vulnerable, still hurting and raw from memories revisited.

He couldn't make love to her now, which meant he probably never could.

His breath snagged as reluctantly, agonizingly, he pulled back and fatalistically accepted what was the truth. She'd reached out to him for comfort.

The effort to acknowledge that truth and act on it sliced right through him.

With two strong hands, he pulled her arms from around his neck and gently pushed them to her sides. "No, Amy, this isn't right."

Her eyes immediately flew open, hurt and glazed. Touching him felt so irrevocably, so strangely preordained, she was stunned he didn't feel the same way, that she'd misread him. Shock lodged in her stomach. He didn't want her.

She felt as if a cold vice had gripped her heart. "What are you saying?"

He wanted to crawl into the nearest hole and cover himself in sackcloth and ashes for causing the wounded expression in her eyes. When they'd opened, they'd been filled with dreamy passion. Now, they were dark and uncertain.

His fault. All his fault.

He either had to be the biggest fool in the world for stopping this or the biggest heel for starting. Either was a good bet.

His mouth clamped into a resisting curve. "Look, Amy, the way I see it is you've just had a bad dream, you're probably a bit shaky right now, and I'm the nearest thing to human comfort you can find at the moment. But I'm not the kind of man someone like you should get mixed up with this way. I'm a soldier for hire, an outsider."

Her limbs trembled as she tried to steady herself. "I didn't ask for your professional credentials," she protested.

Her troubled green eyes glistening up at him almost undid him.

"Maybe you didn't, but I only live for the moment, and I like it that way. If we make love, that's all we'll have—one night of passion, period."

The hurt that raced through her sliced like a knife to her heart. She'd been rejected before—by her husband who hadn't wanted to father another child and so had stayed away from her bed. But this hurt was unlike that. This was an outright rejection of her without any mitigating circumstances.

"Why are you analyzing this so much?" she retorted, pained in a way she couldn't even rationally explain.

If he wasn't going to make love to her without thinking beyond immediate satisfaction, why wasn't she happy? Why wasn't she grateful he was being so honest with her? Eyes shadowing, she pulled herself away from him, feeling irrevocably cold.

He rasped a response. "Because you're not listening to what I'm saying, Amy. I'm a hired gun."

She hugged her arms around herself to block the chill. "What does what you do for living have to do with what's happening between us?"

Crawford wished he could reach his cigarettes without looking like an insensitive bastard. He stretched behind him and found that his fingers just touched them. With supple dexterity, he drew one out. Finding them relaxed him on the surface. For the first time, he understood that making love with his body was one thing, but making love with heart, mind and soul was quite another. She had too much power to make him think along those lines.

He was barely going to get out of this alive, he thought.

"It has everything to do with it," he responded tightly, lifting his dark eyebrows. "Unless you want to believe we're just two bodies meeting in the middle of the night."

Her eyes widened at the veiled slur. Surely the passion she'd felt emanating from him hadn't all been merely an instantaneous reaction to having an available, warm body close at hand? Humiliation fueled her need to cry. Pride stopped it.

"Well, you're right about one thing, Crawford. I'm not interested in a one-night stand."

He flinched as she reverted to calling him by his surname. But he understood her need to put him in his place and treat him like the hired hand he really was.

"That's my point exactly," he responded dryly, lighting his cigarette as he inched himself away from her with feigned carelessness, masking the pain it cost him. His body felt heavy, too heavy almost to move, but he managed to move backward, securing a good few feet between them. He felt he could breath fractionally better with the space gained.

"There can't be any romantic relationship between us, so I thought I'd better quit in case you didn't understand the ground rules." He shrugged, drawing cigarette smoke into his already burning lungs. "I never was one to take advantage of a lady."

Amy's breath came in torturous, sharp gasps. Her face lost its flushed color as it drained from her cheeks.

"You're a real jerk, you know that," she tossed out at him, fury biting into her words.

He didn't want to hear those words on her lips, even if he'd invited them and even if he deserved them. His gaze turned dusky on her. She looked so translucently pale and beautiful, his breath quickened. He felt such an incredible, indescribable loss now that she was no longer in his arms. What words could describe that kind of hollow pain in the pit of a man's stomach? The kind of pain that put your heart's desire in temptation's way, then snatched it away just as you realized the dream could never be? Frustration made him ground his lips together.

"That's what I'm been trying to tell you."

She'd never felt so humiliated or angry before. Without thinking, she raised her hand to strike him, but he caught it just in time, his eyes turning to a turbulent blue.

His nobility was beginning to turn to cold resignation and anguished need.

"Be grateful I'm warning you, Amy. I could have just taken what was offered. At least give me some credit."

Amy's free hand curled into a fist. She couldn't seem to stop shivering. "All right, Crawford, have it your way. I had a nightmare. I wasn't offering you anything. It just happened."

He studied her with shuttered eyes and a racing heart.

He no more believed her than he believed pigs could fly. She was falling for him, and it scared the daylights out of him. But what scared him even more was that he was falling for her.

He clenched his jaw. How rapidly he'd taken her from comfort to surrender to rejection. He was amazed at how short a trip it had been, although he shouldn't have been. Like every other emotion she invoked in him, it flared with astonishing speed.

He stood up, uncurling her hand.

"Good," he said coolly. "Then we understand each other. I'm sorry about the nightmare, and I'm ever sorrier for its reason, but like I said, I think you reached out to me because of that. There are worse reasons for reaching out to another human being in the middle of the night, I'll admit, but a nightmare isn't enough reason for us to get tangled up together. Now I suggest we both get some sleep. You'll think differently about this in the morning, I can guarantee it. By morning, you'll realize that I'm right."

He began walking away from her toward the front end of the cave, where'd he'd been sleeping before he'd heard her cry out. Every step, he discovered, was agony. His heart and body screamed out at him to go back to her. The ache inside him was unbearable and the pressure between his legs was going to take a long time to dissipate.

He forced himself not to look back, telling himself that this was best for both of them.

Amy fell back on the sleeping bag, pulled herself into a fetal position and buried herself determinedly in its downy folds.

She wasn't going to let his rebuff get to her. It had been a long trip from Boston to Marita, not just in time, but in emotional distance. She'd grown a lot since then. She'd buried a child and lost a husband. She'd suffered David's rejection not just of her, but of her hopes and dreams. And because of all that, she'd made a decision to adopt a tiny human being, who, she hoped, would not only need her, but love her as if she were her natural mother.

Hot tears burned in her eyes as she tried to bring herself under control. Damn you, Crawford, she murmured silently at him in the dark. Damn you for doing this to me. For making me feel again when it's the last thing in the world I wanted.

Amy awoke with a start to the sound of an engine turning over. She sat bolt upright, trying to orient herself, but the zipper of the sleeping bag impeded her progress at the same time as it brought back vivid memories of the previous night.

She snuggled down into the sleeping bag, temporarily immobilized. Crawford. A flush spread across her face and with it unrequited need and confusion.

So close, she thought, she'd come so close to getting past that arrogant, mocking look on Crawford's face and discovering the man behind the facade. And that man had been amazing. Tender. Passionate. He'd stunned her with his desire, stirred her beyond anything she'd ever felt before. She'd never experienced that kind of wild wantonness in a man's arms, that kind of aching, as if she had been incomplete before knowing him, before being held in his arms. And it had only been a few kisses, nothing more, but they had dashed her reserve and opened up emotions inside her that she thought she'd permanently shut down.

But she didn't want another man in her life. She'd sworn after her marriage that she was going to go her own way and make decisions that suited her.

She took a deep breath, awakening fully. Last night, he'd pulled away from her. It hadn't been the other way around, she had to remind herself.

Why, though? Did he really believe the reasons he'd offered her? Or were they just excuses to save her pride? If they weren't the latter, why did he seem to think that who and what he was constituted an insurmountable obstacle?

She shook herself dejectedly. She hadn't come looking for this. She was a fool to have succumbed to his rough charm. She frowned, something suddenly dawning on her.

Her heart started to pound as she remembered what Crawford had said about the woman he'd escorted alone.

She charged me with rape.

Her insides tensed. Was that the reason he'd pulled back? Did he think she'd cause trouble for him afterward, the way the other woman had?

Her blush deepened with shame. No wonder he'd extricated himself and walked away from her.

How was she going to face him now?

An apology was the only answer. She had to clear the air as soon as possible.

Teeth chattering, more with nerves than with the climate, she yanked herself out of the sleeping bag, pulled off the nightshirt she'd been wearing and exchanged it for a white cotton dress.

She remembered that Crawford had told her over dinner that there was a nearby waterfall where they could freshen up.

She shivered, feeling she desperately needed coffee before she could handle any kind of conversation with him.

She caught a telltale tangy aroma and glancing toward the fire, saw a pot of coffee already close to perking. At the same time, she also noticed that half the supplies were already gone. Obviously, she'd slept while he'd been doing the lion's share of the work.

He hadn't even thought enough of her to ask for her help, she thought. On top of his rejection of her, that thought stung more than she would have expected.

She exhaled a harsh breath. She'd been rejected and humiliated before by her ex-husband and hadn't died from it.

Walking over to the pot, she saw a terse note attached to it: "Use this to rinse when you brush your teeth."

Bitterly, she crumpled the note in her hand. Not exactly a love note.

She tossed the note into the box of garbage by the smoldering fire and poured coffee into a mug, took a scalding sip, then grabbed her overnight bag and went outside in search of the waterfall.

The day was brilliant.

Startled by a landscape that had been shrouded by nature the previous night, Amy paused at the opening to the cave inhaling the warm mountain air and adjusting her eyes to the startling light.

The rainstorm was long-gone, but it had left behind a shining layer of moisture that resembled a sparkling lace carpet. From her vantage point, the mountain world, so high, wide and broad, looked breathtakingly serene and glorious with its valleys and crevices dusted in dew and painted by a pale, white-gold sun. For a brief moment, it was difficult to believe that this was a country that had known such turmoil and tragedy. Sadness seized her because she knew that it had.

Squinting, she noticed a sleek condor perched on an outcrop, haughty and still. Magnificently preened, it looked ready to swoop, its predator's eye narrow and watchful.

It reminded her of Crawford, she thought wryly.

As it winged into flight, the spell was broken and she turned to the right, following the sound of falling water. She found the small cascade quickly enough and gratefully gave herself a quick sponge bath after brushing her teeth. Then, finishing the coffee, she rinsed the mug out and went in search of Crawford.

After a five minute walk down the incline, she found him. The truck had been moved a few feet. He'd obviously maneuvered it out of the mud.

Walking cautiously, she moved toward the truck, planting her feet squarely on the ground and bracing herself.

Crawford glanced up quickly, a frown on his face. Shirtless, he was bent over the truck, its hood open. In the dawn light, his skin gleamed slick and tawny-colored, stretching over taut muscles. His hair, captured by the light, shone like polished mahogany. Sweat glistened across his tanned, broad shoulders. He looked tempting, exciting, virile.

"Hi," she said.

"'Morning," he muttered.

Butterflies dive-bombed in her stomach. This is crazy, she thought, taking deep breaths to try to control her anxiety.

She wet her lower lip in a nervous gesture. "Why didn't you wake me?"

The throaty, breathless sound of Amy's voice trailed down Crawford's already hot body like a searing brand. Turning and straightening with deliberate slowness, he forcibly blanked his gaze before letting it drift over her with feigned laziness.

In daylight, with the early-morning sun catching the sheen of her hair, she looked like a goddess adorned in billowing white. Light and air seemed to drift around her. His throat went dry.

He wiped his hands on a rag, then jammed the cloth back into his back pocket before slamming the hood shut. Deliberately, he didn't move closer to her.

He shrugged carelessly. "I figured you need the rest."

"Thanks, but you don't have to cater to me."

"Okay," he replied in tight tones. "Next time, I won't."

She shuffled with discomfiture. His remoteness cut her to the quick. "I'm willing to do my share of the work, you know," she continued pointedly, her gaze straying past him to the boxes lined up near the back of the truck.

His eyes, arctic blue in their coolness, narrowed. "Fine. Then next time, you can put the roosters out of their misery, and I'll sleep in."

Amy started at his hard tone. Searching his shuttered face, she tried to find some emotion left over from the night before that would make conversation easier, help her bridge what had happened between them with the realities of the morning. But she could read nothing in his expression.

She took a deep breath. "Look, I'm sorry about last night."

He should have seen it coming, but Crawford immediately felt as if someone had hit him in the solar plexus. What the hell else had he expected?

He forced himself to move with languid grace toward the back of the truck and its pile of boxes. Then, wiping his forehead with his forearm, he turned. Leaning against the truck, he

casually crossed his arms in front of his naked chest, but he wa
unable to keep his eyes from blazing. He didn't even try.

"Okay. I hear you."

Amy fought down a desire to run from his coolness. Isn't thi
what he wanted to hear?

She took a step closer to him, his lean, hard body temporar
ily distracting her. She was grateful that his arms covered the
dark mat of hair covering his chest. She remembered its coarse
sexy thickness only too well against her bare skin.

She stopped barely two inches from him, her lashes flutter
ing upward. "Crawford, I want to talk about last night
Are…are you afraid I'm going to be like that other woman?"

Crawford caught a whiff of feminine soap. On her pale skin
the aroma seemed like the most potent aphrodisiac. He arched
his eyebrows, using all his control not to drag her into his arm:
and bury himself in her and her scent.

Distracted, his gaze met hers. "Other?"

"The lady who…charged…." Amy's voice trailed off a:
Crawford regarded her arrogantly.

"Sorry?"

She squelched a flash of temper. He was being as hard-to
thaw as a thirty-foot-high iceberg. This couldn't be the same
man whose lips had been so gentle, so wooing, so seductively
slow on her skin the night before.

"The lady who…charged you."

Crawford's gaze glittered with understanding. The questior
had caught him off guard. It was the lady part that had throwr
him off, he thought. And the fact that there was nothing re
motely similar between what he'd felt for the errant woman—
which had been nothing but disgust—and what he'd felt for
Amy. What he'd felt in Amy's arms had been so stunning, so
devastating, that even now his head reeled. It was laughable to
even imagine there were any similarities.

Except he didn't feel the least bit like laughing.

"Oh, her." He unfolded his arms and reached for the T-shir
he'd tossed on the roof of the truck, and dragged it down, no'
bothering to elaborate.

Her heart twisted that he hadn't denied the idea.

She faltered, torn between feeling sick and furious. "Listen
Crawford, I'm not going to cause you any trouble the way she

did. I just wanted you to know that," she said quietly. "I'm not like her, but I'm sorry—"

Crawford picked up a bundle of dynamite, his lips grinding together in a fine, bloodless line.

"Fine with me. Look, sweetheart, you made your point." He tossed the dynamite into the back of the truck, venting his frustration. "Let's not belabor it, okay?"

Amy's chest rose in hurt anger. "What's the matter with you? I'm apologizing, aren't I?"

Crawford whipped around with a fury that stunned her. "Yeah, and if you do it one more time, I'm going to let you walk on your own pretty feet to the next village." His hands seized her arms and squeezed tightly before riding up her shoulders.

Her mouth dropped open. She stood motionless, in bare feet, staring at him as his fingers pressed into her skin. The glory of the morning had waned fast, rammed into oblivion by the coolness of his blue eyes and the rugged tilt of his head. But at the same time, a jolt shot right through her at his touch. Dismay and embarrassment flushed her skin.

She felt deflated, annoyed, confused, hurt and also, she had to admit, terribly, terribly rejected. But if she didn't want to get involved with him, then why did she feel so badly?

"Just what's gotten into you, Crawford?"

She watched his jaw muscles tense up to his temples.

"I'll tell you what's gotten into me, lady. I don't like the fact that suddenly you're sorry you kissed me. Doesn't do a lot for a man's pride, you know."

Stunned, Amy's eyes widened on his broad, tense back with disbelief. Despite her thoughts, a wild kind of hope surged through her. What exactly was he saying? That he had some feelings for her, or that he didn't? Was he as mixed-up about what had happened between them as she was? In reflex, her hand snaked out and caught his arm. "Crawford...."

Male annoyance darkened his eyes to storm-blue as he felt her fingers on his arm. "What? Leave it alone, why don't you?"

She thought about doing what he suggested for exactly one second. Until her failed marriage, she hadn't taken a lot of risks because her life had been privileged and secure and she hadn't needed to. But she'd grown in the last few years and become more independent.

She met his gaze head-on, her eyes flashing. "No. You owe me an explanation. First, you're angry with me because we kiss, then you're angry with me because I apologize. I'm not sorry I kissed you. I just wanted to apologize for throwing myself at you. There are no subliminal messages here, Crawford, although God knows, maybe there ought to be."

He turned, not because she had enough physical strength to deter him, but because he knew she was right. He was acting like a complete idiot.

He knew he was letting her carry the whole responsibility for what had happened between them because his own insecurities were tearing him apart. He exhaled a wave of fury in a ragged breath of self-disgust. He was just confused enough to want to leave it that way and have her be angry with him. His gaze narrowed.

He couldn't do it.

He kicked at one of the boxes on the ground, scowling.

"There were two of us last night, so you don't need to apologize. Nobody forced me. Nobody forces me to do anything."

Her voice came out in a quick, soft tremor. "Did you kiss me because you felt sorry for me, then?"

He took a shallow breath, then clamped his mouth around tense words he didn't want to say. It hurt to slam the door on her and on the warmth and softness she held out to him, but he had no right to take anything from her. There'd be too many strings attached.

Finally, he rammed the words out. "No, but so what? I won't deny how much I want you and that there are sparks between us, but some things, Amy, just shouldn't happen."

Amy decided she wasn't going to back down now, either. "Just what are you trying to push past your lips, Crawford?"

"Good God, Amy, look at us, we're as different as night and day."

"So?"

"So. . . I'm not into picket fences and families."

Her temper escalated. "That's pretty presumptuous of you, Crawford. How do you know that I am?"

He laughed hoarsely. "Any idiot could see that you are. Think about why you're here, Amy—to start a family—right?

Last time I looked, families meant homes, security, having a job. There's a child waiting for you in the Manion Range—remember?''

Amy's breath caught. She hadn't forgotten that a child was waiting for her. She could never forget that. Her aching heart reminded her every minute of the day. But for a very brief moment, she suddenly realized she had actually allowed herself to dream about something else—something so beyond her, and so crazy that her heart pounded at the prospect—Sam Crawford. Could a child alone fill that blossoming ache in her heart, no matter how ridiculous it was and no matter how much she told herself she wanted to resist it? Did she, as he'd suggested, want more from him?

She forced a faint humorless smile to her lips. "Is that what scares you, Crawford? That somehow I might seduce you into taking on not just me, but a daughter?''

The comment struck home, silencing him. She could do it. Only too easily. Make him think he was capable of rejoining the human race.

Cut it off now, he told himself. "Angel, I can't even think that far ahead. I don't think of futures, I only think of the present, and the present means getting in this truck and trying to make as much time as we can. How about we get at it?''

Amy exhaled a deep breath as he retreated, but she could hear regret in his voice, and strangely it filled her with wild hope. Was it possible she felt something for him against even her own will? And he for her?

She moistened her lips and tossed back her hair. She'd take this one day at a time, she decided.

"Okay—end of discussion. Are we going to Aruka today?''

He shook his head, relieved they were off the other topic. "Because of the storm, we have to pass Aruka. Instead, we should try to make the next nearest village by nightfall.'' He pulled open the other door on the back of the truck, blocking the vision of her dark mane of hair and wide eyes. "All we have to do is finish loading and pack up the rest of the stuff from the cave and douse the fire.''

Amy could have laughed at the irony of the last line, if the truth didn't hurt so much. With a conscious effort, she calmed herself. She hadn't imagined the gentleness in him when he'd touched her. Whatever reservations were keeping him separate from her were obviously strong enough to override the passion that they'd unleashed in each other the previous night.

She brushed away stray strands of hair, unsettled by the early-morning breeze. She wasn't going to worry. She wasn't going to work this to death. She was going to press on, ignoring the obstacles—just as she usually did.

To his back, she asked placidly, "Would you like more coffee first?"

Chapter 11

Amy caught her breath defensively as a heavy blanket of hot air blasted through the open windows of the truck. Squinting, she looked toward the shimmering, distant, hot-gold horizon, expecting to see a cordon of people hugging the gray mountain wall to the right. She was surprised to see that there weren't any.

She'd become accustomed to seeing men and women walking along the side of the mountain road. Usually, they were in groups, the men, weathered, grime-coated, sometimes in army-style khakis like Crawford, but always armed, if only with handmade weapons.

She closed her eyes briefly, recalling what Crawford had told her. Because the land around the center of Marita had been leveled in order to make it harder to attack, people were either concentrated there or in the smaller villages, higher in the mountains. The people they were seeing were likely moving back to their homesites after months of fighting. Many of the women had fought alongside their men.

Her daughter was one of these people, she thought. These strong, resilient people with their direct, fiery gazes and straight backs constituted her child's heritage.

Some day, I'll tell my daughter about the courage of her ancestors. The long, hard battle they fought for freedom. How I watched them resolutely walk home after winning a revolution.

She rubbed her back against the hard, hot leather, lost in reflection.

Raising a soft drink can to her lips, she took a long, pensive gulp of the sweet cola, feeling lethargic. They'd broken for lunch an hour earlier. She wished she'd moved around more before getting back into the truck, but it had been so hot, she hadn't even tried. Now she was regretting it.

Opening her eyes, she searched out Crawford's face. "Everyone on the road seems to know you," she commented.

Turning his head, he regarded her through his sunglasses. Sunlight formed an entrancing halo around her lovely face. Since they'd left the cave, he'd steeled himself to block out her aroma, the vibrance of her presence and the memory of how right and sexy she'd felt when he'd taken her in his arms. He wasn't, he was discovering, having a great deal of luck.

"Lucky guess."

"They call you by name," she pressed.

He didn't answer immediately. Instead, he focused on the ribbon of road visible through the windshield. The road was narrowing as they climbed higher into the mountains. Below them, a treacherous gorge spun out and down like a ragged sliver of gray ice. He'd seen army vehicles become wrecks in two seconds flat because the drivers misjudged the turns and conditions of the terrain.

He needed to concentrate, he told himself sternly. But the memory of kissing Amy had him aching, tingling...burning...not concentrating on the road.

He needed a smoke.

"That persistence of yours is going to get you into a lot of trouble one of these days, Ms. Blake."

"I'm just pointing out the obvious," she said wryly. "How about a straight answer for a change? How come everyone knows you? They all call or wave at you."

He wished she'd stop digging. But he'd learned that giving her something was the best way to shut her up. He clenched his teeth. "I've been here awhile for one thing, and for another, there aren't too many Americans here. Most of the mercenaries are German, Spanish or Italian, so I guess I stand out. Satisfied?"

His decision to shut her out apparently extended beyond the physical. They'd been driving in virtual silence all day. Retreating from her behind vague responses was about the only reaction she'd been able to get out of him since setting out. Her hands curled into tight, resentful fists. What had she done that was so terrible? Kissed him, enjoyed it, told him so, then apologized? Was that so bad? Hadn't he enjoyed it, as well?

Her stomach clenched in memory. Last night was still a revelation to her. She'd come alive in his arms, felt emotions and stirrings that were so primitive, they'd left her spinning with confusion and need. Now she felt hurt and betrayed that he could block her out so effortlessly, when she couldn't do the same with him.

She blinked wearily, her eyes raw from mountain dust.

Inhaling a hot breath, she wished the questions would stop plaguing her, but she recognized that they likely weren't going to. Crawford had insinuated himself into her emotions, and there was no way to change the fact.

"Maybe everyone remembers you because you helped them in their fight for freedom."

Crawford grunted, the old attitude bristling beneath his words. He took refuge in it. "Not much of lasting value in that, angel. Fame is fleeting, haven't you heard?"

Amy felt her throat tightening with frustration. He wore his moods like shields against her intrusion. It made her feel cold and shut out in a way she couldn't explain.

"Why don't you like to admit that perhaps, just perhaps, you might care about the Maritans and their cause, and that they might be grateful to you."

"I make it a rule not to get emotionally involved with my clients, Ms. Blake—any of them," he replied bluntly.

Amy caught the jibe and flinched. He had to mean her, as well, she thought, deeply offended.

"You've already made that point, Crawford. As usual, you're just evading the issue."

He sucked in dusty air. He could read between the lines as well as the next man. He knew what her probing was all about. She was looking for something to admire in him, most likely to justify her behavior of the night before. Well, he wasn't going to invent it so she could feel better about what had happened between them.

"Which is?" he asked laconically.

"Why you act as if these people mean nothing to you, when they must."

"You know what your problem is, Ms. Blake?" he said with deliberate disdain. "You just can't accept the fact that I'm a soldier who fights because he likes it and gets money for it. To me, whoever is paying my salary is entitled to a good day's work. Period. All you're seeing out there are happy customers."

Amy had to school herself not to glare at him. It was the same old song and dance.

"People choose professions that give them satisfaction," she argued heatedly. Because they care, she wanted to yell at him just to get a reaction, but held her tongue. His body language told her he was already bristling with impatience.

He shot her a warning glance. "I leave lofty ambitions and noble aspirations to the politicians, Ms. Blake."

She opened her mouth to retort, then clamped her lips into a tight line as she saw his knuckles tightening on the wheel.

She sat rigid in the seat. No, she thought, disbelievingly. That wasn't all there was to him. She wasn't going to believe it, because having that image of him suited him, for whatever reason. She wasn't going to let him off that easily.

"You protected me with Garcia. You waited outside the junta headquarters for me even though doing so, no matter how courageous, was likely suicidal. You fly in supplies of milk for children you claim are only a job to you. None of that adds up to a man who doesn't care. You say you're not a family man, yet you've obviously convinced your own family into helping the Maritans. Most men I know like women to think the best of them. Why don't you want me to think good things about you?"

She could get to him faster than any woman he knew, he thought. With her low, husky voice, laced with faith, she could unravel him, if he gave her half a chance.

He looked away from her. Right now, the last thing in the world he wanted to see in her eyes was respect as well as warmth. Only suckers believed either meant anything.

"I gave up caring what people think about me years ago, angel. It takes too much energy."

"You have energy aplenty, Crawford."

He groaned under his breath. He wished he could be the hero she wanted him to be, but he knew better. Heroes died on battlefields and got dust kicked in their faces, and men in love didn't fare much better.

His jaw set into a tense line. "In two seconds, Ms. Blake, I'm going to throw you out of this truck. Do us both a favor, and lay off. Enjoy the scenery, why don't you?"

She stared at him, poised to say more, then decided against it.

He was running away from the truth and from her. But what about last night? she wanted to ask.

Even if he was trying to block out the memory, she'd never forget the look of compassion on his face or his concerned kindness as he tried to chase away the demons of her nightmare.

She blinked, surveying his tough, grim profile. It invited no comment.

Sighing, she closed her eyes, listening to the sound of the engine and the crunching of the wheels on the rough mountain road.

She'd never forget his kiss, either, she realized.

In seconds, cut off from him by his continuing silence, she drifted into a restless sleep.

"Ms. Blake, wake up. We've arrived."

For a moment, Amy felt disoriented, then the events of the past few days came back to her. Her eyes flew open, flinching in reflex at the bright sunlight flooding the truck.

"I'm sorry. I must have dozed off."

Her neck felt stiff as she straightened. She'd drifted to the left, and judging from her position, her head had almost fallen on Crawford's shoulder—but not quite, she realized gratefully. She shook herself into full consciousness. Another inch and she'd have been lying on his lap.

A warm flush crept up her face at the images that conjured. "What . . . what time is it?"

"Six o'clock."

Blinking, she tried to toss her hair off her perspiring neck, but strands still stubbornly clung to her damp skin. Embarrassed, she realized she'd slept close to two hours.

"Where are we?" she managed to say, easing herself into an upright position.

"Cresca." Crawford geared the vehicle down. "We'll stay the night here."

Shifting and stretching to get the kinks out of her muscles, Amy glanced with interest through the windshield, everything beginning to sharpen into focus.

Curiously, she surveyed the town as Crawford brought the truck to a slow stop.

Rows of buildings, halfway between huts and cottages, but lit with what appeared to be electricity, stretched in four quadrants of neat squares. The hydro power had to come from mountain waterfalls, or a generator, she thought.

In the center was a small block of what appeared to be commercial buildings. The new national flag of Marita, fabric boasting nothing more than a solid block of green to depict renewal, flew brilliantly from all of them. She could see a distant cross outlined against the mountain sky, heralding a church.

She inhaled sharply, struck by the absolute silence and lack of activity surrounding her.

Twisting her head, she turned toward Crawford, who was jiggling with the keys in the ignition. "Does anyone live here?"

He yanked the keys out of the ignition noisily. "Five hundred and thirteen people, to be exact, give or take a few because of the revolution."

More than she could see, she thought, frowning.

She scrambled to pick up her tote bag. "Isn't it possible that Orega's men have taken over the town?"

Crawford carelessly jammed the keys from the ignition into his side pocket. "No chance. This is one of Garcia's strongholds and his hometown." She noticed a slight hesitation before he continued, "It only fell once... now it's too well-armed."

Uneasy, she glanced away from him. The town was eerily quiet. Like a heavy summer night before a storm. After all his warnings to her, she couldn't understand how he could be so calm. His warnings suddenly had a setting, a scene, significance.

Why wasn't he worried by the sheer silence of the place?

"But if Orega's men are interested in arms, wouldn't Cresca be a good place to hit?"

Crawford grinned insolently as he ran his fingers through his hair. "Nice to know you were listening, Ms. Blake, and yes, you're right ... but we've been watched for the last two hours ... by men of the village."

She was too relieved to snap back at him. "You recognized them?" she asked in a hushed voice.

He shrugged, his mouth twitching. "Two of them, but I think that's enough." Now she felt annoyed with him. He was enjoying this, she thought, getting her back up. Proving himself right and her wrong. Her dark green eyes blinked up at him.

"Then why didn't you tell me? And where is everybody?"

With impatient effort, he said, "I didn't tell you because, if you recall, you were sleeping, and the villagers are just taking their time, assessing the validity of the sentries' judgment."

Stretching his long legs out from under the steering wheel, he tossed her a look over his shoulder. "There are some nervous people in this neck of the woods and trust isn't given easily in a place like Marita. It has to be earned—so when you get out of the vehicle, do it slowly," he commanded autocratically. With that, he slid out of the truck and moved out of view.

Amy ground her teeth together at his response.

"Thank you, Crawford," she muttered under her breath.

Pulse pounding, she was careful to do as she was told, however. She trusted Crawford's judgment far too much to ignore it, she acknowledged. Opening the passenger door, she stepped outside cautiously, grateful to have her feet back on the ground and the circulation returning to her legs.

Breathing in deeply, she instantly experienced a deliciously pure sensation invading her lungs, like a spring day at its finest.

She gasped in pleasure. "I can't believe the air. It's so fresh, I can almost taste it."

Crawford heard her from his position at the back of the truck and stopping what he was doing, put his head around the corner of the open door, his expression softening and clouding at the same time as he saw the sheer, simple joy mirrored on her face.

"One of the benefits of very little industrialization. If the Maritans could export this air, they'd make a fortune and then all their economic woes would be over."

Tentatively, Amy smiled back at him, but remained motionless next to the truck, feeling as if she were in a deserted old western town.

The buildings were there, but there were no people. It was evocative of an old Hollywood set, unworldly in its emptiness. Dust rolled in balls along the streets. Seemingly abandoned buildings hinted at people hidden within. The silence was so deafening, it possessed a waiting sound of its own.

She wouldn't have been surprised to see a snake slithering across the main street, or Gary Cooper turn a corner.

Crawford returned around the side of the truck, carrying one of the coolers in which he kept the beer.

She ran her hand along the side of her damp neck and raised her eyes to his, once he joined her. "Are you really sure people live here?"

He deposited the cooler on the ground. "Yes . . . just give it a minute. . . ."

He was right. Within seconds, a chorus of sounds—and emotions—sprang through the air, electrifying it.

"Crawford!"

Her eyes widened. It was like the eruption of a volcano as people followed the voices. From the sudden crush, all five hundred and thirteen of them, she imagined. Voices rose in a babble of words. Her head reeled as people suddenly surrounded them on all sides.

She couldn't, of course, understand what anyone was saying, but as men and women pressed closer to them, especially to Crawford, there was no mistaking their pleasure in seeing him.

Crawford responded in fast Spanish to the volley of conversation coming at him. Flustered, Amy turned every which way attempting to return all the interested smiles directed at her. She imagined she resembled a ridiculous, bedraggled Cheshire cat. She was about to attempt a "how are you?" to a small group when Crawford caught her arm.

"Ms. Blake, this is Señor Jaime Romero, a lieutenant in the army, and now mayor of the village, and his wife Rosa."

Slowly, she turned. The woman bustling toward her reminded her of Mercedes, although she was about twenty years older. Buxom, eyes shining with vitality, she beamed and bobbed her head, welcoming Amy in Spanish.

Amy smiled back, acknowledging the other woman. Then, a man in his sixties stepped forward. He was dressed in raw beige cotton that set off his swarthy complexion.

Piercing, almost black eyes locked with hers as he greeted her with a grave smile and spoke in precise but slow English. "Welcome to Cresca, Señorita Blake. We hope you will enjoy your visit to our humble village." He bowed formally as he extended a hand toward her.

He was so big, like a sturdy, weathered oak towering over her, that his firm grasp almost swallowed up her own hand. Immediately, she warmed to him, recognizing instinctively from her years as a politician's daughter that he was a man who'd been born to lead. He possessed the same innate presence that her father and many of his friends exhibited. This was a man who might not seek leadership, but it would seek him, she surmised.

"Thank you. It's very kind of you to let me stay here."

He shrugged with genuine modesty. "We would not turn away a friend of Señor Crawford. Come—my wife and I will show you where you will stay." Taking her by the elbow, he began to draw her through the crowd, all the time giving quick directions to the people who had gathered around. Within moments, she was propelled away from the throng of villagers and away from Crawford.

Glancing over her shoulder, she went to say something to him but saw he'd become enveloped by people.

"This way, *señorita*." Romero translated for his wife as they reached the threshold of a cottage, and Rosa, grinning, bobbing and talking, held the door open. "Naturally, we are short of space, but there are two beds in here. We hope you don't mind sharing the cottage with Señor Crawford. Many of our women fought alongside the men, so they are accustomed to sharing accommodations with men—but of course, if there's a problem..." His voice trailed away delicately as she flushed.

It was just as Crawford had said, she thought, catching her lower lip with her teeth. Put in perspective, weren't her concerns about sharing space with Crawford minor in comparison to the hardships the people of Marita must have had to face in the past year, the compromises they'd had to make? Yes, she decided—but still, to say that sharing space with the intense Crawford was a problem would be putting it mildly.

She shook her head and lied. "No, not at all. I'm very grateful you can put me up at all. I realized that someone must have given up this cottage so I...I mean we...could have some privacy. I appreciate the family's gesture. It's extremely generous. I wish I could repay you in some way."

Romero lowered his voice. "We know who you are, Señorita Blake. General Garcia has alerted most of the villages. We know you will repay us by helping us in our quest for recognition and independence. That is all we ask."

Amy stood stock-still. In her lifetime she'd never been entrusted with anything quite as important as this. It was a heady feeling, she discovered, and it was frightening as well as exhilarating to have responsibility for something with such broad implications. Her heart thumped with another realization. These were her child's people. How could she not deliver? How astute Garcia had been to count on her heart as well as her head in soliciting her aid. And how wise he had been to know his own countrymen would not let him down, either, in his boasts of them.

"I will do everything in my power to get that message back to my father's committee," she replied in a soft voice.

Romero smiled lightly as if he'd expected nothing less. "I am glad the sleeping arrangements are acceptable. Because of who you are, we could not leave you unguarded, so it's wise that you do not stand on ceremony. You need protection, and Crawford will provide it."

Her pulse hammered against her temples as she thought ahead to another night in Crawford's company. Who would protect her from her attraction to Crawford? she wondered. Did she even want that protection?

She straightened her back. This was no one's dilemma but hers.

"Yes," she nodded firmly. "Of course."

Amy drank in the exotic night air. Life could be a revelation, she thought, as she lifted her head, observing everyone around her, their smiling faces lit by dancing, red-blue firelight. After the silence of their arrival, the noise level of the partying townspeople and their children was like the burst of a disjointed verbal symphony, set off by the vibrant strumming of two male guitarists. Jaime Romero had ordered a village barbecue, and everyone—men, women, children, goats and dogs—had come.

None of it, though, she realized would have been possible without Crawford.

The extra boxes in the truck that she'd wondered about had contained food supplies. When she'd returned outside to collect her overnight bag, she'd stood back as Crawford, still surrounded by the townspeople, had unloaded items from the truck, including the extra blankets and explosives. The latter he'd turned over to Romero and some of the men. The group had then carried them toward what she guessed was a storage area.

She'd been right, she reflected thoughtfully. All along, her heart had instinctively known there was far more to Crawford than he pretended. Would a man who didn't care about anything except himself have brought supplies to this small village in the mountains? No one had paid him to do it. No one except the people of Cresca would know he'd done it. He hadn't even told her.

Now, sitting on a collapsible chair around a rough wooden slab the size of a card-playing table, one of the townspeople had carried out to the town square, her heart thumped as she watched Crawford distribute the last of a box of small toys to the children who had gathered around the table. It was the second time that day he'd totally surprised her.

She took a deep breath, slanting her gaze, surveying him. For close to an hour, he'd been letting the children pull on his legs, bounce on his knees or tickle him—whatever they were able to negotiate. Treating him as if he were a favorite uncle, they squealed for his attention at every turn and he accommodated them in patient, teasing Spanish, making them giggle.

She was startled as much by that as by anything. He'd make a wonderful father, she thought in mute amazement. She'd never in a million years have envisioned him in that role, but

with her own eyes she could see how well he related to the chil
dren, and how sensitive he was with them. Gone was the rug
ged, abrasive guide who'd led her to Cresca. It was as if the
hard crusty exterior she'd grown accustomed to was unfolding
like a cactus. Still prickly, but with hidden treasure.

Crawford shooed the last of the children away with a wave
of his hand and turned toward her. Behind him, a crescent
moon crowned the black top of the mountains. In the moon's
aura, he looked tanned, fit and handsome, like a barely civi
lized barbarian. Her breath caught.

"You look like you've seen a ghost," he said, reaching for his
cigarette pack on the table. She blinked her dark lashes, real
izing he was giving her an assessing look.

A faint smile twitched at the corners of her mouth. "Per
haps I have."

He snapped his lighter. "Anyone I know?"

"You."

"Me?" Tossing his pack back onto the table, he laughed
"I'm real, angel, believe me."

She wasn't losing her temper on this one, she thought. "No,"
she replied, smiling. "You're a fraud. I've got your number
Crawford. You can't fool me any longer. You're a regular Kri
Kringle, bringing presents for the children."

Crawford's free hand reached broodingly for his wineglass
Even if it was temporary, it felt good being with her, sitting b
her side while he drank wine and had a smoke. Just having her
by his side gave him pleasure. He wanted her badly, he wanted
all the intimacy it implied, including the closeness and the
openness that a man and woman share when things were really
good between them.

Soon, he realized, he might not even be able to resist her
God help them both when that happened.

Restlessly, he drew his left leg up, crossing it at the knee
"You don't understand expedience, Ms. Blake."

She toyed with the green wine bottle on the table. It, too, wa
courtesy of Crawford. "What's that got to do with all the stuf
you hauled up here for these people?"

"I travel through here a lot. I have to be accepted. If I'm not
I don't have the freedom I need, so I bring things. Ain't noth
ing like a little graft to keep things running smoothly."

Amy felt as if a light blub had lit in her head. He'd caught her so many times before, she thought, just this way, with this kind of attitude. How could she have been so dense? She realized she did understand him. He *was* tough and hard. In the lines of work he'd chosen for himself he'd have to be. Once, though, he'd been idealistic, possibly too idealistic. Now, to protect himself, he turned things off. Except there was still a small part of himself that even he couldn't control. With Garcia, who represented power—which was something she knew Crawford had no respect for—he was combative and disdainful, but the way he treated the people and children of Cresca was spontaneous and kind. Those attitudes were drawn from inside him, perhaps even against his will. And the way the Maritans treated him with affection and respect told her things about him that weren't refutable, no matter what he said.

She suddenly felt as if she'd been struck with another thunderbolt. She *was* falling in love with him, she realized incredulously. She'd likely been falling in love all along, except she'd been too busy fighting with him to trust her heart. But perhaps that's what she'd been fighting.

She drew in a deep, full breath, her pulse racing with the acknowledgement. But outwardly she merely arched her neck and grinned at him, not just with her mouth but with her eyes.

"I see," she said with forced nonchalance. "Well, whatever works."

Crawford froze warily, his cigarette between his fingers, "What, no arguments, Ms. Blake?"

She shook back her hair in a flashing cascade that framed her face.

"Why bother, Crawford?" she replied sweetly. "I never win, do I? You're a law unto yourself."

He frowned. Something wasn't right here. He was about to respond when one of Romero's men suddenly appeared beside him and whispered in his ear. Distractedly, he shook his head as if in agreement to the man's suggestions. Then, he stood up abruptly.

"Romero wants to have a talk with me. Will you be okay for awhile?"

"Actually, I think perhaps I'd like to take a walk and get my muscles working again. Do you think that would be all right?"

"Sure—but don't stray." He paused as he stared down at her.
Weeks from now, she wouldn't be in his life. He wouldn't have
her wide, luminous eyes to drown in or her soft, sexy voice to
stroke his skin and emotions. The thought twisted at his gut,
causing him physical pain. Involuntarily, he reached over and
touched her hair. It felt like cool silk between his fingers. "Stay
within the sentry's range, angel," he ordered hoarsely. "I
wouldn't want to lose you at this stage." With that, he turned
sharply on his heel.

Amy trembled as his hand slipped away, and stared after him
until he'd disappeared with the messenger into one of the cottages.

I wouldn't want to lose you at this stage. The words echoed
in her mind and heart. She harrumphed to herself. He wasn't
going to lose her at any stage, if she had anything to say about
it.

Amy wandered into a wooded area. After she'd gone a few
feet, a guard stepped out of the darkness and, returning her
smile, pointed at another guard about three hundred feet away.
She imagined that was as far as she was expected to venture.
Nodding that she understood, she ambled through the trees,
trailing her hands along the branches. It seemed like a century
since she'd worked flowers, ferns and herbs with her hands, she
thought wistfully, missing the feel of petals and stems between
her fingers.

As she had the previous day, she could smell flowers and foliage she couldn't identify. Their heady perfume filled the evening air with musk and sweetness.

In the distance, she could hear guitars and muted but joy-
ous laughter adding to the magic of the night.

Marita was a wonderful country, she reflected. For the first
time in its history, the Maritans had true freedom. At an exciting pivotal point, it stood poised on the threshold of progress,
able to build from scratch and to shape its own destiny. The
Maritans were magnificent, dark and fiery, filled with hope.

She fervently hoped that all their dreams would be fulfilled,
and that the killing and fighting was finally over. She also
prayed that what little lobbying she could do would help.

Stopping by a log, and plucking a wildflower, she sat down
pensively, brushing the petals against her cheek. All evening

she'd been watching the Maritans. They were wonderful with the children, the families close-knit, protective and loving of each other. But watching them had caused a nagging doubt to take root in her mind.

Did she have the right to take a child from the Maritans, especially when they revered them so much?

Who was she to play God?

"A peso for your thoughts."

Startled by Crawford's sudden presence, she tensed, almost crushing the wildflower. Turning, she regarded him in the night light. The moon streaked silver through his gleaming mahogany hair. His profile was hard and rough in the sharp, unremitting light, but she liked it, she thought, with a shiver. She was getting used to its planes and angles. It was familiar and exciting, a lived-in face, her father would have called it, filled with the evidence of his experiences, sorrows and victories. She wouldn't have had it any other way.

She straightened back on the log, too confused for once by her own thoughts to banter.

"I—I was just thinking about the people of Marita and their reverence for children. Maybe I shouldn't even be here."

Intrigued by this turnabout, Crawford lit a cigarette, the flame of the match shimmering in the scant light. He squinted at her through the smoke. "Why not?"

She returned his look, her eyes, dark and brooding, with none of the usual challenge in them.

"Maybe I don't have the right to take Carmela away from her culture and heritage. Who am I to come here and take her away from her own people?"

His eyebrows drew together in a sharply grooved frown, as he blew out a ring of smoke. "What kind of a life do you think she'll have if you don't?"

Amy answered with slow, heartbreaking regret. "She'll be with her own people, learning their language and customs. She'll..."

He interrupted her, his voice, low and rough. "She'll be one of many Maritan orphans, is what she'll be."

A startled expression flitted across her face as if she hadn't expected support from him. He wondered uncomfortably if she'd thought all along that he didn't approve of what she was doing. "But—"

He wouldn't, couldn't let her finish. "No buts, Amy, th family has already decided they can't afford to keep her. I they're not able to find someone else to adopt her, they won' have any choice except to put her in an orphanage."

He watched as she lay the flower on the ground and clenche her hands on her lap.

Her voice caught as she returned his searching look "Maybe, though—maybe she'd be better there. At least she' be in her own country."

Crawford's lips thinned to a line of sad bitterness. He re spected the sentiments she was expressing and he respected he for having them, but she hadn't seen the truth of it.

He hoped she never would.

"Amy, I've been to those orphanages. Any one of thos children would be thrilled to be adopted by you rather than b there, believe me. They're clean, humane and safe, and th Maritan nuns take wonderful care of them, but trust me, n child would choose them over you."

Confusion racked her. Surely it couldn't be reduced to suc simple alternatives? Adoption or an orphanage?

She was going to be transporting Carmela to another cour try, immersing her in another world, entirely different fro Marita.

Raising her head, the moonlight slanted across her pale fac highlighting her tension.

"There's got to be more to it than that, Crawford. How ca I take her from her roots? Is that fair?"

He tossed his cigarette onto the ground and brought his he down on it. He understood what she was saying and he kne it was a tough decision. Sometimes he'd had to make difficu choices too.

"Stop it, Amy." He took her by the shoulders and tried ease the tension out of her by rubbing his fingers into the so hollows under his touch. "The world has become a global vi lage. Borders keep vanishing. Everyone is responsible for th world's children. It's too late to believe otherwise. You can a ways bring her back here for visits."

She shook her head, her eyes widening. "I'd always planne to do that, but suddenly, Crawford...oh, I don't know...it ju doesn't seem right. It seems arrogant to think I can give her better life." She pulled back a fraction and Crawford's arms dropped.

He watched her twist her hands. They were delicate the way she was. He wanted to capture them in his own, feel their smallness nestled in his, but thinking of the night ahead they were going to be spending together, he knew he couldn't afford to make another move toward her.

He preserved his distance, saying, "Look, Amy, Marita has one of the toughest procedures in the world for adopting a child. Lots of potential parents get turned down. You were accepted. That says something. You can't back out now."

Alarm shone in her eyes. "I don't want to back out. I just want to do what's right."

He kept on arguing. "This *is* right, Amy. You're not taking anything away from Carmela, you're giving her something—a chance at a another kind of life."

"I wouldn't . . . want her to grow up to hate me for . . . what I've done," she replied in a halting voice.

She looked so fragile and bewildered, framed like a cameo by the overhang of the trees, that he wanted to drag her into his arms. His hands knotted into fists. It was so hard to think of anything else when he was with her, except her.

"Nobody could hate you, Amy, even if they wanted to," he said huskily. "You're beautiful, intelligent, courageous . . ."

Her gaze caught his and her heart turned over with surprise and excitement. The raw, vulnerable longing mirrored on his expressive face sliced into her, cutting off her air supply. For a moment she could only look up at him, her temples pounding. It was one of the first times he'd ever been verbally open with her without anger or irritation coloring his words. What was he saying exactly? Was he struggling as she was with the depth of their attraction?

Time seemed suspended as they stared at each other.

Then, the moment was broken at the echo of crunching undergrowth, and Romero came toward them.

Nodding to Crawford, he stopped in front of Amy. "You look so serious, Señorita Blake," the mayor chided as he glanced down at her.

Amy's eyes darkened. Remembering how the people of the town had been so generous and gracious toward her, she felt a fresh wave of guilt.

"I was just—"

In an instant, she felt Crawford's arm snaking around he
and his voice interrupting firmly.

"Ms. Blake was just saying that she is anxious to find he
child and to hold her in her arms. I was telling her that ther
isn't much longer to wait."

"Ah..." Romero's face broke into a broad smile. "How
wonderful it is that you would come so far to adopt one of ou
beautiful children. And how lucky your child will be, Señorit
Blake—part Maritan, part American. We are very proud tha
you would want her so much. It fills us all with self-esteem
Your wanting one of our children is a true sign of respect."

Amy flushed with a start. Crawford's sensitivity had pre
vented her from a grave error in judgment. Had she re
sponded, she would have insulted Romero.

"It's my privilege, Señor Romero," she replied softly.

The mayor beamed. "Good, then perhaps we could ad
some pleasure to privilege. The townspeople would like you an
Crawford to join them in their last dance of the night."

Chapter 12

Amy held her breath, fully expecting Crawford to refuse, but he stunned her by shrugging with a crooked smile.

"Sure, why not?"

Her eyes widened. The idea of Crawford doing anything as civilized as dancing was ludicrous. He couldn't mean it, she thought, she must have heard him wrong—but the mayor's face widened into a broad smile and he extended a hand in invitation. "Good. The musicians are waiting."

Crawford resolutely wrapped her hands into his and as soon as they emerged from the thicket, the musicians started up and the townspeople applauded with delight. Amy smiled with tight nervousness in response. For two days, she'd shared tight quarters with Crawford and had come close to losing her perspective.

She certainly wasn't going to regain it dancing with him, she reflected. She felt her pulse starting to race. Dancing meant two bodies, two sets of arms, two sets of legs, pressed together, swaying in harmony.

She blinked hard, trying to chase away the images. Stop this, she ordered herself sternly.

He edged between the other couples and led her into the throng as the two guitarists segued into a soulful ballad.

Stopping, he turned, facing her, his brooding features clearly delineated in the shafts of moonlight slicing through the sky. He was so close she could have trailed her fingers along the lines of his set mouth. She remembered the feel of it when it hadn't been so hard. She lifted her eyes, her gaze locking with his.

She held her breath for a moment, then let it out. The night suited him—it was a perfect backdrop for his dark, dangerous looks. But it made her think dangerous, disturbing thoughts.

"You look as though you're about to face a firing squad, Crawford."

His mouth twisted into a wry curve. "Not much call to learn the two-step in the mountains, Ms. Blake. I'm not what you would call a dancer."

The blue of his eyes were almost navy as she craned her neck to look up at him. She could get lost in that burning gaze, she thought. Lost and reckless. Emotions started to churn inside her. Against all reason, she wanted to feel his hands on her, his arms around her, his body brushing against hers, even if it was temporary and it was madness.

Heart pounding, she made her eyes remain steady on his. "I'll take my chances, Crawford."

He forced a hoarse laugh. Feeling her body imprinted against his was about the last thing in the world he wanted to take a chance on.

He hunched a broad shoulder with feigned nonchalance. He just hoped he didn't embarrass the hell out of himself. "Your call, Ms. Blake."

He watched the sweep of her lashes upward. "I'm sure you're more than adequate as a dancer, Crawford."

He closed his eyes. Innocent sensuality exuded from every pore of her. He could feel himself drowning in it, drawn against his will to taste its exotic darkness and promise. He didn't have to look at her to know it was there. He could feel it, like a full, gathering wave.

It was only a dance, he told himself. A stupid, insane dance that they were undertaking for diplomatic reasons.

He opened his eyes, a challenge shadowing them.

If *she* could take it, he could take it.

"Well, don't say I didn't warn you."

With that, he pulled her into his arms.

Amy's breath caught, her heart beating uncontrollably. She was getting used to him by now, she thought, the sarcastic edge that always seemed to be lining his voice. But his body against hers was unbelievably alluring, his scent wild and musky, part sweat, part mountain air, part soap and water, but heavy and claustrophobic, closing in on her. Her temperature skyrocketed as she felt herself losing ground.

She drew back a fraction, sucking in hot, humid air.

"I'd like to thank you."

To the best of his knowledge, he hadn't done anything yet. Wishing was as far as he'd gotten.

He raised his eyebrows with elaborate emphasis. "No kidding? For what?"

"I might have blown it with Romero and offended him, if you hadn't stopped me."

Crawford ground down the desire burning inside him and tried to center his thoughts on other things. There were other activities a man could indulge in besides making love to Amy Blake, but for the moment, he couldn't imagine what they were.

He pulled his gaze away from a little boy and girl dancing together and forced his eyes back to her. "Your guilt was getting the better of you. Guilt's a useless emotion."

"I tried to tell myself the same thing when my little girl died, but it's hard to accept."

Crawford saw a mist veiling her eyes. He immediately sobered, the expression in them filling him with a desire to console her.

"You beat up on yourself too much, Ms. Blake."

She smiled faintly, but it didn't reach her eyes.

"Did you really mean what you said about my adopting Carmela, or were you being uncharacteristically diplomatic back there?"

He hesitated. Right and wrong had so little meaning for him that the distinction was irrelevant as far as he was concerned. What he'd always believed to be right had in the long run turned out to be wrong. But he couldn't have let her turn her back on her dream.

"Angel, I've already told you my views on the subject. . . ."

She opened her mouth to speak, but he cut her off as soon as he saw a shadow of denial cross her face.

"Amy, stop agonizing over it," he ordered, moving his arms as if to shake her. "We had a deal, remember? *I* do all the worrying."

She let out a deep breath, and bowed her head on his shoulder, grateful for his toughness. "Okay. Sorry," she mumbled.

He squeezed her hand, trying to ignore the feel of her hair as it brushed the triangle of bare chest above his shirt.

"That's better. I like it when you follow orders."

She glanced up at him and smiled at that.

He smiled back. "Relax," he told her. "Enjoy the dance."

She took a deep breath and wondered how she could. Without conversation, all she could focus on was him. He filled her senses with every movement they took together. Her eyelashes drifted upward in protest, then downward as she gave in to the sensations washing over her. Her breasts were almost flattened against the solid bulk of his chest. She could feel a hard thumping as he took her hand, and covering it with his, pressed it against his heart so the rhythm seemed to travel to the tips of her fingers. He'd lied, she discovered. He was a graceful, long-limbed dancer, moving easily and sensually to the plaintive sounds of the guitars. She was moving, following his lead, but she wasn't sure how—her legs were trembling, and her insides were melting.

The outside world suddenly ceased to exist for her. All that mattered was him. Sam Crawford, renegade.

Suddenly, his voice whispered something harsh and unintelligible in her ear, and he pulled away from her.

Their hands were still touching and she looked at him, startled. "What's the matter?"

His mouth was clenched and she could feel his tension through her fingers. "Pardon the pun, but I'm afraid I'm just not up to this, Ms. Blake."

"But..."

"Look, I don't go in for self-flagellation."

When she didn't answer immediately, he swore under his breath and, using the full strength of his muscled arms, drew her in against him, punishingly tight, so she could feel what she was doing to him.

Amy suppressed a gasp as she realized she could feel every male inch of him, including that part of him that was bulging and ready. Her eyes met his in shock but not repulsion. Something clawed at her stomach in response, turning it over.

"Crawford," she whispered in a raw voice, without stopping to think.

"I warned you, angel," he replied dryly. "The real reason I don't dance well is it makes me think of other things. I get sidetracked."

Everything inside her seemed ready to ignite. If he could want her, maybe he could love her.

Her pulse was throbbing at her temples. She'd never been in a situation like this before, where she'd had to be the aggressor. But if he said yes to making love this time, would it be enough? She needed more than lust between them, perhaps not love exactly, but affection, surely, and gentleness. Some emotional sharing that she could cling to.

She opened her mouth to speak, but the look on his face and the chilling expression in his eyes rooted her to the spot. He hated wanting her. The realization cut through her like a sliver of hard, cold ice.

"I—I understand," she said in a halting voice, even while she thought she didn't understand at all.

Crawford's body was hot and coiled, sparks shooting off inside it, fired with tension. The moment he'd pulled her against him, he'd known what a mistake it was. Her heat and her exotic scent, the feel of her thighs pressed to his need, filled him with torment. His heart was pounding like a jackhammer.

"Do you?" he said, gruffly, shaking his head. "I wonder."

Amy flushed. "I'm not a tease, Crawford. Surely, you're not blaming me because you need a woman?"

Crawford's hands knuckled into fists. He didn't need a woman. He needed *her*. But right now, he needed air more—and fast.

Disgruntled, he said, "No more talking and no more dancing, Ms. Blake. I think we've met our obligations to the natives, so if you don't mind, I'd like to call it a night."

Suddenly, Amy became aware of the quiet that had descended. The lilting plaintive notes of the guitars had drifted away, carried by a hot, dry breeze, and the townspeople were dispersing. A twinge of sadness seized her that the moment between them was over.

"The music's stopped anyway, Crawford," she said softly. All wrong, she thought. She'd handled this all wrong. She set her teeth, wishing she had more experience at seduction. Why couldn't she get through to him that it was all right to want her? Why wouldn't the words come?

He dropped her hands in an abrupt motion. "I'll walk you back to the cottage. Are you ready?" he asked brusquely.

Amy nodded, trying to keep her hands from shaking by pressing them against the skirt of her dress. "Yes."

They waved good-night to some of the townspeople and walked back to the cottage in silence.

The night had an after-the-party feel to it, languid and winding down. As she followed beside him, her lungs couldn't seem to get enough air into them. She thought ahead to the cottage with its two pristine cots.

Now what? she wondered, her heart thumping. Would Crawford shut her out as he had so many times before, or this time, would he accept what she so desperately wanted to give?

They reached the cottage, and Amy paused uncertainly on the threshold. A heavy hush had fallen over the town, and the moon had drifted behind clouds. She didn't know what to do, but Crawford held the door open for her, so she stepped inside.

When he didn't follow, she hesitated, asking in a shaky voice, "Is something the matter?"

With the moonlight framing his muscular frame and weathered face, he shook his head, his eyes hooded, his masculine mouth curving tightly to the side.

"I think I'll walk off some of that wine I had. I'll be back in awhile. There'll be a sentry outside at all times, so you should be safe."

He wasn't coming in. A wild surge of disappointment and gut-wrenching loss seized her as she watched him turn and walk away. But at the same time, she felt a surge of self-recrimination.

Why had she backed off when it was the last thing in the world she'd wanted to do? Why had she let him go? She caught her lip between her teeth.

That's the last time you're walking away from me, Crawford, she promised herself, before closing the door behind her.

* * *

Amy slanted Crawford a look as the truck left Cresca. They'd left the town with more fanfare than when they'd arrived—the townspeople all gathering to wave them off—but ever since she'd gotten up, Crawford had barely said a word to her. She wondered if he'd slept any better than she had. Perversely, she hoped he hadn't.

She'd lain in the narrow, hard cot, listening to the subdued sounds of the villagers burrowing in for the night. A dog had barked in the distance, and she'd seen the shadowy figure of her sentry pass by her window a number of times, but by the time she'd drifted into a restless sleep, Crawford still hadn't returned. She hated herself for it, but she'd tried to stay awake, waiting for him to come in and have it out with him. She finally fell asleep, though, and when she'd awakened in the morning, he still hadn't been there.

Now she was feeling lost as she sipped on a mug of coffee from the thermos that Rosa had filled for them. His silence was disturbing. She missed his banter and aggression. She couldn't take it anymore, she decided. Two hours of being shut out was quite enough.

"All right, Crawford," she challenged. "Just what did I do to deserve the silent treatment?"

His hands corded on the steering wheel, strong and restrained. "Nothing." His voice was even but threaded with a fatigue she didn't miss.

"Nothing?" She flicked her lashes at him, turning sideways in the seat. "Pardon me, but I think I know the silent treatment when I'm getting it." She neglected to add that it had been David's favorite form of censure and that she was a past master on the tactic.

"Give it a break, Amy," he snapped. "I drank too much and had a bad night, that's all."

"I don't think you had any more to drink that I did, Crawford," she responded in a neutral tone.

"Good," he retorted. "Then let's compare hangovers, shall we?"

Amy held her breath. Don't ask, she told herself, but somehow the words were out before she could stop them. "Where were you last night?"

He regarded her laconically through his sunglasses. "Out with the boys. Romero had some homemade brew he wanted me to try."

"Romero said you were supposed to protect me."

His head snapped up. "I don't have to be with you every minute to do that. I did check on you from time to time."

He took a deep breath. In fact, he'd done more than check on her. He'd actually hovered over her bed, a raging debate warring inside his head as to whether or not to act on his instincts. To hell with tomorrow, he'd thought. Sanity had prevailed, however, and he'd gone outside and kept watch with the sentry, sleeping fitfully in a hard chair by the door. The sentry had looked bemused but hadn't said a word once he caught the warning look Crawford had given him.

Now as he looked at Amy and saw the wounded expression on her face, the ache he'd felt last night revisited him, twisting inside him. He had to block her out and keep blocking her out, he told himself, swearing under his breath.

"All right, but obviously something is bothering you. If I've done anything, I'm sorry—"

"Seems to me, you and I exchange an awful lot of apologies the morning after...especially when they're mornings after...nothing...wouldn't you say?" he replied dryly.

Amy flushed beet-red, her eyes widening in protest. They didn't have to be, she thought mutinously. "Maybe that's the problem."

Crawford reacted instantly. He couldn't believe it. He'd played by the rules, a woman's rules, and she was lecturing him. Days of male frustration turned to raw fury.

He might be hung over, he thought, but he wasn't brain-dead yet. He'd call her bluff and get it over with.

"Oh...so if we'd made out last night, there wouldn't be any apologies this morning, is that what you're trying to say?"

Amy's heart beat in her throat. In for a penny, in for a pound, she thought. "I'm not into that kind of analysis, Crawford. How would I know?"

He laughed a low rumble of derision. "Well, I know, angel. Whenever a man makes love to a woman he isn't going to marry, he nearly always apologizes, if not to her, then to himself. It's in the genes."

She could only study him in amazement. He was so unyielding, she thought. She took a deep breath to steady her jitters. "Crawford, why is it so difficult to admit that you wanted me last night, and that you hightailed it out of the cottage because you couldn't handle it?"

His brows shot up. "I've already admitted to wanting you in no uncertain terms, but I've wanted a lot of women in my time, and admitting it won't change a thing, Ms. Blake. If anything, it only complicates matters, and I don't think you need any more complications in your life right now. I know I don't."

"I can answer for myself, Crawford."

"Then answer me this, Ms. Determined-To-Drive-Me-Crazy. Just how many one-night stands have you had in your life?"

"That's not the point," she retorted.

Crawford held his patience in check only by a thread. "It's exactly the point, as far as I'm concerned. You're not the kind of woman who's, shall we say, seasoned at that sort of thing, which means you're liable to get all dewy-eyed on me and start thinking plans. Read my lips, Amy, I'm not into plans for the future. How many times do I have to spell it out?"

Amy caught her lower lip between her teeth. "Maybe I'm not either, Crawford."

"That's what they all say, angel."

Amy felt as if she'd been slapped in the face, but she wasn't about to give up. Yearning shadowed her eyes. She didn't want to beg, but if she had to . . .

"Why can't you give me a chance, Crawford?" she demanded. "Why can't you let yourself get involved with me?"

His hands tightened on the wheel. "There are rules about these kinds of situations, and I intend to keep them. My job is to get you to your little girl, and that's what I'm going to do, period."

Amy couldn't believe her ears. This from somebody to whom rules were mere inconveniences. "Rules are made to be broken, Crawford."

He whirled on her. "Not this rule, Ms. Blake. Now, please, my head is killing me."

She blew out a sigh of exasperation. "All right. I'll be as quiet as a mouse." She leaned her head back against the truck's back rest and then, on second thought, tilted her head and added, "Until lunch time, that is."

His only response was to grunt dubiously.

* * *

They were away from Cresca and moving north again, and
after a detour, the weather was murderous. Amy glanced at her
watch. It was almost five. Her mouth felt dry, her back ready
to break, her legs numb from sitting so long and her arms
prickly from the heat. The altitude was making her feel light-
headed, but she felt the truck slowing down.

Turning to Crawford, she asked hopefully, "Are we going to
be breaking now? Everything I own has either fallen asleep or
is burning up."

He kept his gaze focused forward. Romero had warned him
that his scouts had seen evidence of Orega's men to the far
north of the town, the route that Crawford had originally intended to take, so he'd backtracked a bit, hoping to come up
around them on the eastern side and cut across from there.

He nodded. "There's a spot right around the corner. Then I
thought we could get an early night, and leave earlier in the
morning, maybe beat some of this weather."

"Okay," she replied politely.

Crawford squinted, suppressing irritation. Since they'd had
their discussion about making love, she'd kept her promise and
been reasonably quiet. Now he realized how she'd felt earlier
when he'd been so uncommunicative shortly after leaving
Cresca. Without her snappy conversation, he felt strangely, irrevocably lonely. Three days ago, he would have enjoyed the
isolation, the long drive by himself.

No-win, no-win, he thought with a fierce frown.

He geared the truck down as he steered it into the turn. Amy
let out a sigh of relief as they came to a standstill beside a bank
of trees.

"How about you get some of the supplies out of the truck,
while I scout around?" He'd given up treating her like a porcelain doll. He'd discovered that she was strong and agile and
willing to work.

"What do you want me to take out?"

"Enough food for dinner and breakfast, and the sleeping
bags. We'll have to sleep outdoors tonight. There aren't any
caves nearby, and we're too far from a town to make it."

Amy nodded and got out of the truck, grateful to feel land
beneath her feet. She walked around to the back of the truck,
meeting Crawford as he opened the doors.

"Now, listen," he warned. "I don't want you taking any chances. Here's the rifle. Keep it slung over your shoulder at all times. I'm fairly sure that we're well away from any of Orega's men, but better safe than sorry."

She accepted the weight of the gun grudgingly as he slid it over her shoulder. "How long will you be?"

"Thirty minutes tops, I want to circle all around. Now remember what I told you. Shoot first, ask questions after."

She regarded him gravely. It was ridiculous, she knew, but if something happened to him, she'd yearn her whole life for what had never happened between them—the ultimate physical sharing that for her represented the gift of love she wanted to give him.

Quickly, she leaned upward and kissed him gently on his cheek. "All right, but please . . . come back."

Crawford blushed like a teenager, taken by surprise at her spontaneous open gesture and words. He felt all his defenses, all his arguments, draining away, all driven by the overwhelming sweetness of her.

He couldn't cave in now, he thought.

"I'll be back, angel," he said brusquely.

Amy waited until he'd disappeared from view before setting to work. Wearily she began unloading, the rifle making it hard to get things in and out of the back of the truck. When she couldn't reach the sleeping bags crushed well into the interior because the rifle kept dragging at her as she bent over to accommodate the roof, she slipped the leather strap off her shoulder and leaned the gun against the fender. It was only for a minute, she told herself. Then, she hauled the two bags to the end of the truck and jumped down, turning around to pull them out.

Like a crash of thunder, she heard a sound.

Her right hand on the edge of one of the bags, she whirled, her eyes widening as she saw two men in fatigues descending upon her. She opened her mouth to scream, but one of the men slapped his hand across her face, cutting off her air, then clamped it hard against her mouth and cheekbones. She kicked out, staggering backward, feeling the edge of the truck's floor slicing into her back.

Suddenly, she felt a terrible pain in her head as if a million bricks had exploded. Her body went limp and the world went black. Her last thought was of Crawford and Carmela, her family that as yet hadn't had a chance to happen.

He'd come looking for this, but he hadn't really expected to find anything.

From his position on the ledge, Crawford's lungs constricted against the wall of his chest as he peered down at the camp in the clearing surrounded by heavy underbrush.

He had found something. Soldiers from Orega's splintered army.

Lying on his stomach, he scanned the area through his binoculars. As best as he could tell, it was a small party. Stragglers, likely. Three at the most, he surmised.

He moved the scope slowly. There was only one battered truck and one sentry on guard. From the man's outfit he couldn't confirm that he was definitely one of Orega's because he was wearing fatigues and both sides wore khakis, but it was a pretty safe bet, he thought.

Scanning, he couldn't see any stored weapons or food, so the party was probably only stopping in the clearing and not making full camp. He shifted his large body slightly. There'd been no attempt made to put up a makeshift shelter, which would have indicated a longer stay, or that Orega was with them.

He shook his head. Orega wasn't with them. Orega liked his creature comforts.

"Early dinner break," he muttered cryptically.

Adrenaline pumped through his veins as his blue eyes watched the man leisurely roll a cigarette between his fingers. Where were the others? he wondered, frowning.

Amy.

Tremors of icy fear immediately shot through him. Of course. As long as they were fast and efficient, a party of three is all it would take to kidnap one slight female.

His heart started to pump furiously at his carelessness. How could he have been so blindly, arrogantly stupid?

Orega would never send a large group to kidnap Amy. Big groups attracted too much attention and would slow down the process. Three of Orega's slyest men is all it would take.

God . . . and he'd left her alone! He was at least fifteen minutes away from her. He was a first-class idiot.

How could he have done it? How could he have taken that chance? His fists curled as he broke out into a heart-wrenching sweat.

Thinking of Amy in their hands made his stomach heave with sickening, mind-destroying guilt as his imagination raced graphically in overdrive.

His fault. All his fault.

Damn it, Crawford, think. Think.

He sucked in deep breaths of sultry air, forcing himself to be rational. Wallowing in guilt was only going to compound the problem.

Number One: Chances were they were going to be bringing her back here.

Number Two: If he tried to get back to her, he might miss her. But if he hedged his bets right, he could be further ahead by waiting.

Number Three: At the moment he had the sentry all to himself. Without his partners, the man was easy pickings.

Number Four: He couldn't risk a shot.

His eyes grew dark with anguish as Amy's lovely face flashed before his eyes. It was all he needed to galvanize himself into action.

Murderous rage rose inside him. He still knew how to kill a man with his bare hands if he had to.

You bastards, you're going to pay for this.

He reached for the knife in his boot and began slithering down the incline.

Amy fought her way out of the black shadows reluctantly, her head, her back and her shoulders throbbing. She started to open her eyes, her heavy lids objecting to the light and effort. Slowly, she raised her head, fighting nausea and dizziness. She was in a natural alcove, her legs splayed to the side. Her back and shoulders hurt because she was propped against a jagged rock, her arms tied behind her at the wrists. She could feel the unyielding stone slicing into her. Moaning as she lifted her head, she refocused, trying to ignore the pain.

Watching her were two men, one facing her and the other hunched beside her on his heels. Grenades belted their loose pants and a pair of assault rifles was slung over each man's shoulders. Her eyes widened, large, dark and frightened as she struggled frantically against her bonds.

Her heart pounded with futility. There was no way for her to escape trussed as she was, and there were two of them, and one of her.

What were they going to do with her? Ransom her for guns? Or did they have something else in mind?

Fear exploded inside her as the man nearest to her leaned over and touched her hair. He laughed and turned to joke with the other man while he did so. The other man, sporting a full, greasy black beard, merely raised his eyebrows disinterestedly.

As the first drew closer, a smell of rank decay stung her nostrils, reminding her of a sewer. Her gaze drifted upward, filling with horror as his hand moved from her hair to the cleft between her breasts. His black, wild eyes glittered lecherously at her.

She went to yell but discovered a dirty rag had been shoved into her mouth. She gagged, her eyes flashing with terror as he muttered something harsh and obscene-sounding, his breath burning the side of her cheek.

She felt utterly and totally powerless.

The soldier's hand began to move toward the thin, cream-colored fabric of her shirt, his eyes boring into her, as if trying to solicit a reaction. Every part of her body stiffened and screamed in silent, terrifying protest. Panic and repulsion tore at her, but the second soldier's voice shattered the silence as he poured forth a volley of angry Spanish.

Moving quickly, the second man stood up and savagely slapped the other soldier's hand aside. Amy's heart stopped beating and caught in her throat while the pair argued, but the second man, obviously the senior, won the argument.

While she watched with pulse racing, the first soldier's hand dropped, clenching by his side. Rage burning in his eyes, he stalked away, but he turned to regard her with hatred and frustrated lust in his eyes. Then, he spat on the ground, shooting her temporary savior a venomous look.

If she could have breathed out a sigh of relief, she would have, but the rag in her mouth prevented even that. She cringed, shivering, looking away, wanting to cry, as well, but too proud to do it.

Then, her blood turned lifelessly cold and she jerked her head upward, turning it from side to side, her gaze searching wildly.

Crawford. Where was Crawford?

Oh, my God, had they killed him?

The second soldier shook her and put his palm under her elbow. He yanked her cruelly to her feet. Pain shot across her shoulder blades as he jerked her stiff body around. Using one of the rifles slung over his shoulder to direct her, he aimed it toward a clump of trees, then made a motion with his feet to indicate she was to walk.

A deep lassitude overtook her as she felt her heart breaking for the man she'd come to care about, for the moments they would never share. Suddenly, as vividly as if he were standing in front of her, she could envisage his stern face. His silver-blue mercurial eyes that were always snapping with anger and so many other emotions that he tried hard to conceal. How could she live without his energy, his fierce strength, his quick compassion that even he didn't acknowledge? Regret and tears stung her eyes in hot fury. They must have killed him. If only she'd done as he'd told her and kept the rifle on her, perhaps she'd have been able to save him.

Her heart turned over, splintering, leaving in its wake an excruciating ache. He had wanted her no matter how much he'd tried to avoid the fact, she thought, but she'd never had the chance to show him that the feeling was returned.

Crawford, oh, Crawford. This is all my fault.

She'd never felt so empty and alone in her life. Woodenly, suddenly drained of emotion, she stumbled forward, then her spine stiffened.

If she gave up now, who was going to look after her little girl?

Chapter 13

The twilight was brilliant. A royal purple edged with gold, heralding a classic mountain night. Crawford sat as still as the gray stone on which he had parked himself, his back facing the vantage point from where he'd viewed the camp.

Anyone looking down on the clearing would have seen only one of Orega's sentries, his head turned away from the mountain view. He hoped.

His heart was drumming rapidly, his stomach muscles tangled into knots, his body wired. He'd been sitting for hours in the one spot, plagued by doubts, tortured by guilt.

What if he'd calculated wrong? What if the absent soldiers didn't have Amy, and she was frightened at finding herself alone when he hadn't returned? Would she think he'd abandoned her? What if Orega's soldiers did have her and had decided to take her somewhere else and he'd misjudged?

Had they hurt her? Touched her? Harmed her in any way? Was she even conscious?

His pulse hammered relentlessly against his temples. Closing his eyes, he found himself unable to banish the agony of his thoughts no matter how hard he tried.

Why had he fought her so hard? Now it all seemed like useless energy.

The silence pressed down on him, a mantle of remorse and recrimination he couldn't shake.

He should have protected her better, he should have brought her with him, kept her safe by his side. What kind of man was he that he hadn't protected his own woman?

His woman. That was the second time he'd felt that overwhelming sense of belonging, bonding. Not just her to him, but him to her. It was ridiculous. Primitive.

But it felt insanely right.

He exhaled a ragged breath.

What if the soldiers decided not to ransom her? What if they voted to keep her instead and . . .

"Miguel?"

The suggestive wheedling voice jolted him out of his reverie and reversed his thoughts. Cold, savage anger overshadowed the regret and yearning in his heart. Deliberately blocking the emotions, he gave himself up to the seething rage simmering beneath his guilt and anguish.

You're mine, you scum.

For a moment, he closed his eyes, concentrating all his energies on listening.

More than one person, he estimated.

He took a steadying breath, struggling not to turn immediately and see if Amy was behind him. Grunting in response, he merely waved with his left hand, while his right hand tightened around his Beretta. His mouth was dry, but beneath the khakis, his body felt a trickle of warm, sticky sweat underneath his armpits.

"Miguel . . . we have an expensive package for you to look after," a guttural voice rang out, with laughter accompanying the coarse Spanish. "She is worth a lot of guns."

In measured torment, Crawford held his breath, waiting. They had to mean they had Amy.

He raised his hand again, twisting his arm so that the slim piece of metal he'd attached to his camouflage shirt caught the light. His breath snagged as he caught the reflection of Amy.

She was alive. He offered a silent prayer of thanks, then began to stretch upward with extreme caution, checking the metal piece again. The soldiers had moved to either side of her so that she was standing between them.

The position was better for him. Far better.

Before, when he'd checked, one of the men had been standing directly behind her.

Amy would have been the soldier's cover.

Now, all he had to do was get both of them at the same time. Piece of cake. Like winning the lottery.

He lowered his left hand and reached for the rifle by his feet. The moment his fingers found it, he crouched, whirling, and screamed a command.

"Amy, to the ground!"

For a split second, Amy was unable to move.

It couldn't be, she thought wildly.

But allowing herself to believe in miracles, she hesitated no longer and dropped to the earth just as the two soldiers shouted in surprised rage, and a round of gunshots rang out, shattering the peaceful stillness of the secluded camp. Without being able to use her arms to break her fall, she collapsed facedown on the hard ground, her right cheekbone and jaw taking the full impact. She gasped as a shooting pain shattered her head.

Crawford!

Her heart beating a staccato rhythm in her chest, she twisted, flinching, glancing upward, catching a glimpse of Crawford's tense features frozen into a mask of icy contempt.

One of the soldiers fell on top of her, knocking the air out of her lungs. With a fury fueled by careening emotions, she kicked him away with her feet.

Then there was an unearthly silence. She held herself rigid, barely trusting herself to breath, the acid smell of smoke burning her nostrils as it lingered in the air. Let him be safe, she prayed.

Suddenly, someone was dragging her to her feet and she panicked.

Dazed, afraid to believe, she discovered she couldn't open her eyes. If she didn't look, she'd never have to know that Crawford was lost, she thought irrationally. To look would destroy her hopes. She lashed out, wanting to keen with anguish.

"Easy... angel... easy... it's me."

Her eyes flew open, locking with a familiar sky-blue gaze, shadowed with concern.

"You all right?" he asked in a raspy voice.

She couldn't talk, she could only speak with her eyes, and they shone at him, brimming with tears and relief and a love she didn't even bother to conceal as her body stilled in reflex before shuddering in his embrace, giving him his answer.

"Hold your arms out," he commanded.

She did as she was told.

Moving one hand behind her, he deftly cut the ropes around her wrists with a sharp slice of his knife. With the other, he jerked the rag out of her mouth.

Her arms free, she threw herself at him, her legs unsteady because they were shaking with relief.

"Crawford," she cried. "Oh, my God. I thought you were dead."

Works both ways, he decided, as he caught her tight and held her in a fierce embrace. If there was a heaven on earth, this was it, finding the one you cared for, safe.

"Shh . . . sweetheart, we're both okay."

Stroking her hair and holding her head nestled against his shoulder, he closed his eyes, feeling his body trembling. Like a smoldering fire, the heat of desire for her never seemed to be far away. It would never go away, he thought.

He took a steadying breath, turning off his thoughts. They weren't out of the woods yet.

"Almost," he grimaced. "Those guys have better aim than I would have given Orega's men credit for."

A strangled cry caught in her throat as she saw the blazing red staining his shirt. "You're hurt," she gasped.

No one had ever cried for him before, and no woman had ever made him want to cry with the sheer joy of just holding her, or knowing she existed somewhere on the planet like a beautiful, rare flower. But the moaning of one of the men negated any more thought and regret.

Deliberately, he blanked his mind to anything except escape, his tone becoming urgent. "No time to discuss war wounds, Amy. They only grazed me. We have to get out of here. Those goons aren't going to stay down forever. Can you make it to their truck?"

She nodded happily. At the moment, she could have scaled a mountain. The agony of believing that he might be dead drained out of her. She was dizzy with gratitude that he was alive.

She sucked in deep gulps of air. She let out her breath slowly, rubbing her wrists as she drew them upward. She wasn't going to risk losing Crawford today or in the future, now that he was safe.

"I could fly, Crawford."

"You sure?"

She smiled.

The last crisis seemed to have made her perceptions and determination crystal-clear.

Straining to look up at him, she raised shining eyes to his. "Whatever it takes, Crawford," she whispered.

Crawford washed off as much of the grime as he could in the stream near the cave he'd managed to find. He blew out a tired breath. He'd emptied the stolen—no, he corrected wryly, "requisitioned" truck—of its fuel and abandoned it to the mountains while Amy had hastily packed up their supplies in their own truck. Then, he and Amy had driven like maniacs to put as much distance between themselves and the wakening survivors.

He made a mental note to himself to tell Romero where he'd hidden the requisitioned truck.

He washed his grazed arm gingerly. He wasn't any too sure exactly how many survivors there were. He hadn't bothered to check.

But he wasn't going to lose any sleep over it, he concluded.

His brows drew together thoughtfully. Romero's advice to take an alternate route had been faulty. He had to conclude either that or that there was a spy in Cresca who had escaped notice so far. The latter was hard to believe. Spies had never survived for long in Cresca and their passage out of there wasn't usually pleasant. After what had happened to Garcia's wife and child, the townspeople were particularly sensitive to and savage with spies. Still, he had to alert Romero at least to the possibility.

He sat on the ground and reached for his cigarettes. It was amazing, he thought, shaking his head with weary disdain, that the goons hadn't thought to search for Crawford's truck. They could have saved themselves the long wait while Amy came to before heading back to their own camp. They could have also spared him having a near heart attack wondering whether he'd jeopardized Amy, while he sat on that rock, waiting for them to return.

Idiots, he thought scathingly.

He lit himself a cigarette, the isolation strangely irritating. Normally, when he was alone like this, after a confrontation, he reveled in it, savoring the fact that he had no one to answer to except himself—no bureaucracies, no corrupt governments, no corporations, no family. When push came to shove, he nearly always gravitated toward solitude. It's what he'd done the last decade. Kept to himself, turned off the world and its problems, played soldier, lived from one physical skirmish to the next and then moved on, no strings attached. Now, he didn't relish going back to that kind of existence again. Now, he was beginning to crave a normal life because Amy Blake shone like a beacon, as a reminder of what the best of that could be. Only problem was, he couldn't bring himself to trust that when this was all over, she'd have any feelings for him.

Why did she even want him in the first place?

The only answer he could think of was that this whole trip had the feel of a shipboard romance, and shipboard romances, he reminded himself grimly, were notorious for their intensity . . . and their brevity.

He drew in a long breath of dry smoke.

So once the cruise with Amy was over, then what?

He sure wasn't going to jump ship into her world. And he certainly wasn't about to ask her to join his.

He shifted restlessly. Coming close to losing Amy had heightened his awareness of exactly what his life was going to be like after she returned to Boston. Brutally, agonizingly lonely.

He'd become trapped by his own choices, by who and what he was.

The realization made him rigidly cold. It was just too late for him and Amy. He wanted to tell her that when she'd been kidnapped, his feelings for her had crystallized. Like a man on the gallows, truth had hit him. But then there was always reality to deal with. It was stupid to believe he had a real chance with her or that if he did, the relationship could last. Experience had taught him otherwise. He needed the peace and emotional security as well as the exhilaration she could offer him. But right now, she was probably only responding to the excitement of the moment.

And what could he offer her and her child anyway?

A soldier's life?

How long would the honeymoon last then?

As long as it had with his ex-wife when he'd been a CIA agent? That had been five years, ten months, three weeks and two days. How could he accept that from Amy? He would only be torturing himself if he tried because it would be harder to lose her then than now.

He sighed heavily. What options did he have, ultimately? None.

Above him, a cloudless night shone brilliantly white and eerie. Stubbing out his cigarette, he stretched and started to force his feet back toward the cave.

Amy glanced up the instant he walked back in. Earlier, she'd washed and changed. Her hair, still damp, glistened in the firelight and her gaze captured in its glow shone luminous, like heavy, wet, green grass after a rain. The dark bruises on her head and cheek made her look excruciatingly vulnerable. His throat went dry as he walked toward the beckoning fire. He wanted her so badly, every muscle ached.

"Feel better?" she asked quietly, fidgeting with the medicine bag he'd brought in with them.

"Nothing like a little mountain water to wash away the worries," he quipped.

She stood up, and silhouetted through the firelight, he caught the outline of her body beneath the loose slacks that she wore and the lightweight shapeless top that couldn't conceal the lush, petite curves beneath it. The top was a kind of buttercup yellow that caught the golden shadows in her green eyes.

He felt his heart lurch in his chest.

She smiled up at him, a bottle of ointment in her hands. "How about I bandage that bullet wound?"

If he got any closer to her, he'd be doomed to another night of agonizing frustration.

"I can do it," he replied in a tight voice.

His gaze merged with hers and she felt herself suddenly going warm at the burning intensity she read there.

She fell back on her heels, letting out her breath in slow, uneven gasps. He was wired about something, she thought.

"Don't be silly, Crawford. It'll be easier if I do it."

For a moment, he hovered above her, like an irate lion. Then, he slumped onto the ground beside her, holding out his arm, and growled, "All right, then, if you want to be Florence Nightingale, be my guest."

There was a long silence as she shifted toward him.

"I imagine this is going to hurt," she murmured, taking his arm in her hands and positioning it in front of her and trembling slightly as she shot him a quick look. He wore a strained expression on his face. Whatever tension he had brought in with him to the cave and for whatever reason he was carrying it, she felt it soaking into her and as if she were on the edge of a precipice.

The cave they were in was smaller than the last one they'd shared, more compact, the walls closer, exaggerating her proximity to him. She inhaled sharply, the feel of his skin beneath her sensitized fingers as rock-hard as he was and roughly sprinkled with mahogany-colored hair that caught the shimmering firelight.

She let out a deep breath, wanting to caress that hair... that skin....

She held her hand poised.

"Ready?"

He gritted his teeth as her gentle fingers warmed his skin and sent his imagination reeling.

"Just make it snappy, okay? I don't like a lot of fussing," he ground out.

Her sweet scent, indelibly imprinted on his memory bank, seeped through his senses. Her left breast was inches away from his arched upper arm. He could feel his body reacting immediately as she lowered her head to get a closer look at the bullet wound. He knew this was going to be true validation of the cure being worse than the disease. He closed his eyes, flinching as the ointment stung. He continued to hold his breath as her touch continued, despising what each soothing, hypnotic stroke was doing to him.

"Aren't you finished yet?" he asked impatiently.

"Almost." She glanced tremulously at him, touching her tongue to her lip in a nervous gesture.

She'd looked at him that way before, he thought, and he hadn't survived it then, either.

In that instant, he lost whatever battle he'd been waging with himself.

To hell with it, he thought savagely, his self-control finally exploding.

In a second he'd trapped her hand with his, tossed the ointment aside with the other, reached out and grabbed her.

"Enough of this," he rasped.

Amy gasped as the tube went flying out of her hand.

Then, as quickly as his arms went around her, his mouth came down on hers—hard, punishing, conveying all the frustration and yearning of the past few days. Within a mere second, his tongue had forced her startled lips open and demanded entry.

She went still, stunned. Then, liquid fire trickled through her bloodstream. A spontaneous moan murmured on her captured lips.

She'd only gotten a hint before of what he could do to her, but this invasion was pleasure incarnate. Her hands went limp, her mouth greeted him, inviting him in. Heat exploded inside her as his lips ground down on hers, pulled back, gentled, then plundered again.

She shivered as his fingers splayed across the bare skin of her neck, then snaked through her heavy hair, holding her tight against him.

She realized she loved him; she'd recognized that possibility almost from the beginning, but if she had known this kind of rapture, passion and sense of destiny had awaited her, finally, in his arms, she'd have locked him up somewhere and thrown away the key. Dull, old-fashioned Amy.

The new Amy responded to the demands of his tongue by making some demands of her own.

His breath caught as she welcomed his thrusts, urging him on. He couldn't believe it. He'd expected a warm response. Having kissed her before, he had more than a good idea of what he could expect. But this was beyond his wildest expectations. She was the sweetest, wildest, sexiest woman he'd ever kissed and beneath all of that was a promise that made him want to explode before he'd even begun.

There was no way to satisfy his need of her once and for all, and he'd been a fool to even think he could take this kind of taste of her and survive. If he followed through now, he was banking torment for himself in the future.

He drew back, breathing hard. "Amy, this is the point of no return."

Amy trembled. She'd been here before, she thought. She'd experienced his rejection and doubt, but this time she recognized that it wasn't *her* he was rejecting, but something else—his belief that he had nothing to offer her, when in reality he had everything to offer her.

She tried to calm her beating heart and held up a hand to his face and touched his cheek. She realized she wanted him without reason, without explanation, without promises. She wasn't going to let him off the hook this time.

"I'm not afraid of that, Crawford."

He wondered if she knew what she did to him, every time she moved, every time she touched him.

With a quick motion, his own hand reached up and gently moved hers away.

In an uneven voice, he replied, "Amy, I want you to be absolutely sure you know what you're doing."

Amy held her breath, experiencing a moment of panic. What *was* she doing? Was this right to do? Was it right to push him? Next to her breasts, she felt his heart pounding, and close to her thigh was evidence of his arousal. His body wanted her, she could feel his naked need, closing around her, blinding her. In her heart, she instinctively sensed that need slicing through his emotions, as well. But he was still holding back, denying himself and her out of some peculiar sense of nobility. She couldn't let him. She wouldn't. Not this time. Not ever again, if she had her way. Her insides trembled with recognition. What she felt for this man transcended the physical, but the physical wanting was so much sweeter for it.

"Don't you want to make love to me?" she whispered, stunned by her boldness. Even with her husband she'd never been this aggressive, but she'd never wanted David as much as she wanted Crawford. Was this, then, what love really was? This spiraling, out-of-control, rocketing need that tore at your insides and gave you courage to say these kinds of things?

Crawford tried to wrench himself away from her, his brows drawing together darkly. "Want...oh God, Amy, don't...don't do this to me. I've never wanted a woman more in my entire life."

She moved closer to him, lifting her face to his, her breath causing a murmuring breeze as it fanned against his skin. "I'm here, Crawford.... I'm not going anywhere."

He gave it another shot. "Amy...I'm no good for you. You've got your whole life ahead of you. I'm burned out, finished. I can only give you now. I can't give you a future. I can't promise anything, and I won't."

Amy's heart turned over. Why was he so hard on himself? To her, he was the consummate male—virile, strong, seasoned by life and its experiences, principled and caring, but hiding it all behind the facade of tough soldier. If only she'd seen that sooner.

Perhaps she had.

"I'm not asking you for an eternity, Crawford, I'm only asking you for one night...*this* night."

He moved woodenly, his arms dropping to his sides. "Amy, even if...we...did..." He appeared to be struggling with conscience and words as his voice trailed off, "...we're in the mountains.... There aren't exactly corner drugstores up here...."

"Oh..." She blushed with embarrassment as reality intruded. Suddenly, she felt like a neophyte, or a sheltered teenager. Except teenagers probably knew more than she did about these things. The first and last time she'd made love to a man, it had been with a man she was married to. "I—I've only ever been with my husband," she said in a hushed, self-conscious voice.

Crawford stood above her, taut and tense. "I've got fifteen years on you, easy...that's a lot of living, Amy."

Her eyes slowly locked with his. He wouldn't hurt her, she thought. He wouldn't put her at risk. If he'd wanted to, he could have already done that. Instinctively, she believed in his morality with all her heart. "Just tell me it's okay, and I'll believe you, Crawford."

He hovered, staring at her, torn between a million emotions. He could get off the hook, this very moment, he thought. He could retreat behind excuses, but her faith in him tore at him. He didn't have enough resistance left. She was everything he'd ever wanted in a woman, dark and sultry, cool and hot.

Everything about her had brought something inside him back to life.

"I would never endanger you, Amy."

Amy's breath caught in her throat and snagged in a dozen different places. This was it, she thought. Even if he didn't love her, she'd have this night to savor and remember.

"Then, there's nothing to stop us, is there, Crawford?"

Except conscience, he thought.

Hands, breath and heartbeat took the place of conscience as his mouth settled on hers again. Nibbling on her lower lip, he felt her sucking for air, parting her mouth as if to prove her welcome and surrender. Her involuntary action allowed him to search gently inside with his tongue.

So sweet, he groaned silently. Oh, God, so sweet.

He moved one of his hands to her throat, playing its tender curve with his thumb while catching the quickening of her pulse. At the same time, he deepened his kiss, exploring and tantalizing with his tongue.

Amy inhaled sharply, stunned. She hadn't known that a kiss could be so total or that her throat was so sensitive. She began to feel hot and trembly all over, as Crawford's fingers tormented and teased the delicate, suddenly taut skin. She felt as if her body were floating away from her, then drifting back toward her, heavier, and more sultry. He seemed barely to be touching her, and yet she wanted to arch backward and cry with the sheer pleasure of his rough, calloused hands caressing her.

He pulled his lips away from hers and looked into her eyes, his own gaze dark, filled with a hot-blue intensity and smoky hunger. Her breath caught at the naked need mirrored on his face.

"Do you have any idea what you do to me?" he moaned in husky voice, grabbing one of her hands and pushing it down so that it cupped his arousal. "What you've been doing to me the last few days... what you did to me the first time I saw you?"

Amy shivered, feeling out of control, as if she were on a roller coaster that wouldn't stop. The air around them seemed to have cocooned them in a hot, seductive haze.

She couldn't speak, she couldn't think as she felt the full power of his need beneath her fingers. He pressed himself closer, imprisoning her hand against the hard bulge between his legs. She bowed her head, clutching her free arm around his neck, seeking his mouth again.

With a hiss, he ground his lips against hers, hot and urgent, his breath musky and exciting as it mingled with hers and his hand slid down her neck toward the cleft between her breasts. Wild sensation flooded her as his hand traveled toward her breast, cupped its thrusting fullness in his palm and began to caress in slow, measured circles of tingling heat.

Then, his hand ceased its intoxicating pleasure and moving quickly, he picked her up in his arms and carried her, his mouth still locked with hers, toward the sleeping bag in the corner. He slid her down the length of him, with seductive slowness so she could feel every lean, hard inch of him and gently pulled his lips from hers.

She gasped, still clinging to him. "Oh . . . Sam."

He looked down at her with glittering, sexy eyes. He'd wanted to see this expression in her gaze. Did she know that it was driving him crazy? he wondered.

"I'm going to undress you, Amy. If you want me to stop you'd better tell me now, before it's too late."

It was already too late for her, she thought. She couldn't stop. She wanted this fierce man desperately with every fiber of her being.

"I-I can't stop." Her face flushed a vivid crimson.

A low sound echoed in the cave, and she realized it was his soft, strained laughter. She felt his fingers underneath her chin, tilting it tenderly toward him.

"Good, because I can't, either. I was just being noble."

Her heart caught in her throat, thrilled by his response.

His eyes glowed teasingly as he caught the hem of her shirt and paused, "Any bra?"

"No bra."

He smiled seductively and yanked the shirt over her head. Next, he pulled the slacks down her legs while she helped him, then his fingers, trembling slightly, edged under the elastic of her white bikini panties. She moaned, closing her eyes. In seconds, as she held her breath, he had eased them down to her ankles. Then, while she stepped out of them and tossed them to one side, he peeled off his own shirt, slacks and underwear.

Her pulse jackknifed as they faced each other. She felt the air breezing over her skin, and his warm, heavy gaze sweeping over her as she stood, naked, trembling, waiting for him, bathed in firelight and dancing shadows.

All traces of humor left his face as his eyes, slitting into dark slivers, soaked her in from her high, pert breasts to her creamy legs and up again to the mound between her thighs. "My God," he murmured with reverence and desire in his voice. "You're absolutely beautiful."

So was he, she thought, her breath snagging. There wasn't an ounce of fat anywhere on his sleek body. His chest was broad, a mat of mahogany-colored hair trailing down to his tight waist and ending in a narrowing ribbon above his arousal. That he was more than ready for her there was no doubt.

But before she could respond, she felt his hands snaking up her arms and found herself lying on the sleeping bag, his thighs pressing against hers, his chest flattening her breasts.

She gasped. She could hardly breathe, but she didn't care. She felt no discomfort, only a wild resurgence of need as the full weight of his body imprinted itself on hers. But it was a need that he seemed determined to stoke.

In moments, his hands were roaming her body. They seemed to be everywhere, their rough, male texture exciting her inch by inch. Before his fierceness had always been verbal. Now it was concentrated in his hands and body, but added to it was consummate skill and tenderness. He seemed to know when to be strong, when to be gentle, when to tarry and when to move on. She whimpered, reaching out with her own hands, digging into his back with her short nails, delirious with the sensations he was eliciting from her. His mouth came down on one of her breasts, and positioning his teeth around one nipple, he tugged gently until it was swollen in his mouth before he settled down to sucking its ripeness between his lips.

She could barely think. She suddenly felt as if she were being drugged. With age-old primitive instinct, she inched upward, her hips automatically rising. In response, his hands moved under her, cupping her buttocks, bringing her closer to that part of him that was engorged and bulging against her.

Yes, she thought mindlessly, as the tip of his need nudged a secret place. But this wasn't mindless, she realized. This was acknowledgement of how much his strength and passion had come to mean to her. She knew who he was. She wanted him.

Crawford was totally, completely and irrevocably lost in her. Her response to him was something he could only have guessed at. In her wild, innocent sexuality, there was freedom, a simplicity that tore at his insides. He so ached with the need to possess her, he was literally shaking with the emotions that were driving him and through him, fueling his physical passion. He wanted to wait, to prolong the pleasure for both of them, but it seemed as if he'd waited his whole life to experience this. Years without softness slammed against his consciousness. Rational thought seemed a million miles away.

All he could do was feel.

The desire to put himself inside her and drive himself home bordered on insane hunger. Taking deep breaths, he slowed himself down, willing his body to obey despite its aching need. Taking his hand, he palmed it against her mound. Then, hearing her intake of breath, he straightened his fingers and gently inserted them inside her to see if she was ready for him.

"Sam . . . !"

She moaned his name, the sound of it on her lips, searing him, her eyes widening in shock as her muscles contracted around his fingers and she arched even higher.

"Do you like that, sweetheart?" he asked in a raw voice.

"It's—it's wonderful," she whispered, feeling his fingers stretch slowly inside her. Then she gasped as his thumb found an even more tender spot.

"I want this to be wonderful for you, Amy."

She closed her eyes, tossing back her head. Never had she felt such a deep, burning ache. His hands, his body, his scent seemed to be all-encompassing, consuming her, blocking everything else out of her mind.

Crawford's heart was pounding. He felt her shuddering and writhing beneath him, knowing she was as ready and as desperate as he was. For a brief moment, unsure as to where he got the self-discipline from, he hesitated.

"Amy . . . I could get you pregnant."

Her response came out in halting words. "I—I can't get pregnant, Sam."

Her response puzzled him, but he was too far-gone to pursue conversation, so he blanked out what she'd said. Withdrawing his moist fingers, he gently moved her thighs apart and slipped inside her as far as he could go.

Amy moaned, locking her legs around him, pressing her hands against his lower back, drawing him in so he could fill her more. Cupping her buttocks in his hands, he lifted her, allowing full, total penetration. Holding her that way, he began to thrust, slowly, torturously, exquisitely. Unbearable pleasure began to build inside her like a rising volcano. Through her own body she could feel the power and the yearning in his.

Then the volcano began to erupt inside her, wild, out of control, hot and intense. She stifled a cry as he caught her rhythm, matched it and thrust into her time and again, until she wanted to weep with the incredible sensations spiraling inside her. She could feel his muscles straining, his heart beating next to hers as the final explosion began not just for her, but for him. She heard his muffled gasp as total ecstasy shuddered through both of them together, each of their climaxes fueling the other.

Then total release came, stunning them both with its rightness and intensity.

Chapter 14

Crawford stared into the flickering shadows caused by the dying fire, his heart and mind burning with regret. What he'd done with Amy was unforgivable. A mistake of the highest order.

Cradling her next to him, he wanted to cry with frustration as the warmth of her curved, supple, enticing body pressed trustingly against his, reminding him of the savage sweetness they'd shared—a sweetness which he had no business taking advantage of.

He'd ruthlessly satisfied the crawling, aching need that had been driving him for days. Even now, as his hand stroked the satin, lush cascade of midnight hair that fell across his chest, his body throbbed with desire again. And it shouldn't. Making love with her was supposed to have ended his need.

He swallowed a groan. Why, in God's name, hadn't it?

He wanted her more desperately this moment than he had before, but it wasn't hard to figure why. She was a special woman with her quickness, her sensuality, her loving willingness and guts to traipse around the mountains to be mother to a little girl. He was as drawn to her emotionally and intellectually as he was physically. She was the perfect fantasy for a man's dreams.

But the reality had certainly surpassed *his* fantasies. He exhaled slowly, brushed back a strand of hair from her forehead and gently kissed her bare, moist skin. How was he going to let her go now?

He had to.

Suddenly, she stirred, and her eyes opened, dark, dusky and drowsily happy. "Sam . . . ?"

He shrugged tightly, still continuing to hold her when everything logical in his head said he shouldn't. "Who else?"

Amy smiled. As she'd drifted between sleep and consciousness, she'd reveled in the feel of his solid body holding hers. It made her feel safe, secure, cherished.

She snuggled closer to him. "I don't think I ever want to move again."

When he didn't respond, she looked up at him. His face was unsmiling and his jawline tense. Alarms went off in her head. "What's the matter?"

He reached to the ground for his pack of cigarettes.

"I'm not very good at this, Amy. I haven't had a lot of practice."

She watched him shift slightly so that he was partially turned away from her. She held herself rigid. She wasn't going to whine, she promised herself.

"Not good at what?"

He put one naked leg back on the sleeping bag and frowned, grinding his teeth together.

"This—you know—afterward. Talking, explaining."

Moments ago, she'd felt wonderful. Now she felt as if someone had thrown a bucket of ice water on her, but she kept her voice calm. "What makes you think you have to explain anything?"

"I feel I should. I feel I should explain that our—our making love doesn't change anything."

She knew she'd been harboring a deep belief that if they crossed the physical barrier, he'd see that they could have a chance together. Had her belief then been ridiculously romantic? Men could separate love and sex, women couldn't. Had she fallen into the oldest trap of all? Was she going to lose him, after all?

Despite her breaking heart, she forced words past her dry lips. "Didn't last night mean anything to you?"

Crawford raised his eyebrows in silent shock, stunned that she could even entertain such an idea. The night and its joys and pleasures had been incredibly, magnificently special. It would be brilliantly etched in his memory with all its nuances and passion for his entire future. But so too would be the pain at now knowing what he'd be missing and the knowledge that he'd hurt her.

He'd have been further ahead not to have opened the door on those memories by creating them in the first place, he thought bitterly.

But he couldn't lie to make up for that. Standing up, he pulled on his shorts and slacks.

"Of course it did, Amy. I . . ." He struggled to give her honesty, without building up her hopes. He was furious with himself. How could he have allowed unbridled passion to destroy his objectivity?

Impatiently lighting a cigarette, he inhaled a raw ribbon of smoke. "God help me, Amy, I've never experienced that kind of fulfillment with a woman before, but I still think it was a mistake."

A fragile, vulnerable look came into her eyes, slicing into him, more than even her anger would have. She looked so breathtakingly lovely, outlined in a seemingly mysterious light, filled with glows and shadows, that he quickened with need.

"Sam, I'm not asking for a commitment."

"You deserve one, Amy, but I'm not the marrying kind, you know that. I did it once, and I failed at it miserably. My wife's complaints were legitimate. I was independent when it suited me, and when I came home, I came home only long enough to get renewed for the next job. I'm not about to fall in love again and to disappoint another woman, and I'm certainly not about to be tied down. I haven't changed, Amy."

Amy flinched, her eyes filling with tears as she reached over to pull her dress in front of her. "Who said anything about love?"

He laughed without humor. "Amy, you're the kind of woman a man falls in love with and marries. It's written all over you. Family, security, home."

"I'm not Alice in Wonderland, Sam, with a set of instructions you just follow. I'm an individual."

"So am I, Amy, except that *I'm* a loner."

She pulled the dress over her head and eased it down her hips before getting up. Facing him, her eyes clouded.

"Sam, you weren't alone when we were making love last night. You were warm, giving, tender, but we were together. I think you want to love and be loved as much as anyone."

She was getting too close to the truth, he thought.

"All men are different in bed, Amy. We're a political lot when it comes to sex—it's a long tradition."

A tiny gasp slipped past her lips. "I can't believe you were the way you were last night just because sex was suddenly available."

He wet his lips and blew out a long sigh. "No, you're right. It was far more than that, but, Amy, what I gave you last night is as much as I've got to give. There isn't anything else."

Loss slipped into her voice. "So, that's it then, is that what you're telling me? A one-night stand just like you predicted...."

"Don't, Amy, don't reduce it."

"I'm not the one reducing it—you are."

The tremor in her voice almost undid him. He interrupted with a quick verbal volley before he could relent.

"Amy, you and I can't have a future together. It's that simple," he said flatly.

She remained motionless. She could have almost accepted the logic of that, she thought, if he hadn't been so wonderfully considerate and caring making love. The totality of Crawford's giving, his passion and the affection he'd demonstrated had sucked the breath from her. She was convinced that his lovemaking was his way of communicating his feelings for her. After all, he was a physical man. If she could be sure she was right, then maybe she could convince him that he was wrong about their not being able to share a future. But he had to believe in them, too. She couldn't create a life for them alone.

Her mind was in a turmoil, her heart aching terribly. She'd never love another man the way she loved him.

"I think you should let me have some say in that."

His eyes turned remote, his mouth firm. "No, Amy, it's my decision first, not yours." He shook his head. "I never did promise anything—remember?"

She was a fool, she supposed, to have put so much faith in one night. She dug her fingers into her palms, determined not to cry, but she couldn't imagine a lifetime without Crawford's unrelenting severity; that oh-so-familiar well-angled and rough-planed face; the quick mercurial eyes; the energy, courage and hardheaded convictions that made her feel so alive. She wasn't going to give up.

That had to be the way to win him over, she thought. Give him room, she told herself.

She forced herself to meet his gaze head-on. "You're right. You were straight with me, but you're not going to make me regret what happened. What we shared was wonderful. I'll never forget it."

Crawford held himself perfectly still. In a desperate way, he wished she'd push harder, find a way for them when he couldn't identify it—but that was hardly fair. His jaw tightened with anguish and gut-twisting regret. Was there something else, though, that he could do with his life? Another job that wouldn't put him in a straitjacket? Maybe if he called one of his buddies at the CIA...

He sighed, feeling something tearing insidiously at his insides. He identified cold reality and memory as they slammed against his consciousness.

He shrugged with bitter humor. "What would you want with a beat-up soldier, anyway?"

Everything, she thought, her heart breaking a little.

"I don't know, Crawford," she replied, attempting a smile. "Maybe I just think you're salvageable."

He wasn't, he thought. "Amy," he said huskily. "I'll never forget what we shared, either. I just wish...oh hell, I don't know what I wish."

Her smile turned wry. Don't push, she reminded herself. He'll come around. He has to. "Maybe it'll come back to you over breakfast. We *are* going to have breakfast, aren't we?"

Amy was just finishing her coffee when Crawford cleared his throat and said, "Uh...by the way...last night when you said you couldn't get pregnant...was that the truth or were you just...being..."

Amy felt her heart suddenly hammering in the back of her throat as her fingers tightened on the metal mug. "Accommodating?" she interrupted in a dry tone.

He tensed, immediately on the alert. The expression in her eyes had changed dramatically. The question had been hovering on his lips since early morning, but this had been the first opportunity he'd had to pursue it that felt right. Now he had a feeling he should have left the question unasked.

"Sorry—did I say something wrong?"

"I—no, Crawford, I wasn't being accommodating...."

He watched her, his jaw tight. "Look, I guess gentlemen shouldn't bring these kinds of things up, and if you take the Pill or something, it's really none of my business—"

She felt a rush of weakening warmth flush to her face. Sooner or later, she thought sadly, it always comes up.

"You might as well know the truth, Crawford," she said in flat tones. "You've asked often enough."

He frowned with confusion at her strained voice. "Asked what? Look, Amy, I don't need to know anything. I just didn't want you to think that I was putting all the responsibility onto you, that's all."

Pulse racing, she shook her head. What if Crawford reacted to the truth the way her last date had? What then would be the point of hoping for a future together if he didn't know the truth?

She unfisted her hands even though they were shaking. "No, I want to explain."

Male instinct made him protest. "Amy—"

She looked up at him, pain glistening in her luminous gaze. Why had this dominated her life so much? she wondered.

Her chest rose in a quick movement. "I don't take the Pill, but I still can't get pregnant."

"But you were pregnant...I mean you said..."

She twisted her mouth, sad lines fanning around its edges. "I know, yes, I was pregnant, once, but I discovered that my husband didn't want children, or at least he didn't want them at the time I got pregnant. He wanted me to get an abortion." She stopped momentarily, her eyes distant as she recalled the calculating expression in David's eyes.

He regarded her, stunned. "Why in God's name would he want that?"

She tilted her head. "It wasn't convenient for him. His career was just taking off. He'd been born poor, so success and material things were very important to him. He'd struggled to get a law degree, he owed money for that, and he wanted to enjoy the benefits of the good life before we had children.''

Fury and sarcasm merged. He tried to quell both and failed. ''I didn't know kids cost that much.''

She didn't smile, but she did offer him a grateful look before she glanced down at her hands clasped on her lap. ''No, I didn't think so, either, but he persisted. Pushing for an abortion drove a wedge between us. It was as if my little girl and I were on one side, and he were on the other.''

She inhaled a sharp breath. That had hurt the most, she remembered. The rejection she felt for her innocent child, as yet unborn, had been devastating.

Crawford took advantage of her pause to fantasize graphically and wonderfully about throttling her ex-husband.

''Go on,'' he said quietly.

She drew in a deep, controlled breath, but he recognized the pain and loss in her eyes as she spoke.

''Then I had the accident. David was, of course, terribly upset, but I began to realize that he was also relieved. What he couldn't seem to understand was that we had lost our daughter, our child, a proof of our love, but—'' she forced a hoarse laugh ''—inadvertently, he got off the hook forever because I had also lost the ability to have children. The accident had caused internal damage.''

''You're—?'' he paused delicately.

She lifted her gaze and finished for him tonelessly, ''Sterile's the word, Crawford. I'm sterile.''

She'd wanted children, and some guy with his neurotic priorities whacked out of shape had cut her off from the support and love she'd needed. Pain clenched inside him for her.

''That must have been hell for you,'' he murmured quietly.

She unlocked her hands, her throat feeling dry as she continued. ''The worst of it was that we were two people living in the same house, one ecstatic that his life hadn't been disrupted, and the other, mourning, wondering if the grief would ever go away. I'll never forgive him for not sharing that grief with me. She wasn't just my child. She was *our* child.

He could see her, he thought, standing in an elegant home, mourning her child, desperate for her husband's love and understanding.

For a moment, he didn't trust himself to speak as anger surfaced inside him at the faceless man who had shut her out. No one deserved to be a mother more than she did. Killing was too humane for the man.

"So, you left him," he prompted in a soft voice.

Pride and controlled anger was visible on her face then. "I didn't feel like I had any choice. How could I live with a man who couldn't share my grief? It was two years before I wanted to date again, but finally when I did, the man I became involved with dropped me because I couldn't have children. Ironic, isn't it?"

"He said that?" he asked in a voice filled with disbelief and outrage. He'd been too long out of civilization if that was accepted conversation.

She gave a choked, humorless laugh. "In so many words, if you read between the lines. I was damned if I did and damned if I didn't." The hurt of the memory was fading now, she discovered. She turned her head slightly toward him. "That's why I'm here. I can't have any biological children, but I still want to hold a child in my arms and watch her grow up. I didn't see any reason why I couldn't have that—with or without a husband."

Crawford held his breath, rage splintering through him at the husband who had let her down and at the others who'd demanded more of her than was physically possible, as if she were nothing more than a broodmare. For the first time in his life, he felt ashamed of being a man. And how much better was he? Every chance he got, hadn't he challenged her about having her own child, when all along she couldn't have one through no fault of her own?

If he'd ever wondered before if it were possible for him to feel like a bigger jerk than he already did, his question had just been answered.

He held out a hand in guilty resignation. He wanted to offer her more physical comfort but knew he couldn't afford to. He couldn't touch her without getting into trouble, he thought.

He said the only thing he could. But it came from the heart. "Amy, I'm sorry."

She closed her eyes, then opened them and offered him a faint smile. "Thanks, Crawford." She paused, then shifted in the seat toward him, asking softly, "Would it matter to you?"

"What?" he said distractedly. "That a woman I was interested in couldn't have kids?"

She nodded, holding her breath.

He frowned, slightly insulted. "I don't suffer from those kind of macho illusions, Amy. I've seen too many kids abandoned by people who only had them out of a sense of ego. Adopting's just as good. A kid's a kid."

She let out the breath she'd been holding. She had her answer, she thought. Somehow she'd known it in her heart all along. "They're quite a responsibility, Crawford."

"So is life." Crawford shook his head in disgust. "God, men can be first-class jerks."

But *he* wasn't a jerk, she thought. As surprised as he might be, she knew far more about men than she imagined he gave her credit for. She'd been watching her father's friends since she was a little girl. Expressions of feelings might come out all wrong with Sam or they might not cross his lips at all—but she would never have doubted for a minute that they were basic and honest when he finally articulated them. She loved him as much for that as what he'd just said.

Oh, Sam, give me a chance.

"Some men aren't," she said quietly, closing her eyes, then opening them again.

Crawford downed the last of his coffee with an angry grunt. "I still feel like I ought to apologize for the species."

She shook her head, a faint smile coming to her lips. My fierce, beloved Crawford, she thought. Thank you for that. "That's a nice gesture, Crawford, but it's all in the past. All I want to do now is think about the future."

Amy tilted her head backward and raised her eyes. The afternoon mountain sky was a brilliant blue, a heavenly mantle of color, serene and crystal-clear.

Holding her breath, she basked in the warmth of the golden-white sun and waited for Crawford to return.

He'd been gone about fifteen minutes, checking on the condition of the truck and refueling. The rifle felt heavy against her arm. This time, she'd done exactly as he'd told her and kept it slung across her shoulder.

Her mind drifted. Maybe Crawford couldn't love her until she showed him a way they could live together. She knew that had to be the major factor separating them. He needed his freedom and his independence. She recognized that. But she was prepared to give him both. She'd even share a tent with him, if she had to... and if, of course, he'd let her.

"All ready?"

Startled, lost in thought, she glanced up. Crawford positioned himself in front of her. Even in his remoteness there was a blatant sexuality about him that he couldn't conceal.

"Okay." She returned his smile.

"Got everything?"

She nodded. Her knapsack was already on her other shoulder and she'd packed away their utensils, clearing away the remnants of their breakfast shortly after he'd left, leaving no traces, the way he'd shown her.

As they walked to the truck, she asked, "How far away are we from the Manion Range?"

"Another day."

Less than twenty-four hours. In twenty-four hours she'd be with Carmela. Her heart thumped every time she thought of how close she was to her child.

This time tomorrow, I'll be holding her in my arms.

But this time tomorrow, she'd be that much closer to losing Crawford. And five days after that, she and her child would be back in Santa Clara. Would she even see him again after that? Would he just say goodbye to her then?

She caught her lower lip between her teeth. She wouldn't let him. By then she'd have thought of something.

Twenty-four hours could go by so quickly, Crawford thought. He sat in the truck, concentrating moodily on the road, looking for the landmarks that would tell him they were near the Manion Range, and trying not to think of the woman beside him.

It still stunned him that she wanted him with such sweet, determined passion. Perhaps she even loved him. Women like Amy Blake didn't tend to want a man they didn't love, at least a little bit. He wished with all his heart he could love her back with the kind of commitment she deserved, but what was the point of even trying if he could offer her nothing?

He swallowed back a dry breath, wondering if sainthood were ever conferred on agnostics. He'd endured and survived their previous night together without making a move on her, but it hadn't been easy. Of course, he'd had to park himself and his assets at least fifty feet away from her to achieve the impossible. In retrospect, how he'd gotten through the night knowing it was likely their last together alone before she had Carmela to take care of was anyone's guess, he decided.

He inhaled a ragged breath. Sainthood was damned hard. He winced at the irony of the thought. He was quite sure he was the only one in the world who could see any bleak humor in it. And even he didn't appreciate it that much. Underneath his attempts to make light of what he was going through, he knew that a raw ache was digging itself into his gut and lodging there, building in intensity. This time, even his crusty approach to life's disappointments couldn't vanquish the thought that soon, too soon, the lovely, irresistible, feisty Amy Blake would no longer be in his life.

He heard her shuffle anxiously beside him. She knew they were drawing near the village to which the Alvarezes had taken Carmela. He could only guess at the emotions running through her. Respect laced through him for the umpteenth time. She'd risked a lot for this moment. "Are we almost there?" she asked quietly.

For a moment, he took his eyes off the road and regarded her through his sunglasses.

This time tomorrow, she'd be a mother, and he'd have no choice but to keep his distance from her.

He tried to shake the depressing thought off. "Just about."

He felt her tense a fraction, but she merely nodded and returned her gaze to the road. With an effort, he resisted stopping the truck and kissing her one last time before they reached the village.

But then it was too late as he saw the crest he'd been waiting for and dreading.

He shifted, closed his eyes briefly, then said evenly, "Well, Ms. Blake, one of your dreams is about to come true. This is it—the Manion Range."

Looking up immediately, Amy took a deep breath, a quick surge of anticipation shooting through her like an electrical shock. She opened her mouth to answer, but found she couldn't. It had turned as dry as sand.

She was finally here.

Her pulse started to race and her body tremble as Crawford turned the truck into the primitive town. She glanced around. Like Cresca, Manion consisted of quadrants of buildings. Some were homes, she imagined, and others likely devoted to local government and whatever commerce the Maritans in the town were involved in. Above, ribbons of sunlight slashed across the face of the mountains and bathed the town in clouds of pale gold.

Sentries had already stopped them to ascertain who they were, so the town's dirt streets weren't empty. Children, adults and animals were in evidence everywhere.

Her stomach somersaulted as she heard a baby's cry.

Was it Carmela?

My darling girl. At last. Oh, how I'm going to love you.

"How are you doing?"

Crawford's voice cut through her, jolting her out of her reverie. Tearing her gaze away from the town, she turned and offered him a wan smile. "I think I'm shaking like a leaf."

Crawford maneuvered the vehicle through a gathering throng. "What's to worry about?"

A million things, she suddenly thought, as she saw the bodies milling around the truck and regarding her curiously. Maybe she hadn't prepared enough for this. Maybe she was going to be a lousy mother. She hadn't given much thought to the realities of motherhood. What did she really know about being a mother? Her head whipped back to Crawford, alarm showing in her eyes.

"Why did I think I could do this? What if the Alvarezes don't like me?"

"I'll shoot them," he replied dryly.

Her eyes widened, his attempt at humor going over her head. "What if they think I'm too old? What if they think I'm too young. What if—"

"Hold it." Frowning, he stretched out his right hand and tried to lace his fingers into hers. They were knotted into tense curls. Methodically, he forced them open. He'd never seen her this unsure of herself. But there were probably a dozen faces to Amy Blake he'd never seen or would get to see. It was going to hurt like the dickens to give her up.

He shoved the thought to the back of his head with effort.
"They're going to love you, just wait and see."

Her green eyes, as bright as emeralds, flashed in protest.
"Yes, but—"

"Amy, trust me." His fingers squeezed hers. She clung to
them as if they were a lifeline, but her insides stopped being so
taut and instead turned to jelly.

"Oh, God, Crawford, suddenly I'm so scared."

"I would be too, angel," he offered soothingly. "Relax,
okay? Everything's going to be fine. As soon as you have her
in your arms, all your doubts will disappear."

"You don't know the first thing about it, Crawford. You're
fabricating, just to shut me up," she challenged, all nerves
again.

"That's right," he conceded. "But if I didn't say anything,
I get the feeling you'd chew my head off for that, too. It's a no-
win situation, angel."

This was insane, she thought. She squeezed his fingers. "I'm
being ridiculous, aren't I?"

"On a scale of one to ten, I'd say you were off the board."

"You won't leave me, will you, Crawford?"

He shook his head, releasing her hand. "I'll be with you the
whole time. We'll be like Mutt and Jeff. Come on, let's get out
of this thing, before my butt falls asleep again."

Deftly, he parked the truck on a slight incline and set the
brake, his blue eyes scanning the town. He had a feeling he'd
met the Alvarezes once, he thought, and would probably rec-
ognize them if he saw them. His suspicion was confirmed as he
spied a couple moving through the crowd heading in the direction of the truck from one of the cottages.

"There are Carmela's guardians now, and if I remember
correctly, Alvarez speaks English." He pointed the couple out
to Amy with an inclination of his head, then pausing, he looked
down at her, his blue gaze merging with hers. "Not much
longer, Ms. Blake, and you're going to be a mother. You
okay?"

Amy took three deep breaths to relax her insides as she
glanced away and peered through the windshield at the approaching pair. She was suddenly terrified. "I guess so," she
answered.

Crawford's boots kicked up dust as he got out of the truck. Immediately, he was surrounded by chattering Maritans. Looking altogether like a rescuing soldier in his khakis, he calmly and quietly moved the people back and headed toward the passenger side of the truck.

"Next to the revolution, we're the most exciting thing that's happened to Manion in years," he told her as he helped her down, trying to relax her. "The Range discourages even Maritans from making the trek up here."

"But we made it all right." Amy stayed close by his side as the Alvarezes drew near. They looked serious until they caught sight of her, then their faces flashed with relief and broke into broad smiles. Behind the couple, she noticed a group of children. Eight, she remembered them saying they had in their letters.

"The weather was on our side. Much of the time weather makes the Range impassable."

The man spoke as the couple stopped in front of them.

"Señor Crawford...Señorita Blake...welcome to Manion."

Smiling, Crawford took the man's proffered hand, then introduced the couple to Amy.

"Señor and Señora Alvarez. Señorita Amy Blake."

Always, Amy thought, the Maritans had such wonderfully expressive dark eyes. The Alvarezes were in their late thirties, handsome and erect like most of the Maritans she had met. *"Buenos dias,"* she managed to say with a faint smile. She was too nervous to attempt more.

They each pumped her hand in turn, grinning happily, unconcerned by how quiet she was.

Sensing her growing tension, Crawford casually looped her fingers into his without looking at her. He tilted his head quizzically, regarding the other man. "I thought I remembered you, Andres. How are you and your wife?"

The other man beamed. "Excellent, Crawford, especially now that we see Señorita Blake." Quickly his smile faded. "We weren't sure that she would get our message. We have been very worried about her, and one of our scouts told us some of Orega's men are prowling again. So terrible...." The strapping man shook his head in scorn. "They are savage barbarians...they do not deserve to live."

This wasn't the moment to bring up the fact that Amy had been kidnapped by the men, but the mercenary in him couldn't resist some kind of response. His eyes cold and hard, he raised his eyebrows. "They'll be destroyed in time, don't worry, Andres."

"We pray for such a miracle," the other man replied soberly. Then his face softened as he turned toward Amy and waved his hands out expansively. "Well, the moment we've all been waiting for is upon us—enough talk of the revolution! I'm sure Señorita Blake is anxious to see the child she has come for."

"I'm sure she is, too," Crawford said quietly, as he turned toward her, holding her hand firmly.

Glancing down at her, he felt bittersweet longing lodge in the pit of his stomach. She looked like a startled deer, not much more than a child herself, but he knew nobody was going to be a better mother than she was. "How about it, angel?" he murmured huskily. "You ready for motherhood?"

She'd never be ready, she thought, her heart jackknifing. But ready or not, she couldn't have walked away now.

A child. Her child was waiting for her. Her beloved Carmela.

She exhaled a long, slow breath. For a very brief moment, her heart felt torn in two. One half of it was bursting to finally hold her child in her arms. The other half was aching because this was almost the end of her trip. Maybe, too, it was the end of her relationship with Sam.

Oh, God, I love them both. I want them both.

She straightened her shoulders. Deal with one crisis at a time, she told herself. Nodding, she said in a soft voice, "Yes, I would like to see my little girl, please."

"Follow us," Señor Alvarez directed, leading them through the onlookers toward one of the nearby cottages.

Once they'd reached the threshold, Crawford stopped and delicately extricated his hand from Amy's tightfisted fingers.

The expression on his face was serious and gentle.

"I knew I said I'd be with you, but I think you should be on your own from here on in."

Her eyes widened luminously on his. "Sam—" she protested.

He shook his head firmly, his eyes a silvery hooded blue. "Amy, this is your moment, not mine."

Her lashes fanned upward. How could she have ever thought he had no sensitivity? She focused on him with clear eyes. She'd never have made it here without him. This was going to be one of the most important moments in her life. She'd lost one child with no man by her side. This time, she wanted the man she loved to be with her as she found another.

Her lips clenched stubbornly. She wanted Crawford. If her dreams turned out the way she wanted them to, he was going to be as much a part of her future as Carmela.

Please, dear God, help me make it all happen, she prayed. "No, Sam, I can't go in alone. I want you to share this with me."

Crawford frowned with confusion. Why would she want him with her? He could only imagine what lay beyond the door and how much finding her child meant to Amy. It felt sacrilegious to share the meeting with her, and yet, he knew he wanted to be there, to see her face, to feel her joy, if only to know that she had found what she was looking for.

She deserved this moment on any terms she wanted it.

Let her have it, he thought, as a lump caught in his throat.

He feigned a shrug. "You're the boss, angel."

Amy forced herself to remain calm as they entered the cottage. Crawford, because of his size, had to duck. She held fast to his hand and strength, and blinked, adjusting to the darkness. The Alvarezes discreetly stepped aside while she got her bearings.

Surprisingly, it was cool inside the cottage, and smelled like wildflowers. She breathed in deeply, pleased that her child had been surrounded by the scent of flowers.

There wasn't much furniture—a table, a few beds, a hearth centrally located, but in the corner was a cradle, set away from the windows to avoid the sun. Her heart turned over quickly once, and then certainty overcame her.

Her baby. Her child.

Clinging to Crawford, Amy moved forward toward the primitive cradle. When she looked down and bent over, her heart skyrocketed. Nestled in a cocoon of handmade sheets and blankets was the most beautiful child she'd ever seen. Or was it just Amy's love that made the baby appear beautiful? She didn't care, she thought. The child's face was partially turned to the side, but her profile was sweet and delicate.

"Oh, Crawford, isn't she perfect?"

Without waiting for an answer, she dropped Crawford's hand and bent down. This was her child, her baby. In that instant, she felt as if they had been destined for each other. Without thinking, without hesitating, she touched Carmela's forehead and in a startling instance, the baby's eyes opened, and she turned her head on the pillow, directing her dark, serene gaze on Amy.

At the look of innocence and trust on her new daughter's face, Amy's pulse slammed against her veins. Brown eyes merged with her green gaze. An eternity of emotion seemed to pass between them. So this is what it felt like to be a mother. This blossoming and overflow of love.

Awed, Amy bowed her head, and pressed a trembling kiss to Carmela's forehead. Her eyes filling with happiness, she murmured, "Sweetheart, if you only knew how long I've waited for you, but that's all over, now. We're going to be together from now on." And Crawford, too, she vowed, once we convince him.

Mrs. Alvarez suddenly materialized beside her, speaking excitedly in Spanish.

Uncomprehending, Amy blinked. Bewildered, she looked behind her to Sam for assistance and he translated gently.

"She's telling you to pick her up, Amy."

Amy glanced back at Mrs. Alvarez who, with a smile on her face and a lot of nodding and waving, directed Amy. Amy closed her eyes, thinking of the child she had lost. That was yesterday, she thought, and there would always be a place in her heart for the child she'd never held. But Carmela was now, and alive.

Biting her lip, she turned from both Crawford and Mrs. Alvarez and touched her little girl. In that moment, Carmela raised her hand, and fisted it around Amy's.

Amy's heart jumped into her throat. The child's eyes suddenly flashed open with pleasure, and Amy's arms clasped around her.

Oh, my baby, my own. I've waited so long.

Over the head of her child, she searched out Crawford. Glowingly and confidently, her gaze locked with his, gratitude and love glistening in her eyes.

His breath caught at the beautiful ageless image of mother and child she presented. He'd always remember the moment she became a mother, he thought.

She deserved to be a wife, too. But not his. She could do better than him. Even what they'd shared so far was over now.

He felt all the black humor, all the arguments, all the resistance in him sneaking back and slashing through him, mocking him for ever having attempted to think he was going to get away from Amy Blake in one emotional piece.

She smiled at him, and then the Alvarezes crowded around her, communicating with her in the universal language of hands and gestures—and the spell was broken.

He heard Amy's quick, sweet laughter as she picked up Carmela, and his pulse raced. So many things he was going to miss.

He growled under his breath as his eyes filled with tears. If he didn't get some air, he was going to turn to mush.

Turning abruptly, he slipped quietly out of the cottage before anyone could notice.

Chapter 15

Amy took a deep breath as she walked up the stairs of the Palacio for the second time that day. It was hard to believe she had been back in the capital city for an entire day. It was even harder to believe that during all that time, even though she and Crawford lived in the same house, she hadn't seen him, even once.

Her heart ached terribly at the thought. They'd spent close to ten days together and now it was as if he had never existed, as if they had never shared one night of wondrous lovemaking.

She'd never felt so lost and alone in her whole life.

The loneliness had begun to weave its way into her consciousness as they'd left the village, and it became full-blown by the time they'd arrived back at the Mendozas.

They'd stayed overnight in Manion before starting the trek back to Santa Clara. Crawford had said it was best to leave the Alvarezes quickly, and seeing the mist filming the couple's eyes, she'd agreed. She, like Crawford, hadn't the heart to prolong the pain of their sacrifice. She'd faithfully promised to write and keep them informed of Carmela's progress. She'd also discreetly told them that the money she'd given to Giselda would be theirs within a week. When she'd left the Manion

Range, the images of the smiling but teary-eyed Alvarezes and the rest of the village were firmly etched in her brain. But in all the time from then to returning to Santa Clara, Crawford had been distant, except when Carmela had needed attention—and then he'd been ever-present, as awed by Carmela as Amy was. The presence of her child had focused attention away from their relationship. She'd felt torn but unable to do anything except to concentrate on her baby. She hadn't wanted to block him out, and she'd tried not to, but somehow they'd become guide and client again.

Her breath caught as her eyes opened and she looked down at her new child. Carmela was communicating by gurgling with pleasure at all the new things her bright, clear dark eyes captured in their gaze. If nothing else, though, Carmela *was* perfect. Delightful, curious, sweet. And Amy was learning how to be a mother and to understand what it entailed without being scared all the time that she was doing something wrong. She was slowly learning the nuances. The little sounds to listen for and what they meant. The telltale expressions in the alert eyes. How to hold her baby so they were both comfortable. Her heart swelled with love every time she looked at her child. She hadn't thought it possible to feel such pure, unadulterated love for another human being.

But had she gained one person to love, only to lose another?

She wanted to go to Crawford and ask him to share all the love she was feeling, but she knew that he was leaving shortly on another assignment. Somehow, there seemed even more love in her heart for Crawford now that she had Carmela, but how could she explain that to him if he wasn't around to listen to her?

General Garcia frowned at the noise. Passing by his office door, he opened it, and he blinked to focus on a sight framed by the afternoon sunlight drifting in from his office windows.

A smile, almost of relief, lit up his face and eyes.

"Señorita Blake, I thought I heard a child. Please—come in and let us see your little treasure."

Relieved, Amy flashed the guard a quick, apologetic smile before following Garcia into his office. Earlier in the day she'd made a report to Garcia about the kidnapping, had given him her impressions of Marita and had renewed her commitment to lobby her father for the country's recognition. But then, another guard had been on duty. This second one had seemed far more suspicious than the first and she'd become somewhat flustered.

She stopped midway into Garcia's office. "I'm afraid my Spanish is hopeless. I'm not sure your guard even understood what I was trying to say. I think he was debating with himself whether he ought to whisk me away. Thank goodness, you heard Carmela."

"Revolutionaries have extremely acute hearing, Señorita Blake." He neglected to add that he heard the cries of children in his heart, both day and night. This cry, though, he could enjoy and would.

"Please, *señorita,* have a seat." He directed her to a bank of easy chairs by the window and she selected one, settling down, the child burrowed against her, buried in a quilt of wonderful blue and yellow flowers.

He took a deep breath. Once, one of his children had a similar quilt.

"So, Señorita Blake." He watched her from under hooded eyes, his heart breaking a little at the classic image she presented of mother and child as she unnecessarily rearranged the quilt around the baby in her arms. "Thank you for bringing Carmela so I could see her." Curious, he raised his eyebrows. "Where is Crawford, by the way? I half expected him to be with you."

She shrugged, but her voice choked as she replied. "I don't really know...."

Garcia narrowed his deep-brown eyes, shrewdly steepling his fingers together slowly and reading reluctantly between the lines. Psychoanalysis wasn't a particular strength of his, but as a leader he was wise enough to know when he ought to attempt it.

"Tell me, Señorita Blake, exactly what does that mean?"

Amy licked her lips. "Well, I haven't seen much of him," she confessed shakily. "And I understand that he's leaving in a few hours on another assignment, so I guess he and I have said good-bye."

Ah, he wondered, since when would that be a problem? There was only one time when it might be. He suppressed a sudden, knowing smile. He'd imagined as much when Crawford had nearly torn him apart at the Mendozas. It suited, he thought. Crawford was bound to fall hard. It was how he did everything. It was equally expected that he would resist.

Garcia's mouth thinned to hide his amusement. Now he understood why, according to his aide, Crawford was so anxious to get out of town again. The male flight pattern was something he was quite familiar with. "Likely he's around," he said casually. "Probably replenishing his supplies."

Amy took a deep breath. "Actually, I think he's avoiding me."

Or the truth, Garcia reflected. He allowed himself a smile. Leaning back in his chair, he regarded her lovely shadowed face.

"When I was a young man, *señorita,* we used to hunt mountain lions, not to kill, mind you, but I discovered that it takes time and patience to track them."

Amy swallowed the hard lump in her throat and thought of how much time she'd spent, how much patience she'd already exercised and how at least one of those things had run out. "And what if you don't have time, General?" she asked bleakly.

"Well, then that does make it a bit difficult to corner them. But you know, Señorita Blake, while we're on the topic of Crawford, just as a matter of interest, of course, I thought you might like to know that *I* have to approve all travel plans, and for some strange reason, I appear to have lost the paperwork for Crawford's upcoming trip."

Amy studied him with a confused expression on her face, then the meaning of what he was saying dawned on her.

She stared at him in absolute amazement, then a broad, open smile spread across her face. She could have leaped across the desk and hugged him.

Her gaze sparkled as she fell in with the charade. "Really, General, I wonder where it got to."

He shrugged, a serious expression on his face. "I have no idea. It's very difficult to keep up with desk-bound bureaucracy when you've been a fighting general."

Amy's heart filled with hope. Time, she thought. Just a little time. That was all she needed.

She wanted to jump up and down with excitement. "How long, General, do you think the paperwork might be lost?"

He considered the matter with mock gravity. It would be wonderful to get something over on Crawford for a change. "I'm not really sure. Do you suppose two or three days might be sufficient?"

She could hardly contain her joy. "Yes, I think so... provided, of course—" she arched her eyebrows at him playfully "—you don't get shot at dawn because of it."

His eyes twinkled. She was a real delight, he thought. "No fear of that, Señorita Blake." Standing up, he returned her smile and walked toward her. "Now, let's do something important, shall we? Let's take a look at your baby."

Crawford stormed up the curved staircase of the Palacio past two astonished chatting guards and marched into Garcia's office.

The general looked up from his desk in surprise. Nobody barged in on him without an escort of some sort. When he saw Crawford, he quelled a quick smile and shook his head at the two guards who'd followed in on Crawford's heels and had raised their rifles to his head. Disdainfully, Crawford didn't even bother to turn.

Dubious, one of the guards started, moving forward. "General—"

Garcia waved him aside. "It's all right," he said in a measured voice. "I was expecting Crawford. Please—close the door behind you."

Standing up, he faced the other man and waited for the door to be shut before greeting him laconically. "Well, Crawford, I see you are safe and sound. I'm not sure whether to be grateful or not."

Crawford's eyes flashed blue fire. "Cut the crap, Garcia. I've got a couple of bones to pick with you."

The general raised his eyes in a dramatic sweep. "You nearly always do, Crawford. What is it this time?"

"First, I'd like to know where the paperwork is that will let me travel, and how you could let Amy Blake go up into those mountains knowing that Orega's men might be looking for her?"

So hotheaded, Garcia thought. So precipitous. It was amazing to him that the lamentable U.S. trait had proven so successful over there.

"First of all, Crawford, the paperwork has been delayed because my informants tell me that some of Orega's men are approaching the Manion Range, and I can't risk your going up there again."

Crawford snorted. "Whom do you think you're talking to, Garcia? I can handle those idiots. What is this?"

Garcia ignored the rhetorical response. "And as for your second question," he replied patiently, "that was only a possibility, Crawford, and a very slim one at that. But I agree it was most unfortunate that—"

"Unfortunate? It was criminal. You have a bad track record protecting women, General."

Garcia's stomach somersaulted and he paled beneath his dark skin. Fragments of memory exploded inside his brain, sucking the breath out of his lungs.

"I could have you executed for that, Crawford," he replied in a deadly rasp.

"Yeah, right." Crawford leaned over the desk and slammed his hand on it. "Except you've got it wrong, Garcia. I'm the one who ought to shoot *you* for risking *her* life that way."

Darkness swirled around Garcia, bleak and heavy. He could see himself shrouded in it, seeing two figures clearly, pinpricks of light focused on the horror he didn't want to witness. Blinking, he fought his way through it and raised his eyes toward the other man, grateful that the images were, if not vanishing completely, at least receding enough for him to be able to focus on Crawford's angry features.

He spoke carefully. "She was protected at all times, Crawford. I sent a contingent of men to follow her."

"Like hell you did!"

Garcia folded his arms in front of himself, feeling the pounding of his heart subsiding. Thank you, God, he prayed.

"Tell me, Crawford, how did you manage to get the door fixed on your truck the night of the rainstorm?"

Crawford fell silent, then blew out a frustrated breath.

"Damn you, Garcia. It would have been reassuring to have known."

Garcia offered him a cold smile. "That would have spoiled everything, Crawford. I promised Amy Blake freedom to see this country on her own terms without interference. I believed it was vital that she have that opportunity. Had I told you and

had she found out, she would have believed that you, amazing
as it probably seems, were part of an organized plan to restrict
her movements.... So you see, I ensured that she have that
freedom even as I ensured that she be protected from any dangers.''

It made sense, Crawford thought begrudgingly, but then
Garcia had never been stupid. It was one fault, unfortunately,
he never could attribute to the man. ''Bloody nice of you,
General, except what happened to your so-called contingent
when Ms. Blake was kidnapped?''

Garcia's lips thinned. He wondered how Crawford could get
anything accomplished, considering the amount of energy the
man spent on challenging anything in his path.

''They were temporarily diverted by some of the kidnapping
party. However, one of them was able to secure additional aid,
but by that time you had come to the rescue, so to speak.''

Crawford shook his head in disgust. ''Pretty risky stuff,
General.''

Garcia sighed under his breath. ''I would have preferred that
Amy Blake not travel alone, but then...'' He continued in a dry
voice, ''She did have you, after all, and as ridiculous as it might
sound, I had faith in your ability to keep her safe. And I was
proven right.''

His eyes narrowed, Crawford regarded the general. Except
for the incident involving his family, Garcia had always enjoyed a reputation for being dedicated, honorable and astute.

Crawford hated to back down, but he decided to let it go.
''All right, General, we'll let it go at that—for now.''

Garcia unfolded his arms, bowing mockingly. In some peculiar way, he realized, he would miss Crawford. ''Such graciousness astounds me, Crawford.''

Crawford shrugged, grinning. ''It's the American way.''

Garcia's eyes glinted with wry amusement. Yes, he thought,
he would definitely miss this American. Such arrogance was to
be admired in some ways.

He straightened and held out a hand to Crawford. ''I'd like
to wish you luck, Crawford, and to thank you for everything
you've done to advance Marita's quest for independence,'' he
said formally.

Crawford regarded him with surprised sarcasm. ''I'm not
going anywhere, if you remember, General.''

Garcia almost laughed out loud. He wondered if all Americans were as dense as Crawford could be in matters of the heart. No Latin male would ever make the mistake in judgment that Crawford was making.

"Well, yes, of course," he replied diplomatically. "But—just in case—I'd also like to thank you for, uh—" he cleared his throat "—all the unofficial aid you've given my people."

Crawford felt uneasy. What was this? The golden handshake? "A couple of milk cartons, General, nothing more. My friends could easily afford them."

Garcia arched his brows. The tough simplicity with which Crawford could overcome obstacles had always drawn the general's respect. He, himself, unfortunately had always agonized too much.

"Still—" he said, lifting one shoulder carelessly "—thank you."

Crawford adjusted the assault rifle hanging loosely from his shoulder and shot Garcia a suspicious look. "If you're thinking of spiriting me away in the middle of the night, your goons had better think twice about it."

This was almost too good to be true, Garcia thought with amused amazement.

"Crawford, you're paranoid. Why would I go to that much trouble when I could have had one of the guards shoot you right now?"

Crawford frowned. "You're making me nervous, General. I think I liked you better when we were arguing."

Garcia chuckled. "You know what your problem is, Crawford? You need enemies in order to function and channel that anger of yours. If you don't have something or someone to fight, you're uncomfortable. You don't know how to accept life when conflict isn't there for you, or to trust that things aren't about to blow up in your face, so you attack first."

Crawford felt like someone had speared an arrow into his consciousness. Was it true? Had he taken all his anger and disillusionment and translated it into physical combat? Was that so wrong? Is that what he was also doing with Amy—rejecting what she had to offer because he was afraid he'd lose a part of who he was? Afraid he'd lose the anger that had become almost a part of him because it was a shield against life and heartbreak?

Was he afraid to trust she really had any feelings for him?

"You think too much, General."

That wasn't the first time he'd been accused of that, Garcia thought. Trying to intellectualize violence, trying to rationalize, trying to negate feelings. He gave himself a mental shake. Emotions weren't a general's prerogative. Generals weren't supposed to feel.

He blew out a breath of heavy air and replied softly, "Revolutions require both brains and brawn, Crawford. But before you go, I want *you* to think about something. You chose to leave Amy Blake alone when you went scouting, is that not correct?"

"Sure . . . but—"

Garcia interrupted with slow, knifelike precision. "There's always a 'but' in life when men make choices, Crawford. I too, have had to make choices, but—perhaps our choices, yours and mine, weren't so different. Just think about it. By leaving her you put her at risk, and yet you left her in order to reduce that risk. But still, you felt terrible guilt, isn't that true?"

Crawford held himself motionless. He could well remember the agony of doubt and guilt he'd experienced when he'd realized that Amy had been kidnapped. But he'd found her.

He'd been lucky, he thought. Maybe the general was trying to tell him he hadn't been so lucky.

He moved forward with involuntary curiosity. "Garcia—"

Garcia smiled faintly, surprised he'd said as much as he had, and surprised at the unlikely source of absolution he'd selected. "Just something to think about, Crawford."

Crawford pursed his lips and leveled a straight look at Garcia. Hadn't Amy, with her instinctive ways, suggested that there was more to what had happened to Garcia's family than was obvious? What, after all, did he really know about what had transpired at Cresca? he reflected. Even Romero hadn't been all that forthcoming.

The general, after all, had a point about Crawford's actions with Amy, so who was he to judge?

He shrugged. "General, as they said in the good old U.S. of A., the jury is still out."

Garcia's eyes locked with his. "Not a bad expression, Crawford, not bad at all. Well . . ." He dropped his hand and retreated behind his official position. "*Buenos dias*, Crawford."

Crawford took the general's hand and shook it. He was surprised that he hadn't noticed until now how firm a handshake Garcia had.

He threw back his head cockily. The paperwork would come through sooner or later, he thought. It had to. He was counting on it. He needed some external stimulus to stay away from Amy Blake. "See you around, General."

Garcia swallowed back his laughter. The man really didn't know what was about to happen, he thought incredulously.

Suddenly, the general laughed. It was the first time in years, he realized, that he'd laughed with such innocent spontaneity.

"Crawford, I don't really think so. I think—as I believe the British would say—you've met your Waterloo."

"Right, I'm coming." Crawford snapped at the knock on his door, as he pulled the last of his things out of the suitcase and piled them back on the bed. Now that he'd had a chance to think about the delayed papers, he was seeing red again.

Impatiently, he strode across the room and yanked the door open.

Amy stood there, her gaze locking with his. "May I come in for a minute?" she asked.

He shrugged, his pulse racing at the sight of her. For a moment, he couldn't breathe. He hadn't seen her for over twenty-four hours. He'd thought that would be enough time for him to acquire some objectivity about her, but in a torrent all his feelings for her fired through him. He'd never be able to be objective about her. Even from the beginning, he hadn't been able to. She'd gotten under his skin and stayed there.

"Sure, why not?" He lifted his eyebrows at her empty arms. "Where's Carmela?"

She smiled nervously, following him into the room. "I'm afraid Carmela is going to end up with a lot of relatives. She's downstairs with Mercedes and Raoul. They're like doting grandparents. I'll be lucky if I can get her back."

"So..." Closing the door behind her, he folded his arms across his chest arrogantly, desire, love and yearning bottoming out in the pit of his stomach as he regarded her. There was a special glow to her now that she was a mother, a confidence that was softer, gentler somehow. It was just his luck it only made her seem more provocative. "What can I do for you, Ms. Blake? Come to say good-bye?"

She took a deep breath. It's now or never, she told herself. Just out with it, she thought.

"Not exactly. I came to tell you that I love you and I want to marry you."

He stared at her in absolute amazement.

"You can't be serious."

"I'm very serious."

His heart pounded. "Just how do you think we'll pull that off?"

Amy felt panic surfacing inside her, but kept her voice deliberately light. "We'll get a blood test, hire a minister, get a church or go to city hall. We'll do it however you want. It doesn't matter to me, as long as you're there."

Silence fell between them. Just for a moment, he allowed himself to believe it was that simple. That he could have her for the rest of their lives. Then he shook his head adamantly.

"No."

He saw her eyes widen luminously as she struggled to fight the hurt shadowing them.

"Sam, you don't mean that."

"Angel, it's easy to walk down an aisle, I know. I've done it and so have you. The difficult part comes after that, making a marriage work. I failed once. I sure don't want to fail again."

She wanted to run and cry her heart out, she thought. But she'd made up her mind she wasn't going to. He wanted her, she was sure of it. Otherwise, he wouldn't still be fighting her so hard. He wouldn't have held her that night after the storm with such concern and compassion. He couldn't have made love to her with such intensity and tenderness if he didn't care. He was just too stubborn and gun-shy to admit it.

"Is-is it because you don't love me?"

His breath quickened at the back of his throat. At that precise moment, with her expressive eyes fanning upward, any man would be a fool not to love her. Her femininity and loveliness were the kind of things a man dreamed of. But maybe it wasn't a question of whether he loved her. Maybe it was just a question of *allowing* himself to love her.

His response came out a hoarse sound. "I don't think that's the issue here, Amy."

He hadn't said he didn't, she thought. She took a long breath, determined not to let him off the hook. "I think you are for me the way I care for you. From the very beginning, I felt something for you, Sam, and I sensed that you did for me. You could at least admit that."

He held up a hand, his blue eyes darkening.

"Look, all right, I'll admit it. I don't know if it's love or not on my part, but I think there's a very good chance that what you're feeling for me is gratitude that I took you to find your little girl—"

"I'm grateful to Garcia, but I'm not in love with him," she interrupted quickly.

"All right, all right, but we were literally thrown together for two weeks. It's only natural that things would...happen between us."

Hope soared in her heart. He was arguing with her, not retreating. She was going to convince him yet that being together was the only possible solution for both of them.

"Sam, what happened between us happened because—and I know it probably sounds silly—because whenever you're near me, I feel like there's magic in the air. When I'm with you, I feel totally and completely alive. I've never felt that way with any man before, and I know I'll never feel it again. I've had my losses and disillusionment, too. But if we can give each other magic, then I'm not going to give you up without a fight."

That was one of the things he adored about her, he thought, her innocent feistiness. He doubted he'd ever be able to control her. He doubted he'd want to.

Still, this was wrong. All wrong. He wasn't good enough for her. "Amy, just think about what being married to me means."

She replied reasonably. "It means I'll wake up with you beside me. I'll have someone to love, to care for, to fight with, to grow old with."

His eyes turned a turbulent blue. He wished she wouldn't do this to him. "Look, I know you don't like to anticipate problems, but, sweetheart, I know what those problems are. Even if you can ignore them, I can't."

"So, why don't you tell me what they are?"

He inhaled a ragged breath. Listing problems, he thought, was something he was very good at. "If I remain a soldier, you'll hardly ever see me."

"My father traveled ninety percent of the time he was married to my mother. They were in love until the day she died."

"You'll be living in one part of the world, and I'll be living in another."

"Then I'll live in your world."

Horrified anger burst inside him. "No, you won't. Just remembering what I felt like when I knew Orega's men had you just about destroyed me."

"Then come back to my world."

He gave her a fierce look. "There's nothing I can do in your world. I've tried everything. I worked for the U.S. government and saw more corruption than I care to remember. When I couldn't put up with it anymore, I put a suit on and joined the corporate world in international development. The corruption I saw there made the CIA look like a picnic. There's absolutely nothing I can do in this world that I can stomach, except what I'm doing now."

She returned his look with a level look of her own. "Then find something else, something new."

Suddenly, he recalled one of their first conversations. He'd lost ground then very rapidly, he remembered, in a similar kind of exchange. He could feel the earth moving out from under him again. He wanted to groan with frustration.

"Like what?" he snapped.

She tossed back a stray strand of hair with her hand. "Marita's going to be developing rapidly in the next few years. Why can't you be a bridge between foreign investors and the Maritan government? You know how to do that, and there are *some* ethical business leaders in the industrialized world. I know, because I've met many of them through my father. Come back with me to Boston and try it, that's all I ask."

She was doing it to him again. But it had appeal, he thought. A lot of appeal. It's something he hadn't thought of.

"I don't know, Amy...I—"

Gaining momentum, she barreled ahead. "This is my little girl's country. I'd like to think that someone was fighting for her people. Just think—you'd still be a soldier, but in a different way."

"Amy, that's too romantic."

"Is it?" she replied in a calm voice. "Well, I happen to think you are a romantic filled with ideals and convictions. Only a

mantic would react to the horrible things in life the way you
. Why shouldn't the romantics have a run at it for a change?''

"Amy..."

Moving closer, she stopped in front of him, and tipped her
ad back to look up at him. He stood frozen, unable to move,
muscles rigid. Suddenly, it didn't seem like a game of wits
y longer.

Her voice was serious and low. "You can help Marita, Sam.
u can put it in touch with companies that could develop the
d of import/export business that goes along with invest-
nt. I trust you to do it, so does Garcia, and I know my fa-
r will."

He ground his teeth together behind closed lips. That kind of
st was hard to live up to. "Amy, I don't like being tied down.
a rebel."

Her eyes fastened on his, a fiery green, flecked with warm
lden shadows. "I—we—Carmela and I won't tie you down,
romise you. The world needs rebels. If you cop out and don't
rticipate in the development of Marita, then you abandon
s country to the possibility of idiots doing it. They could be
same idiots that you've already sworn you hate, the kind of
ots who might try to exploit the Maritans. Tell me, can you
with that?"

She knew the buttons to press, he thought grimly.

Just on principle, he gave it one last arrogant shot. "Let the
ots have the world."

nstead of being annoyed, she merely smiled at him ten-
ly. Weakening, she thought, he's weakening.

She rose on tiptoe to plant a kiss on his cheek, then mur-
red, "I didn't come here to hear you say that. You're a car-
person, and I know deep-down inside you do care about me
Carmela—don't you?"

He scowled. Losing wasn't something he did graciously.
ou talked me into taking you into those mountains, and now
l've doing it again, aren't you?"

"Not talked, Sam," she corrected, inching closer and put-
a hand on his chest so she could feel the sound of his heart
mping beneath it. "Browbeat. You're a tough customer, you
w."

He groaned as he felt her body molding against his.

"Is this what I can expect my life to be like from here on in?" he muttered.

"Oh, I imagine. Taming you is going to be a lifelong job. Does this mean you're saying yes?"

Crawford closed his eyes and tightened his arms around her. If this was love, he thought, he could probably handle it. He thought of the years ahead, loving and cherishing her. The right words couldn't come to his lips, but maybe one day, he thought. . . .

He pulled back and frowned. "Okay, I'll try it, but don't expect much."

She smiled to herself. Because she'd expected so much, she' found him. He wasn't saying he loved her, but she knew he would, sooner or later. Waiting was something she'd discovered she was very good at. "Okay," she murmured.

He regarded her suspiciously. "If I come back to Boston where are we going to live?"

"Anywhere you want as long as the three of us are together. I have a house in Boston. If you want to start there, we can."

He bit his lower lip as she nudged up against him. "I hope it isn't one of those frilly houses with French furniture a man can't sit on."

She grinned, her eyes shining. "No, it's very simple, with greenhouse in the back where I grow my flowers. It's got lots of sturdy furniture."

Instantly, it dawned on him what he was being given. A home, family, unconditional love. He was finally going to have a home with her and a new daughter, who had captured his heart as much as her mother had. His throat seized up as he realized the depth of his need for Amy and all she had to offer. He couldn't imagine himself in the role of the man of the house and all that it entailed. But, suddenly, he also couldn't imagine himself not in the role.

Her home. His home. Carmela's home. Their home. A second chance for all of them.

A choke caught in his throat. He suppressed it. "I'm probably going to be one of those husbands who's underfoot all the time," he warned, his eyes gleaming. "I don't have any hobbies, you know, and besides, I hate hobbies."

Tears of happiness shimmered in her eyes as she lifted her face to his. Worrying, she thought, never did get her any where. She'd found what she was looking for by just trusting and believing.

With all the love she harbored in her heart for him, she pressed her warm lips to his and whispered, "Then we'll just have to find a hobby for you that you do like. Starting now."

Epilogue

The child's eyes feathered open, fanning spiky black lashes upward in a slow curve. In the mountains, children often teased one another about riding to happiness on the wings of a condor. But even though she was flying, there was no condor, only a gleaming piece of machinery made up of nuts, bolts, and millions of pieces of metal that somehow allowed it to soar. The airplane was a symbol of progress, a herald of the future for the country she was leaving. It was also taking her to a new life filled with love and affection and new adventures.

Her gaze drifted with innocent curiosity as she lay curled between two sleeping adults. Each touched her—the woman's hand rested on her arm, warming her skin, and the man's shoulder created a curve she could snuggle into.

Her tiny hands opened as if to catch the contentment of the moment and then they closed, capturing it in small fists.

She sat very quietly, not demanding attention. It was as if she knew there would always be enough for her.

Others on the plane had commented on her sweet personality. There was an angelic quality about her, they'd said. And she was so incredibly quiet and peacefully still, never crying through the long wait to get onto the plane, never fidgeting.

One traveler, unable to resist, had put his fingers between her curling, inquisitive fingers so she could squeeze them, and had repeated those same kinds of words. It was as if she possessed infinite patience and faith in the future, and had finally found something she'd been waiting for, he'd said.

Her reaction to what he had said had apparently surprised him.

She'd gurgled delightedly as if she actually understood his words—and agreed with him.

* * * * *

HE'S AN

AMERICAN HERO

A cop, a fire fighter or even just a fearless drifter who gets the job done when ordinary men have given up. And you'll find one American Hero every month only in Intimate Moments—created by some of your favorite authors. This summer, Silhouette has lined up some of the hottest American heroes you'll ever find:

July: HELL ON WHEELS by Naomi Horton—Truck driver Shay McKittrick heads down a long, bumpy road when he discovers a scared stowaway in his rig....

August: DRAGONSLAYER by Emilie Richards—In a dangerous part of town, a man finds himself fighting a street gang—and his feelings for a beautiful woman....

September: ONE LAST CHANCE by Justine Davis—A tough-as-nails cop walks a fine line between devotion to duty and devotion to the only woman who could heal his broken heart....

AMERICAN HEROES: Men who give all they've got for their country, their work—the women they love.

IMHERO5

Take 4 bestselling love stories FREE

Plus get a FREE surprise gift!

Special Limited-time Offer

Mail to Silhouette Reader Service™

3010 Walden Avenue
P.O. Box 1867
Buffalo, N.Y. 14269-1867

YES! Please send me 4 free Silhouette Intimate Moments® novels and my free surprise gift. Then send me 6 brand-new novels every month, which I will receive months before they appear in bookstores. Bill me at the low price of $2.71 each plus 25¢ delivery and applicable sales tax, if any.* That's the complete price and—compared to the cover prices of $3.50 each—quite a bargain! I understand that accepting the books and gift places me under no obligation ever to buy any books. I can always return a shipment and cancel at any time. Even if I never buy another book from Silhouette, the 4 free books and the surprise gift are mine to keep forever.

245 BPA AJH9

Name	(PLEASE PRINT)
Address	Apt. No.
City	State	Zip

This offer is limited to one order per household and not valid to present Silhouette Intimate Moments® subscribers. *Terms and prices are subject to change without notice. Sales tax applicable in N.Y.

UMOM-93R   ©1990 Harlequin Enterprises Limited

**Relive the romance...
Harlequin and Silhouette
are proud to present**

by Request

A program of collections of three complete novels by the most
requested authors with the most requested themes. Be sure to
look for one volume each month with three complete novels by
top name authors.

In June: **NINE MONTHS** Penny Jordan
                                  Stella Cameron
                                  Janice Kaiser

**Three women pregnant and alone. But a lot can
happen in nine months!**

In July: **DADDY'S
             HOME**   Kristin James
                                  Naomi Horton
                                  Mary Lynn Baxter

**Daddy's Home... and his presence is long
overdue!**

In August: **FORGOTTEN
           PAST**   Barbara Kaye
                                  Pamela Browning
                                  Nancy Martin

**Do you dare to create a future if you've forgotten
the past?**

Available at your favorite retail outlet.

HARLEQUIN®   Silhouette

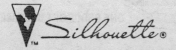